Readers everywhere are discovering the
fast-paced excitement of the Colton Parker Mystery series.
Here's what they're saying about Brandt Dodson's *Original Sin*...

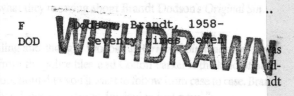

"Compelling... the narrative grips you and won't let go. Colton Parker was
plucked from the police blotter and thrust onto center stage. He's a hard-
nosed, blue-collar gumshoe with the folks-next-door case-to-case. Brandt
Dodson has fashioned a gritty, fascinating first novel."

Mark Mynheir, former homicide detective
and author of *Rolling Thunder* and
From the Belly of the Dragon

"Crisp. Wry. Honest. PI Colton Parker is as unexpected as a bullet
hole in a brand-new Brooks Brothers suit. You're gonna like this
gumshoe!"

Clint Kelly, author of *Scent*

"*Original Sin* is a terrific read, packed with characters—both savory
and otherwise—you couldn't forget if you tried. I'm looking forward
to the next book!"

John Laurence Robinson, author of the
Joe Box Mysteries: *Sock Monkey Blues*
and *Until the Last Dog Dies*

"I love a good mystery, and *Original Sin* by Brandt Dodson has all the
elements of a good mystery: a PI the reader can identify with, a believ-
able cast of characters, and a plot that's right out of the daily paper.
High recommended!"

Linda Hall, award-winning author of *Dark Water*,
Margaret's Peace, and *Katheryn's Secret*

"*Original Sin* is the first in a series that promises a bright future.
Fans of Robert Parker's 'Spencer' series will feel right at home.
Recommended."

Aspiring Retail Magazine

"This is a terrific beginning to what promises to be a great series of
mysteries with a touch of inspiration. Rating: 4½ daggers."

The Romance Reader's Connection

A COLTON PARKER MYSTERY

SEVENTY TIMES SE7EN

BRANDT DODSON

HARVEST HOUSE PUBLISHERS

EUGENE, OREGON

Cover by Garborg Design Works, Minneapolis, Minnesota

Cover photo © Jesper Markward Olsen / iStockphoto

Photo on page 273 © Susan Gerth

SEVENTY TIMES SEVEN
Copyright © 2006 by Brandt Dodson
Published by Harvest House Publishers
Eugene, Oregon 97402
www.harvesthousepublishers.com

Library of Congress Cataloging-in-Publication Data
Dodson, Brandt, 1958-
    Seventy times seven / Brandt Dodson.
        p. cm.—(A Colton Parker mystery; bk. 2)
    ISBN-13: 978-0-7369-1810-7 (pbk.)
    ISBN-10: 0-7369-1810-8 (pbk.)
    1. Private investigators—Fiction. 2. Missing persons—Fiction. I. Title II. Series.
    PS3604.O33S48 2006
    813'.6—dc22   206001341

Printed in the United States of America

06 07 08 09 10 11 12 13 14 / BC-MS / 10 9 8 7 6 5 4 3 2 1

To Karla

Acknowledgments

Without the following people, *Seventy Times Seven* would
have not been possible. Their efforts have been invaluable
in making this a better book. My thanks go to...

My wife, Karla, for allowing me to ignore the chores and stay at the keyboard.

Bob and Linda Lenn, for their friendship and page-by-page review.

Jeff and Ruby Goldberg, for being who they are
and for their many suggestions.

Christopher and Sean, for allowing Dad the time to write.

Nick Harrison, for his patient editing. Nick,
your suggestions are always on target.

And to all the professionals at Harvest House. You have answered my
many questions and given freely of your time and wisdom.

CHAPTER ONE

His name was Lester Cheek. By any measure, it was the type of name that should have held him back. In fact, it was his name that ultimately propelled him forward.

In school, his build was slight, his posture stooped, and his teeth protruded. He carried a slide rule, wore pants that were far too short, snorted when he laughed, and kept black-and-white glossies of Albert Einstein and Jonas Salk taped to the inside of his locker. In short, Lester was his own worst enemy. But it was the name Cheek the Geek that had cut him most deeply and kept him from his goals and from the kids he sought as friends. Those same kids who became his perpetual tormenters.

He was the butt of jokes and the target of schoolyard bullies. He couldn't find a friendly face—not among the boys, not among the girls, and not even among the other less socially gifted students of Tremont High. The other rejected kids who were on their own quest for acceptance found it in their united rejection of Lester Cheek.

But as time moved on and the kids grew into adulthood, the cliques of high school soon gave way to the stark realities of life. Most of the kids in Lester's class went on to average lives with average problems. Others did less well and found themselves on the wrong side of the tracks—

or the wrong side of the law. But none of them had had to endure and persevere the way Lester had. None of them had to overcome the obstacle of a name like Lester Cheek. None of them had grown in the way that Lester had, and none of them had done as well.

At twenty-five Lester opened the Pottery Shack and sold everything pottery, from cups and bowls to lamps and wall hangings. At first it was a small operation, just Lester and a couple of part-time employees. But eventually one store grew to three, then ten, then thirty. And by the time he was fifty, Lester owned more than forty Pottery Shacks in malls and strip centers throughout the midwest. But he was still Cheek the Geek, and he was alone.

That is, until he met Claudia. She was older than Lester by five years and considerably more worldly. But that was okay with the pottery merchant. After all, Lester was in love, and he wasn't alone anymore.

The couple married and developed a circle of friends. The latter was due mostly to Claudia's effervescent personality because Lester still chafed from years of relentless scorn. But with Claudia at his side, the pain from years of abuse had begun to recede, and life was finally good for Lester Cheek.

And then suddenly Claudia disappeared without giving a reason or offering an apology. And Lester was alone again. And he hired me to find his wife.

I met him at his north side estate on the hottest day in Indianapolis history. The air did not stir. It was as thick and lifeless as solidified blood…and still the thermometer continued its relentless climb. Even the birds had ceased their singing. The only sounds on the Cheek estate came from the inground sprinkler system.

As I climbed out of my car, I was greeted at the door by a tall, thin Hispanic-looking woman who ushered me into the living room, where I found Lester sitting on an expensive Italian leather sofa.

He stood and smiled pleasantly as he extended his hand. I shook it, and after the brief salutation, he asked Consuelo to leave us alone. As soon as she did, the light went out of Lester's eyes as he collapsed onto the sofa again.

"How long has she been gone?" I asked as I took a seat opposite him.

He sat with his head bowed and shoulders slumped, a man trapped in the maze of life with no way out. "Bout a week now," he said, his voice breaking. "But I keep thinking she's coming back. She's *got* to come back."

Thirty-six years had passed since high school, but Lester was still a geek. Still small and still stooped. But I heard no snort when he laughed, for there was no laughter now. Lester had proved to the world that he had worth and that he belonged. Yet somehow he was still alone, abandoned by the only one who had ever seemed to care.

"Were there any problems?" I asked.

He shook his head. "I didn't think so. I thought everything was going well. We were doing great, the stores were doing great."

"How long have you been married?"

"Five years last month."

"And no problems?" I asked again.

He shook his head. "No sir."

"There are always problems," I said.

"If there were, I didn't see them."

"It's possible," I said. "It happens."

"I know. I just hope it didn't happen this time. I don't think I could live with myself if something was wrong and I didn't see it."

I looked around the room. From what I could see, the house was elaborate. The living room was done in a Southwestern decor with some very expensive, original artwork on the walls.

"Georgia O'Keeffe?" I asked, nodding at one of the paintings on the wall.

"Yes. Know her?"

"I know of her," I said. "She's been gone for some time."

"Claudia picked that out. She always had a taste for art."

"Me too," I said. "Can't afford much of it, though. Still, I suppose it doesn't hurt to look."

"You like Georgia O'Keeffe?"

"Sure," I said. "Among others."

"Do you have a favorite?" he asked.

"Several. I would rank Norman Rockwell near the top. I even like the guy who did *Dogs Playing Poker.*" The humor was lost on Lester. "But if I had to pick a single artist, it would be Kinkade."

Lester nodded. "The Painter of Light," he said. "Claudia likes him too. We have some of his originals in the house."

I noticed an elk's head mounted over the fireplace.

"Hunt?" I asked, standing and moving to the trophy.

He shook his head. "No, I bought it. Thought it might look nice in the room."

"It does," I said.

He remained sitting on the edge of the sofa, rubbing his hands together between his knees. His shoulders were slumped and his eyes were focused on the floor.

"Did she leave a note?" I asked.

He shook his head.

"Has she phoned?"

Again, he shook his head.

"E-mail?"

"No. Nothing."

"Have you called the police? Filed a missing persons report?"

He nodded. "Yes. I called them. But they said that she left on her own accord and there was nothing they can do. Her luggage and clothes and makeup are gone."

"Were you home when she left?"

He shook his head again. "No. When I come home from work, she usually comes to the door. This time she didn't. I looked all over for her—" his voice broke again. "But she wasn't here." He paused to gain control of himself. "I didn't know what to do, so I called my attorney.

He said it would be wise to prepare for a divorce. But if I was committed to finding Claudia and working things out, I should hire a private detective. He gave me your name."

"And that's how I got involved."

He nodded as he fought to subdue his emotions.

I made a mental note to find out more about the attorney and thank him for the referral. "Does Claudia have any friends?" I asked.

He breathed slowly before answering. "Yes. Most of our friends are her friends."

"Does she have any particularly close friends? Someone she might be staying with or who might know where she is?"

He shrugged. "There's Melanie Green. She and Claudia are quite close. They usually play tennis a couple of times a week. Have lunch. Work on the board of some charity for a while."

"Which charity?"

He paused, working his hands. "Let's see..." he said, glancing upward the way people do when trying to recall something. "It was...Mothers Advocating for Children—MAC."

"When did Melanie see Claudia last?"

He rubbed his hands together again, keeping his gaze toward the ceiling, "That would have been last week, just before Claudia disappeared. Claudia had a television interview about the charity. After the interview, she and Melanie came back here, had lunch, played some tennis in the back, and..." He looked up at me. "I want her back, Mr. Parker."

"I know."

"I *need* her back." The pain in his eyes was familiar to me. I saw it every morning in the mirror. But in my case, my wife had not left by choice.

I moved back to the chair I had been sitting in. "I can't make her come back."

He looked at the floor again as he nodded. "I know," he said softly.

"I'll find her. But what happens after that is not in my control."

He nodded again.

"Has she been acting differently lately? Anything unusual?"

"No."

He paused the rubbing of his hands as he thought. "No. Except that a lot of money has been withdrawn from our accounts recently. More than usual."

"How much?"

"About twenty-five thousand over the past month or so."

"Twenty-five thousand?" I asked, trying to mask my incredulity. It was more money than I had been able to accumulate in a lifetime of struggle. "Didn't that alarm you?"

He looked at me again. "No, not really. I've done quite well over the years, Mr. Parker, and Claudia enjoyed nice things. I was happy to indulge her."

"Sure," I said, "but twenty grand is a lot of indulgence."

He nodded. "Like I said, it was more than usual."

"When did you discover the withdrawals?"

"Just the other day. I take care of the business and have always given Claudia enough to run the house, along with a personal account. But since she left, I had to assume control of the checkbook again. That was when I discovered the withdrawals."

"More than one?"

"Maybe. I didn't go back any further. That was when I called you."

"I'll need amounts and dates," I said.

He nodded as he began to work his hands again. "I'll have a copy of the check register sent to you today."

"I'll need phone records, credit card receipts, an address book, and a picture. A recent one."

"I'll have them delivered today."

"One more thing," I said. "Did she have any enemies?"

He shook his head. "No, not Claudia."

"Do you?"

"Of course. You can't be in business, and be as successful as I have been, and not have made enemies along the way."

"Are any of these enemies angry enough to cause harm to you or Claudia?"

He nodded. "Some of them."

"I'll need a list," I said.

He began to work his hands faster than before. "It'll take some time, Mr. Parker. It is quite a long one."

CHAPTER TWO

Late August in Indianapolis usually means the kids are back in school, the state fair is over, and there's enough humidity to drown a whale. This particular day in late August was no different.

I drove to Indianapolis Police Department headquarters to talk to detectives about the disappearance of Claudia Cheek. By the time I arrived, my shirt was soaked, and I was beginning to stick to the seat of my car.

I took the elevator to the detective's squad room and found Harley Wilkins, captain of detectives, sitting at his desk. His shirtsleeves were rolled up and his tie undone. In all the years that I'd known him, I had never seen him with a fully knotted tie.

"You look hot," he said.

"Sorry," I said, "but I'm not interested."

He snorted.

I sat in the chair next to his desk. "Who's working the Claudia Cheek case?"

"Who's Claudia Cheek?"

"Wife of Lester Cheek."

Wilkins shrugged.

"Owner of the Pottery Shack."

He shrugged again.

"The Pottery Shack *discount chain?*"

He shook his head.

"Huge chain… 'Your one-stop pottery shop'?" I said, quoting their well-known slogan.

A flash of recognition. "Oh yeah," he said, "*that* pottery shop. So what about her?"

"She's missing. That's why I'm here. I spoke with her husband and he said your guys had already determined that she left of her own free will."

"Yeah. And?"

"And I want to know what they know and how they reached that conclusion."

Wilkins leaned back in his chair. It creaked under the sudden shift in load. "What you want to know is if she left on her own free will or if my guys suspect something else."

"Right. The husband said that her clothes, makeup, and luggage were missing."

"What else do you need?"

"Certainty. I want to know if your guys suspect anything else."

"If they did, don't you think we'd be working on it?"

"I'm just trying to be thorough."

He leaned forward again. The office was heavy with humidity, and beads of perspiration had formed on Wilkins' forehead, giving his black skin an ethereal sheen. "And you don't think we are?"

"I've heard that on some cases you can be quite thorough."

I had been in his office for less than three minutes, and the look on Wilkins' face told me I was already punching all the wrong buttons. I was going nowhere and getting there in record time.

"And I suspect this is one of them," I said. "I just want to know if they picked up on anything that might hint at trouble in the Cheek marriage."

He wanted more.

"I suspect that Mr. Cheek isn't being as forthright with me as I need."

I didn't really believe that, but Wilkins was leaving me with nothing else to say.

The detective studied me for a minute and then swung around to his keyboard. After hitting a few strokes and reading the monitor, he picked up the phone.

"Ellis? This is Harley. You investigated the disappearance of a Claudia Cheek last week, remember? What can you tell me about the situation?" There was a pause as Wilkins took notes. "Uh-huh. Any marital problems?" Pause. "Okay. Anything to suggest that this was something more than a walkout?" Pause. "Okay."

"Ask him if he looked into Lester Cheek," I said. "Was he, or is he, involved in anything?"

Wilkins shot me a glance that told me he knew how to do his job.

"What about the husband?" he said into the phone. There was another pause as Wilkins scribbled. "Okay. Thanks." He hung up.

"Well?" I asked.

Wilkins tore the note from his pad and set it down on the desk. "It's all right there," he said, thumping on the note as he slid it toward me. "Everything they've got. The wife left with her stuff, some money, and her car. No forced entry, no threats, no communications of any kind, and no trouble."

"And Lester?"

"Clean. Not particularly well thought of, but clean."

"He said he had enemies."

Wilkins nodded. "Yeah, probably. Jealousy mostly. If you have something that someone else feels they're entitled to, you're viewed as the enemy. Whether they're motivated enough to snatch his wife—who knows. My guys didn't find anything like that." He paused to study my reaction the way any good cop does. "You've met him. What did you think?"

"I liked him. Felt sorry for him."

Wilkins snorted again. "Don't. He's worth a hundred mill, easy. He can buy all the sympathy he wants."

I saw Melanie Green's name on the sheet.

"What about Melanie?"

"Ellis told me that he interviewed the last friend to see Cheek's wife before she disappeared, and she—the friend—is just as surprised by the wife's disappearance as is the husband."

"You'd think the husband would have heard something by now," I said. "A phone call, a letter—something. Some kind of goodbye, even if it's a notification of divorce."

"It's only been a week," Wilkins said. "He'll hear. From what I understand, he's no prize. She probably married him for his money."

I shook my head. "If it was money she wanted, she could have left years ago."

Wilkins paused to think for a moment. "Yeah, that's true," he said. "Another man?"

"Sure," I said. "That's usually the case, isn't it?"

"Well," Wilkins said, leaning back again and crossing his arms behind his head. "If that is the case, then she's no prize either."

"No," I said, "but now she has lots of money."

CHAPTER THREE

After leaving IPD headquarters, I telephoned Melanie Green and asked if we could meet. She said we could and that she was heading downtown to shop at the Circle Center Mall. She suggested we meet at the Palomino for lunch, and I agreed. After ending the call, I checked to see if I had enough money for lunch. I didn't, so I found an ATM, got some cash, and parked in the garage attached to the mall.

I was early, so I killed time by visiting a bookstore, a music shop, a gift shop, and back to the bookstore again. By the time I realized that I was a few minutes late, I was deep into the third chapter of a Ken Follett novel.

I jogged across the street and told the maître d' that I was there to meet with someone. He smiled and escorted me to a table near a window that looked out onto Illinois Street.

Melanie Green was sitting at the table and had already ordered a glass of white wine. She was dressed in a sleeveless, lime green top with white slacks and matching earrings. Her hair was as copper as her tan, and nicely done. She smiled, flashing a perfectly aligned set of crystalline teeth. This lady had the whole package.

"Mr. Parker?" She extended a hand without getting up.

"Colton Parker," I said shaking her hand.

She gestured toward a chair. "Please have a seat."

"I apologize for keeping you waiting," I said as I sat.

She waved me aside. "No apologies necessary. I just arrived and was enjoying an excellent glass of wine." She looked out the window and watched as the people outside moved about. It was a lot like watching an aquarium...only from the inside. "It *is* hot out, isn't it?" she said.

"Yes it is. Humid too."

"That it is," she said as she sipped the wine. "But you didn't call me to talk about the weather, did you Mr. Parker?"

"No," I said. "I didn't."

She set the glass down and watched the people for a full minute. "You want to know if I know where Claudia is?"

"Yes."

"I don't." She looked at me. "And if I did, I wouldn't tell you."

A server came to the table. "Are you ready to order?"

"You first, Mr. Parker," Melanie said. She picked up the glass of wine and began to sip from it again as she turned back toward the people outside.

"What do you recommend?" I asked the server.

He told me and I took his recommendation. Melanie ordered a salad and another glass of wine.

"Why won't you tell me?" I asked.

"Because she can do better than—" She paused, trying to think of just the right word. "Better than that horrible little man."

Just the right word? "So why don't you just put it out on the table, Mrs. Green? Tell me what you really think of Lester."

"Have you met him?" she asked.

"Yes."

"It's reasonable to assume, then, that he hired you?"

"That would be a reasonable assumption," I said.

She smiled at me over the rim of the glass. "I knew he did." She sipped from the glass again. "What do you know about Lester, Mr. Parker?"

I told her what I knew.

"Now let me tell you what I know about Claudia," she said. "She is of the highest element."

"Meaning what?"

"Oh please," she said, dismissively. "Don't give me that."

"Give you what?"

"That 'arrogant broad who's too good for everyone else' routine. It's a little trite, don't you think, Mr. Parker?" She sipped some more wine. It was loosening her tongue, so I opted not to say anything. Why work for what will fall into your lap?

The waiter brought lunch. "If there's anything else you need..." he said.

"We're fine, Roger," Melanie said, glancing at the server's nametag. "Now make like a good boy and leave us alone."

Roger did as he was told.

"Now where were we?" she asked as she moved the salad with her fork. "Oh, yes. I was telling you about Claudia."

"Of the highest element," I said.

"That's correct," she said. I was beginning to notice a slight slurring of her words. "Claudia cares about people. You know? She serves on committees and chairs organizations that are..." She paused to sip more wine. When she set the glass down, she did it with enough force to indicate that she had misjudged the distance to the table. "That care about people and this city."

"Does she care about Lester?" I asked.

"He's a troll. All he cares about is making more money. Works all the time. That's why she left, if you ask me. She cares about the community. Cares about people. But that...little man...all he cares about is himself." She looked around the room and lowered her voice as she jabbed her fork at me. "Did you know that he isn't very well liked? By anyone?" She leaned back with a smile. "It's true. The man has no friends. Doesn't like people." She nodded. "Yes sir," she said, before sipping more wine. "He just wants to be left alone. Not like Claudia at all."

Chapter Four

Considering the bar bill Melanie racked up, I was more than pleased when she picked up the tab for lunch. I was also concerned about her ability to drive, but when I saw her phone home for a ride I knew that despite the alcohol, she still had the good sense to ask for help.

I left the parking garage and headed south of the city toward the Garfield Park area. Callie would be home from school soon, and I made it a practice to be there when she arrived.

We lived in half of a rented duplex that sat on the periphery of Garfield Park. The land was named in honor of assassinated president James Garfield and was located on the near south side of the city. The park underwent a restoration a few years prior to our move to the south side and now boasted winding walkways, a pool, and a bandstand. A former recreational area that had been allowed to slide to the underbelly of big-city life, the park was once again a gathering place for parents and their children. Unfortunately, the duplex that my daughter and I now lived in had not been part of that same urban renewal.

A single-story home in serious need of repair, our half was slightly less than a thousand square feet, with two bedrooms, two baths, a half basement, a small kitchen, and a living room. Despite its small size, the house was comfortable—at least as comfortable as I could make it—and provided enough room for the two of us.

It was shortly after Anna's death that Callie began to change. At thirteen, she and her mother had been developing the rapport that can be critical for any young girl on the verge of becoming a young woman. Callie's interests in school and sports, especially soccer, had always been high, and she had always excelled at both. But when Anna died, Callie's grades began to drop, and her interest in soccer began to wane. Her circle of friends began to change too. The sudden upheaval in her life resulted in a level of stress she was unable to manage. It finally reached a climax as she took an overdose of medication that resulted in a trip to the hospital. The doctors had called it a "cry for help." To me it was a cause for alarm. I didn't think young girls attempted suicide. Yet I was confronted with one who did. And she was mine.

After her discharge from the hospital, she began seeing a psychologist. These visits confirmed my own suspicions that Callie held me responsible for her mother's death. I didn't blame her. It was an issue I had also been wrestling with. Anna hadn't taken the news of my termination from the FBI lightly. We had argued, and she stormed out of the house. Callie witnessed the argument and the subsequent arrival of the police to tell us of Anna's fatal accident. The die was cast. Callie was like a plane that had lost a wing in flight. She went into an emotional and spiritual tailspin while I blindly fought for control. Since those events, I had been reluctant to leave her side.

I arrived home just a few minutes after leaving the restaurant. At precisely three thirty I saw the bus pull up in front of the house, and I fought to restrain myself from going outside to greet her.

The bus' retractable stop sign was fully extended with its dual red lights blinking as Callie moved from her seat to the door of the bus. I could see her squint as she stepped into the brilliant sunlight with an overloaded book bag strapped to her back.

After she was off and the bus pulled away, I darted over to the sofa and grabbed the sports section of the paper. By all appearances, I was deep into the news when she entered the house.

She sighed as she moved past me and down the hall.

"How was school today?" I asked.

No answer. I soon heard her bedroom door slam shut. Within seconds, the stereo was blaring.

Well, Parker, I said to myself as I set the paper aside, *that went well.* I got off the sofa and went into her room. "You okay?" I asked over the blare of the stereo.

She was lying facedown on the bed, drumming in tune to the music with a pencil. An open textbook was in front of her.

I reached across her to the nightstand next to her bed where she kept the stereo and turned it off. "I asked if you're okay."

The familiar mixture of sadness, rejection, and anger creased her face. "I'm fine."

Years of law enforcement, first with the Chicago PD and then the FBI, had provided me with the necessary tools to ascertain whether a suspect was being truthful or not. I was detecting the latter here.

"You're not being straight with me," I said, sitting on the bed next to her.

"Is this where the rubber hose comes in?" she asked.

If I thought it would work. "Callie, I can't help you if you don't talk to me."

"I'm fine," she repeated.

I searched her eyes as I waited for more. Nothing came.

"Okay," I said. "Do your homework. Dinner will be ready in a couple hours."

I eased off the bed and glanced over my shoulder as I left the room. She reached to the nightstand and turned the music on again. Although she had opened a book, her mind was clearly somewhere else.

Chapter Five

Callie was as quiet during breakfast the next morning as she had been during dinner the night before. Questions about schoolwork, friends, or other interests were met with a nod of the head, a shrug of the shoulders, or a one-word answer.

After seeing her off to school, I cleaned up the table, washed the dishes, and headed for the office. I needed to go over the paperwork Lester had sent me, and being in my office when I did it made me feel as if I was at work.

My office, like my house, my car, and the clothes on my back, had been selected primarily for economic reasons.

It was located on the third floor of a three-story building in the Fountain Square section of Indianapolis and overlooked the fountain the area was named for. Like Garfield Park, Fountain Square had been scheduled for significant restoration, a plan that never fully materialized. Despite that, the office was ideal for my needs. Less than five minutes from home and less than eight minutes from IPD headquarters and the nearby interstate system, it provided me easy access for the needs of both my professional and personal lives.

Ten minutes after I got to the office, I was sitting with my feet up on the desk and a box of paperwork on my lap. Among the items were credit card receipts, several check registers, cell phone bills, and a box of loose receipts Lester had found and lumped together. He had sent Claudia's address book too, as well as some names that he had indicated was a list of enemies. It wasn't as long as Lester had made it out to be. I recognized most of the names.

He had told me that Claudia had withdrawn twenty-five thousand dollars "over the last month or so." Apparently he hadn't bothered to go back much further than that. From the registers and receipts I was looking at, she had withdrawn closer to five times that much. And most of it wasn't recorded in the register. I was using ATM receipts and bank statements to create a collage of Claudia's activities.

For a period going back six months, I had found withdrawals for $5000 in February, $10,000 in March, $10,000 during the first week of April, and another $20,000 at the end of the month.

Then there were two withdrawals in May for a combined total of $10,000, a single withdrawal in June for $10,000, and two more withdrawals in July and August for a combined total of $56,000 for those two months. That was including the $25,000 that Lester had uncovered.

"Well, well, Claudia," I said, "you've been a busy little bee, haven't you?"

I stood and adjusted the fan in the open window, trying to catch whatever bit of breeze might come my way. None did.

I sat back down and began to go through the credit card purchases. After an hour of reading about purchases at Nordstrom's, the Home Shopping Network, and a plethora of upscale restaurants, I noticed two things that stood out.

The first was a $1000 debit item from Easy Travel, and the second was a cash advance of $5000. Both items had been charged two days before Claudia disappeared.

I called Lester at his office and was forced to listen to some droll music before he came on the line. I could hear a PA system in the background announcing the "deals of the century" to his customers.

"Lester, it's Colton," I said when he came on the line. "What kind of car does Claudia drive?"

"A Jag XJS."

"Could you get me the VIN or the tag number?"

"She took the car, Mr. Parker. I—"

"One or the other should be on the insurance face sheet. If not, it will be on the title."

"Okay. I'm not home, but I can leave and get it for you."

"No hurry, just—"

"Yes, Mr. Parker, there is a hurry. I want to know where my wife is. I want to know if she's okay."

"Sure," I said. "I'll wait here until I hear from you."

I hung up and started going through her cell phone records. As I did, I found several recurring numbers. I recognized one of them as Melanie's. The others were unknown to me, so I matched them up to her address book. Most of them were listed as friends, fellow board members from Mothers Advocating for Children, or neighbors. A few didn't match up to any listing in her address book. One number, though, kept reappearing— an out of town number she had called frequently over the past several months.

I called Mothers Advocating for Children and asked to speak to the head advocate. If Claudia was as deeply committed to the organization as it appeared, it would be reasonable to assume she would maintain some connection with it, despite her absence from Lester's life. After all, a failed marriage, regardless of the reason, doesn't necessarily include a dismissal of everything else. If Claudia hadn't been in contact with MAC since her disappearance, it could possibly signal an *inability* to stay in contact. That could alter the view that she had simply left Lester.

I soon had a pleasant-sounding female voice on the line. I asked to speak to Claudia Cheek. When I was told Claudia wasn't in, I decided to push a little harder.

"Do you expect her today?"

The voice said no.

"Tomorrow?"

Again, no.

When I asked about the last time Claudia had been seen at MAC offices, I detected hesitancy on the other end of the line.

"I'm a private detective," I said, giving my name. "I've been hired to find Mrs. Cheek." I then asked the woman if it would be possible to meet with her, and she agreed. I told her I would be by within the hour.

I hung up and was about to leave the office when the phone rang. It was Lester.

"Mr. Parker, I have the VIN and the license plate number."

"Shoot," I said, reaching for a pen and pad.

He gave me the VIN as well as the tag. I thanked him and hung up. Then I called the Indianapolis office of the FBI. After a few transfers, I had Mary on the line.

"I need some help," I said.

"Haven't we been telling you that for years?"

"I need to know if a VIN has registered for new plates or if the vehicle has been sold within the last week. I gave her the VIN, the tag number, and the type of car.

"What have you got?" she asked.

I told her all I knew.

"She probably left, you know. Someone who is that universally disliked isn't going to be able to hold on to someone like her for long."

"I admit he seems a little out of the ordinary," I said, "but he really is a nice guy and seems to really love her."

"I'm not saying he isn't, Colton, but sometimes peer pressure can be too great."

"Maybe."

There was silence on the line for a bit. "How's Callie?"

"Okay," I said.

"How are you and Callie?"

"Not so hot," I said. "Barely acknowledges that I'm around."

"I thought that moving away from Anna's parents and moving back in with you would help the two of you to reconnect."

"It's a start," I said. "I didn't really expect it to be easy."

"Give her some time, Colton. Let her see that you care. She'll come around."

"I hope so," I said, "or I'm going to begin thinking that I'm no better at relationships than Cheek the Geek."

Chapter Six

I met Selena McCoy at the office of Mothers Advocating for Children. The office was located on Main Street in Speedway, Indiana. Speedway was an incorporated town located west of Indianapolis but still in Marion County. The Indianapolis Motor Speedway, home of the Indy 500, was located in Speedway, which had confused me after my initial move from Chicago. It seemed the race could have been more aptly named the Speedway 500.

I parked in the slanted parking stall and dropped a coin in the meter. When I entered, I saw a large room filled with several desks of women who were answering telephones and entering computer data. An attractive woman with an air of authority was directing the operation of MAC in a professional yet friendly manner. I correctly assumed her to be Selena. I introduced myself, and she shook my hand with a firm grip.

"Come back to my office, Mr. Parker," she said. "We can talk there."

She led me through the large room to the rear, where her office was located. It looked out onto the main room we had just passed through, and was economically decorated. I sat in a blue plastic chair opposite Selena's desk.

"Now, how can I help you?" she asked.

Selena was about thirty and tall with a trim figure. She was dressed in a blue suit and had the poise of someone many years her senior.

"Mrs. Cheek is missing. Her husband is concerned and has asked me to find her."

She nodded her understanding. "Yes, the police were here last week asking about her as well."

"I need to know all that you can tell me about Claudia," I said. "For starters, what kind of employee was she?"

She smiled. "She wasn't an employee, Mr. Parker. This is a volunteer organization. I'm the only true employee."

"I see."

"Claudia was a jack-of-all-trades. She worked in the office, did some of our television promos, and organized our fund-raisers."

"What does MAC do?" I asked.

"We advocate for children. We lobby the legislature on children's issues, such as the school lunch program, safer toys, and safer playground equipment. We do everything from advocating for sound adoption policies to making sure that school zones are safe."

"And Claudia was..."

"She was a strong advocate for children. She told me she had lost one of her own and was unable to have any more. That sense of loss drove her to do what she did. And," she said as she looked over my shoulder, acknowledging a woman standing in her doorway, "we were the better for it."

The woman came into the office and slid a sheaf of papers in front of Selena. She signed them and handed them back with a smile, and the young woman left the room.

"Were you aware of any problems?" I asked.

She raised an eyebrow. "Problems?"

"Marital," I said. "She hasn't been home since she left, and all indications are that she left of her own free will."

She paused to think and then shook her head. "If there were problems of that sort, I was unaware of them."

"Did she express any sense of…" I paused, trying to think of the right word. "Restlessness? As if she felt it was time to move on?"

She tented her fingers and paused to think. "No, although she did ask me once if I was happy."

"Happy?"

"Yes. I asked her what she meant by that, and she said she just wanted to know if I felt at home. You know, if I truly enjoyed what I'm doing."

"Do you think that she was? Happy, I mean."

She pursed her lips. "Yes, I think she was. But she always seemed like something was missing. Not in her marriage, though. As I said before, if there was a problem there, I didn't pick up on it. At least, nothing that was particularly overt."

"Covert?" I asked.

She eased backward in her chair. "Maybe. She had been receiving some calls from someone. A man. He seemed to be interested in speaking only with Claudia, no one else."

"Do you remember his name?"

She shook her head. "No, I can't say for sure that he ever gave us a name. Only that he wished to speak with her. If she wasn't in, he wouldn't leave a message."

"Did she speak with him?"

She nodded. "Yes, I believe she did. But, as I say, she never showed any signs of marital stress."

"Could the man have been her husband?"

"Lester?" She laughed. "Heavens, no. We all know Lester. He's been in here before."

"You said that Claudia had lost a child."

"Yes. And that could be it, of course. Claudia has a dynamic personality. Very outgoing. And yet, there's a sense of underlying pain. As I said, it seemed personal. Do you know what I mean, Mr. Parker? The kind of pain that is deep and untouchable by anyone else. The kind that leaves a scar?"

I told her that I did. "Did she fit in with the others here at MAC?"

She smiled. "Oh my, yes. She not only fit; she was very much a leader. She had the respect of everyone here."

"Anything else? Anything you can think of that could give me a handle on where she might have gone? Or why?"

She paused to think. "No. I can't think of anything else."

I stood and extended my hand. "I appreciate your help."

She rose to take my hand. "Please find her, Mr. Parker. She's too valuable to the children of Indiana. We need her."

"So does her husband," I said.

CHAPTER SEVEN

So far, I had learned that Claudia was a well-liked woman with a vibrant personality and that she truly cared for children, probably because of the loss of her own child. She gave no indication to anyone that she was unhappy, yet she had left a loving husband. At this point, I didn't have much to go on, which was typical for a Parker investigation. At least one that was this fresh.

But I did have Lester's list of enemies. It wasn't something that a typical client would acknowledge having, much less be willing to share. The fact that he did share it, though, was one of several reasons I believed that he wasn't responsible for his wife's disappearance. The fact that he would hire a private investigator and then share what most people in his position would consider to be an embarrassing bit of information, showed a real commitment to finding her—particularly when all the evidence pointed to the strong possibility, if not outright likelihood, that she left of her own free will.

Of course, if Lester was craftier than I gave him credit for, the list could be a ruse to make him appear to want to find his lost wife while fingering his enemies for her sudden absence. Killing two birds with one stone could solve two headaches for the pottery merchant and elevate his position from rejected nerd to caring husband. It was possible. But I didn't consider it likely. Given what I knew of Lester's childhood, I had serious doubts that he would bring harm to the one person in his life who had seemed to care and to accept him as he was without reservation. But, of course, the fact remained that she was gone. And for now, my assumption that she cared for him appeared to be all wrong. Either way, Lester wasn't completely off the hook, and neither were his enemies.

The list that Lester had given me consisted of ten names of people he considered angry enough with him to cause harm. But apparently, not angry enough that he was keeping track of all of them. Two of the names on the list had died more than a year ago. Three others were out-of-state, a phone call to another established that he was out of the country, and one had recently been elected to Congress.

Congressmen have enemies too, of course, political and otherwise, but anyone elected to that office would probably find ways to deal with their enemies in ways that did not involve the commission of a capital crime.

The first of the remaining names on the list was Douglas Chatham. Chatham had been an Indianapolis staple for decades. An attorney who had been blessed with a sense of drama, he loved the television camera and was often seen in high-profile cases as he berated the opposition while extolling his client's virtue. The fact that his clients were often accused of everything from mugging handicapped children to torching homes just for the fun of it didn't seem to matter. If taking their case could generate some coverage, which of course generated more clients, he would advocate their cause. In the thirty years he had practiced law, Chatham had built a solid reputation as a stellar attorney but a less than stellar citizen. Interviewing him seemed to be my next logical move.

The law firm of Chatham, Kern, and Brubaker was located in the upper levels of the Hyatt Regency in downtown Indianapolis. I was able to make the drive in less than ten minutes.

I parked in the garage that was attached to the Hyatt and took the elevator to the second floor. Dressed in a Hawaiian shirt with the tail hanging out to cover my gun, I was acutely aware of how little I fit with the "dressed for success" types in the elevator. *Maybe,* I thought as I stepped out of the elevator and onto the second floor, *that could explain my lack of success.*

The atrium of the hotel was visible from all of the floors above, and as I glanced downward, I could see that it was abuzz with activity as people spun in and out of the doors to shop for flowers or cards or books. Guests went up and down in the ornate glass elevators to their rooms or to the restaurant that sat atop the building. At the Eagle's Nest, diners could get a four-star meal and a visual tour of the city as well. Anna and I had once had an anniversary dinner in that restaurant. But now she was gone, and I had neither the money nor the desire to spend an evening at the Eagle's Nest. It underscored the fact that I was alone. I no longer fit in a couples' world.

The offices of Chatham, Kern, and Brubaker overlooked the atrium below. When I entered the offices, I saw that the reception area of the firm was subdued and tastefully done. The smoke gray carpeting was plush and was nicely offset by the mauve and silver wallpaper. The receptionist was a dandy too. Blonde, with long, silky hair and full, pouting lips, she looked like a model off of the cover of any one of a dozen magazines in the gift shop below.

"Can I help you?" she asked.

"My name is Colton Parker," I said, displaying my ID. "And—"

"I'm sorry, Mr. Parker, but we have our own team of investigators. However, if you would like, I could put your name on our list. If an opening should arise, we could certainly call you."

"I'm not looking for employment," I said, "I'd like to speak with Mr. Chatham."

She recoiled with all the subtlety of someone who had just been slapped with a pork chop. "You don't want to work here?"

I shook my head. "No offense, but I really don't. I'm investigating a missing persons case, and I would like to ask Mr. Chatham a few questions. Ten minutes, tops."

She continued to look stunned as she picked up the phone. "I have a gentlemen here," she said, turning to me as she arched her finely plucked eyebrows.

"Colton Parker."

"His name is Parker," she said. "Colton Parker. He's a private investigator, and he wants to speak with Mr. Chatham about a missing persons case." She paused. "He said ten minutes tops." Another pause. "Okay, thanks." She hung up.

"Wants me to go right in?" I asked.

"Actually, he asked if you could have a seat. He's on the phone right now, but he agreed to meet with you for five minutes. He's a very busy man."

"Sure," I said.

I took one of the six seats in the reception area and began thumbing through a newsmagazine while I waited. For the next hour and a half, I listened to the soft chimes of an expensive phone system, followed by the "Chatham, Kern, and Brubaker—how may I direct your call?" answer of the receptionist. Still, I was able to put the time to good use and got the kind of education that's only available in a professional's waiting room. I read nearly every magazine available and got caught up on the latest diva to hit the airwaves. I also learned how to apply foundation if I ever decided to start wearing makeup, and I was introduced to the ups and downs of mutual fund investing. By the time I was ushered back to meet Chatham, I was a virtual know-it-all.

Chatham stood and extended a hand as the receptionist handed him my card. He glanced at it, smiled, and said, "Mr. Parker, I'm Douglas Chatham. Have a seat."

I shook his hand and sat.

He positioned himself in the big, high-backed leather chair behind his desk and made a sweeping gesture of looking at his watch, just in case I forgot that I only had five minutes. "How can I help you?" he asked.

My tenure with the bureau had led me to cross paths with many attorneys. Although the profession generally gets a bad rap, and they all seem to use the Shakespeare quote ("The first thing we do, let's kill all the lawyers") to serve themselves up as the underappreciated martyrs of society, most of them are good men and women who are trying to do a job. I wasn't getting the impression that Chatham was one of those good men.

"You know Lester Cheek."

He leaned back in his chair. He was a big man, overweight big, with thinning gray hair and a round belly. He looked like someone who had spent too much time in the chair and not enough engaged in physical labor. He was dressed in a light blue shirt that had white collars and cuffs, with a silk tie that was anchored by a glimmering gold tie clasp. He wore suspenders.

"Cheek," he said, as he stared at the ceiling and drummed his chin with the fingers of one hand. "Cheek, Cheek..."

I sighed. "Cut the act. It wasn't a question. You know Lester Cheek."

He remained in his "let me see if I can recall" posture but leveled his narrowing eyes at me. "Who did you say you are?"

"Colton Parker, trepid investigator." I said. I now had his undivided attention. Who could ignore anyone who was trepid?

"And what is it that you want?" He covered his mouth with a fist to stifle a cough.

"I want you to tell me about your relationship with Lester Cheek. I want to know why he considers you his enemy, and I want to know if you have any knowledge of the whereabouts of Claudia Cheek."

He looked at my card again. "His wife is missing?"

"Yep."

"Surely, you're not so stupid as to imply that I had anything to do with it."

"Actually, I guess I am that stupid. Or brazen. Depends on how you want to look at it and what my investigation eventually turns up. Right now, I'm looking for your take on Lester and why you two don't exchange Christmas cards."

He smiled as he went into his "aw, shucks" mode again. "Lester and I have had our differences. No question about it. But I haven't seen or talked to the man in a year or more. Nor do I care to."

"What happened between you two?" I asked.

"Nothing specific. I just view the man as a worm."

"Everyone I talk to sees him as a worm," I said. "Or a troll, or a dolt. Why does he mention you specifically as an enemy?"

He started to speak, then stopped, as he began to twiddle his thumbs over his ample belly.

"You only gave me five minutes, counselor. What do you say that we make the most of it?"

"I have filed several suits against the man," he said.

"For what?"

"Name it. Employee issues, slip and fall claims, unsafe working conditions. Things like that."

"That it?"

He shook his head. "No."

"Personal?"

He nodded. "I had a run-in with him over some land development. I, along with several other investors, wanted to develop our land for housing. Cheek wanted to open another pottery store. So…" He eased back in his chair and folded his hands across his ample middle. "We did battle."

"Sure."

"Anyway, he won."

I looked around the office. "You didn't set yourself up like this by being a victim," I said.

"No, I didn't. I'm actually quite capable in matters of the law. But Lester is connected. To be precise, he's loaded and connected. I couldn't fight his friends." He coughed again, but less violently this time.

"And the lawsuits?"

"Not personal. They're legitimate. I just happen to keep an eye out for him to mess up. When he does, I want to be there to clean it up."

"He got something you wanted," I said, "and now you want a piece of him."

"Something like that," he said. "He may have won on the land issue, but it'll cost him in the long run."

I stood. "Counselor, I would like to say that you have restored my faith in the law, but you haven't."

"Mr. Parker," he said, "I will need to have mine restored before I can restore someone else's."

CHAPTER EIGHT

I pulled out of the parking garage and headed north on Illinois Street. I wanted to talk to the next "enemy" on Lester's list, and that led me to the offices of Wrang and Associates, an architectural firm.

So far I had learned that Lester could be aggressive in his business practices and may even be capable of skirting employment laws, which sketched him as not being a particularly caring individual. All of this seemed to fit with Melanie's impression of him. But over the years, I've learned that impressions can be wrong, and someone can be aggressive in business but a real pussycat at home.

The Wrang and Associates building was far less impressive than the Hyatt. A one-story building with an asphalt parking lot, it appeared to have once been a house that had undergone several conversions. One vehicle was in the lot—a large Ford F-350 pickup.

I entered the reception area of Wrang and Associates and found a receptionist who was somewhat less attractive than the one at Chatham, Kern, and Brubaker. This one was tall, about six two, with a receding hair line and a full handlebar mustache. He was solidly built, with large hairy forearms and hands to match.

"Can I help you?" he asked.

I went through the usual routine of displaying my ID and telling him why I was there before asking if I could speak to Randall Wrang.

"You're speaking to him," he said as he stood to copy some paperwork.

I looked around the room. Though far less elaborate than the law offices, it was nicely furnished, with an aquarium in one corner, a television mounted in the ceiling in another, and a couple of potted plants in the other two. The tables held several magazines, mostly *Architectural Digest* with a few *Field and Stream* and a couple of *Bow Hunter* interspersed.

"No receptionist?"

He shook his head. "Not as of this morning. She quit." His face was awash in green light as the copier began to hum. "Wanted a raise, but I couldn't swing it. So..." He folded the lid of the copier closed as it continued to produce copies. "Here we are."

"Sorry," I said.

He shrugged. "What can I do for you?"

"I need to ask you about Lester Cheek."

His expression went flat. "Do you want an opinion?"

"Whatever you've got," I said.

"I don't care for the man. At all." He paused to look at me like he was seeing me for the first time. "Now, if I may ask, why do you want to know?"

"His wife is missing. I've been hired to find her. He has indicated you as one of his enemies."

"I'm not an enemy. I just don't like the man."

"What's the difference?" I asked.

"An enemy means harm. Someone who doesn't like you just doesn't care."

"Why don't you care?" I asked.

"Take a look around. See this office? See any receptionist here?"

"Sorry," I said, "but I don't follow you."

"I had a contract to design the Pottery Shack stores. I had designed several of them, and then all of a sudden, he yanks the deal."

"Broke the contract?"

"I lost a good part of my business and my reputation. When you lose a contract that size, other customers want to know why."

"I'll bite," I said. "Why did you lose it?"

He shrugged again. "Don't know. He just said that he wanted to go in a different direction. I told him we could design any direction he wanted. But he said no. And that was that."

"And that's why you're doing double duty as CEO and receptionist?" I asked.

He nodded as he slid into the chair behind the desk. "Yep."

I looked around the office. "You busy?"

He shook his head. "I have a couple of houses in Terre Haute, a church in Muncie."

"His wife is missing," I repeated.

"I don't care. I don't like the man, and I don't wish him well in anything he does. I hope she takes him to the cleaners."

CHAPTER NINE

I picked Callie up from school an hour before she was scheduled to end the day. She had an appointment with her psychologist, and we were running late.

As soon as we entered the doctor's office and checked in, the receptionist led us back to a large conference room. I was told to have a seat and make myself at home. Callie was taken to another room, where she would meet with Dr. Sebastian. I would meet with him following her evaluation.

I was alone in the conference room for nearly forty-five minutes. The receptionist brought me a Coke, and there were several current magazines to choose from. Unlike those in Chatham's office, however, these periodicals seemed more oriented for Sebastian's clientele. I was working the "Can You Find the Hidden Pictures" puzzle in the most recent copy of *Highlights* when the receptionist asked me to follow her to Sebastian's office.

When I entered, Sebastian stood and extended a hand. A big man who resembled the actor Sebastian Cabot, the psychologist had an amiable personality that instantly put me at ease. He offered me a seat.

"Callie is the next room," he said. "I thought we should talk without her present."

"Sure," I said.

"Callie is in trouble."

I'm a straight shooter. I like it when others shoot straight with me. "How much trouble?" I asked.

He crossed one leg over the other and folded his clasped hands around one knee. "I would say, at the outset, that I do not feel she is at risk for another attempt."

I was relieved, though not completely. I understood that Sebastian's assessment, based on education and experience, wasn't guaranteed to be correct. "That's good," I said.

He nodded. "Yes. But I would say that she *is* at risk for additional problems."

"Such as?"

"Well, let's back up. Callie has experienced some traumatic events. Tough enough, I would say, for any adult, let alone a young girl who is entering the formative years." He readjusted his position, uncrossing his legs and recrossing them the other way. "These early teen years are often critical in helping a girl to become the woman she will be someday." He paused to see if I was with him. I was, so he continued. "So when something of this magnitude occurs—in Callie's instance, the death of her mother—it can shake up her sense of well-being. And, given the other issues she has talked with me about, I think she may be losing her overall sense of self. It's that loss of her self-image that concerns me the most."

"What do I do?" I asked.

He smiled. "Well, unlike what you may see on TV or the movies, I'm not going to tell you that Callie hates her mother. On the contrary, from what I was able to gather during our visit today, this young lady very much adored her mother."

"Yes."

"And her love for her mother, along with the closeness they had, has left her feeling the void all the more deeply."

"Yes."

He paused to study me. "You two are not close." It wasn't a question.

"No."

"You're having a hard time finding your center with her."

"Yes." I shifted in my seat.

"Callie is thirteen. I would say that, at this age, it's important for her to have an anchor."

I shifted again.

"You will be that anchor."

I nodded.

"Or someone or something else will be. Do you understand, Mr. Parker?"

"Yes."

"She tells me that she's close to her grandparents. Do they see her often?"

"She was living with them for a time after Anna's death. I had just started the business, and—"

"You are a private detective?"

"Yes. I had just started the business and didn't have the money to provide for her. I had just lost my job, and our financial position was precarious."

He nodded.

"I also felt," I continued, "that the change in schools, so soon after Anna's death, would be equally upsetting."

"And yet you took her in to live with you earlier than you had planned."

"Yes. After her attempt, I felt that her need to be with me outweighed her other needs."

"Children see what we do, more than they hear what we say. Would you agree?"

"Sure."

"Your statements to Callie that you weren't in a position to care for her, followed by the fact that you took her in to do just that, are confusing."

I hadn't thought of it that way.

"I think the best thing you can do, Mr. Parker, is to be consistent.

Children, even thirteen-year-old girls, need consistency. It provides them with security. And, given the events of her recent life, consistency is what she most needs."

"Consistency," I said.

He nodded. "She told me that her mother was a Christian."

"Yes. Anna converted to Christianity shortly before her death."

"And you?"

I shook my head.

"Well, Mr. Parker, I too am a Christian. And although I won't attempt to convert you," he paused to smile, "I would suggest that you see to it that Callie sees her church friends and participates in the church structure as much as possible."

"Because of Anna?"

"That's one reason, sure. The other is that it provides a sense of stability. She told me that she attended church with your wife regularly. Continuing the same things she did with her mother will help her feel secure. And right now, she needs that rock—that sense of security— more than anything else."

"I understand," I said.

"Does she have a female she could confide in? Her grandmother, perhaps?"

I told him that Callie and her grandmother, Corrin, were close. And I told him about Mary and her love of soccer. I told him it was something she shared with Callie.

He nodded. "Tap them," he said. "Her grandmother is her connection to the past and to her mother. Mary can support her dreams for the future and help her grow into the young lady you and her mother meant for her to be. And she will need to rely on you too."

"She can," I said.

"I know she can," he said. "The main source of her strength, of her sense of well-being, will come from you. She needs to know that regardless of what happens, you will not be shaken. That you will not move."

He rose and extended his hand. I rose to take it.

"I want to see a lot of Callie over the next several months. I'm certain we can help her get on the right track."

"Of course," I said.

"And, Mr. Parker…"

"Yes?"

"I will be praying for her as well."

CHAPTER TEN

Dinner that evening was a pizza, ordered in, with breadsticks and cheese sauce. Not exactly nutritional, but easy. Another reminder of how far I had to go to be the father Callie needed.

After dinner, we worked on homework. Judging by the reception I was getting, she would much rather have done it alone. Guessing by the answers we were coming up with on her algebra, she probably would have been better off.

After the homework was done and the dishes put away, I tried engaging her in conversation. That didn't work. I saw a game on TV and offered to let her stay up later than usual and watch the game with me and share a bowl of popcorn. That didn't work either. Finally, as bedtime approached, she announced that she was tired and had a big day at school the next day. She said good night and went off to bed.

I flicked on the TV, and except for the game, I saw nothing that interested me. In fact, I didn't see anything else that should interest anyone. So I decided to work on the checkbook. Or rather, the checkbook worked on me.

When the bills were paid, I had a total of $218 in savings, not counting the small nest egg I had managed to build from the sale of the home that Anna and I had owned. I had sold the house in order to finance the

---

business and to keep it afloat until it could become self-sustaining. That didn't seem to be happening too quickly, which was causing the small nest egg to become even smaller. Our dwindling savings, along with Callie's mounting medical bills, were causing concern for me, but not one that I could share with her.

After finishing the checkbook, I sat in the living room and flipped through the channels again. I couldn't afford cable, so I spent most of the evening surfing the six channels that were available. I found two game shows, the baseball game I had offered to Callie but which no longer held any interest for me, an old movie that interested me even less, a talk show with two adversaries arguing over which direction the senate ought to go in the next election, and a special on the lifestyle of the ant.

I got up from the sofa, leaving the television on for the noise, and went into the kitchen to get a Coke. I had popped the can and poured the soft drink over ice when the phone rang.

"Colton?" It was Frank, Anna's father. "Corrin wanted me to call. She said the youth group at the church is going to take in a movie this weekend. They were wondering if Callie would like to come along."

"Sure," I said. "Of course, I'll have to ask her, but I'm sure she'll want to go."

"Corrin and I think it will be good for her. Help her to reestablish some old ties. Get back into the swing of her normal life."

I agreed. And I was grateful. Given Sebastian's suggestion to keep Callie's life as consistent as possible, an activity with friends, even if they weren't old friends, was the kind of thing that could help her find her center again.

"You'll let us know soon?" he asked.

I told him that I would and hung up.

Back in the living room, the narrator on the TV was telling me about the treacherous world of the ant.

"They live a life of challenge," he said. "And, like a team, they work to bring in the harvest, where all can enjoy the bounty. Although one ant is strong, when facing the challenges of his world by himself, he is weak.

But when he learns to be part of the whole, to work in harmony with the other ants, he is strong. Each of them, relying on the others and working together, help their neighbors to live life, provide for their young, and become contributing members of their community."

Although one ant is strong, when facing the challenges of his world by himself, he is weak.

As I stood in the living room among the pictures of Anna, I became acutely aware of how small I was and just how isolated I had allowed myself to become.

CHAPTER ELEVEN

The next morning, I drove to the west side of town and found the last "enemy" on my list.

His name was Andrew Carne, and he had been a member of the Indianapolis city council for almost ten years. Based on everything I had read, he had been a straight arrow. Known for being stalwart in his work, he could sometimes alienate others on the council with his inflexibility and unwillingness to compromise. That meant he was a loner. A lone ant. *A lot like me,* I thought as I arrived at his home.

"Come in," he said after I identified myself.

He led me into the living room. It was nice, with a full-wall stone fireplace, a cathedral ceiling of rustic-looking cedar, and a large rug on well-maintained hardwood flooring.

"So," he said, motioning for me to have a seat on the sofa as he sat in one of two recliners, "you want to know about Lester Cheek."

"I want to know your take on him. He has listed you as an enemy. I'd like to know why," I said.

Carne was tall and thin with equally thin hair. His features were angular, and his fingers were long and bony. His Adam's apple bobbed when he talked, which gave him an Ichabod Crane appearance.

"You're not here for that," he said. "I have enemies too. You can't be in politics or business as long as Lester and I have been without having enemies. Why are you here, specifically?"

"His wife is missing. He listed you as an enemy."

"Is he accusing me of having brought harm to her?"

"He isn't accusing anyone of anything. I'm just trying to be thorough," I said.

He rested his arms on the arms of the chair and began drumming his fingers. "I don't like the man. But I don't consider myself an enemy. More of an adversary."

"There's a difference?"

"In politics there is," he said. "An enemy is someone who you wish or need to annihilate. In politics, adversaries are people who may oppose your position on one issue but who may very well be your strongest ally on another. People like Lester tend to see anyone who opposes them, regardless of the venue, as an enemy. He's withdrawn. Isolated. Not what you would call a people person. The result is that many people don't know him, so they don't like him. He doesn't cultivate friendships."

"It becomes self-perpetuating," I said.

"Exactly. A person like Lester soon begins to feel as if the whole world is in concert against him."

"Why does he mention you specifically?" I asked.

"Probably because the man was instrumental in my downfall. I tried to block an initiative that he wanted to see go through the city council. It was nearing election time, so he threw his considerable money and weight behind my opponent."

"And you lost."

He nodded. "Yes, I lost. Now, Lester sees me as someone who wants revenge. Nothing could be further from the truth. I'm quite happy now, being out of politics. Although I will admit I didn't see it that way at the time."

"Did you make any threats against him?"

He laughed. "Heavens no. You don't make threats in politics—you might need to work with that person later. I was in that game too long to go making threats." He shook his head. "No, I just took the defeat and went on with my life. Now I have more time with my wife and grandchildren. Losing that election was a blessing."

"He has friends on the city council?"

Carne nodded. "I think the better term would be business associates. As I said, Lester builds very few friendships. But he's a very effective businessman, Mr. Parker. Nothing illegal that I know of, just aggressive business tactics. But unfortunately, the extent of his friendships lie within the mutually beneficial aspects of them."

"Scratch my back and I'll scratch yours?"

He nodded. "Yes. I would say that that's about right."

"Do you know Douglas Chatham?" I was fishing. I wanted to see if any of the enemies on Lester's list knew each other. I wanted to see if any case for collusion or conspiracy could be made.

Carne chuckled. "Oh, yes. I know Douglas. His efforts prompted me to try and block Lester's initiative."

"How's that?" I asked.

"Well, Chatham had planned a new road through some property that he owned along with some other investors. Lester wanted us to leave the land alone so he could build a new pottery store across the street."

"But wouldn't a new road help his business?"

"Not in this case. If the road had gone through, new housing developments would have sprung up, and the area wouldn't have been zoned for commercial use. It was a quirk of fate, but the way it played out, the land was more valuable to Chatham and, I believe, the citizens of Indianapolis. At any rate," he said with a sigh, "Lester won, and Chatham has been chafing ever since. It's one of the reasons I was glad to get out of politics."

"What about Wrang? Do you know him?"

He smiled. "Oh, yes. He put all of his eggs in Lester's basket. He tried to build his firm solely on Lester's business. When Lester found another architect, Wrang lost his shirt. He's fuming."

"Could he be a threat?" I asked.

He nodded thoughtfully. "Maybe. His association with Lester certainly cost him a good deal of money."

"What happened between Lester and Wrang?" I asked.

Carne sighed. "Well, as I said, Lester is an aggressive businessman. And he can write a contract like nobody's business."

"I don't follow," I said.

"Lester wanted Wrang to design the stores. Ten of them. So he offered Randall a nice contract to come to work for the Pottery Shack."

"As an employee?" I asked.

Carne nodded. "Yes, that's right. So when Wrang designed the first of the stores in his contract, Lester wanted an expanded version of the same design. That's not uncommon. Businesses like Lester's usually will maintain the same motif. It helps them to establish an identity of sorts."

"Sure," I said. "A lot of fast-food places do the same."

Carne nodded again. "That's right. Then, when customers move to a new community, they see the same design and immediately identify it with the product and, hopefully, the same quality of service."

"Sure. Makes it easy to establish a connection with new customers in a dynamic market."

"Correct. Well, at any rate, when Randall had completed the basic and then the expanded design, Lester fired him."

"Why?"

"Since Randall was an employee of the Pottery Shack and not a contractor, any design that Randall drew now belonged to Lester. So—"

"Lester didn't need him anymore, and Randall was out in the cold. He'd sold his business, and now he'd lost his employment and his designs—"

"So he had to start all over. Which he did," Carne said. "Unfortunately, there was some bad blood between Wrang and Lester, to say the least. So, when Randall started to get the business off the ground, Lester let word leak out that he had fired Randall. With Lester's visibility and leadership in the business community, Wrang and Associates soon became just Wrang."

"No associates," I said.

"That's correct."

I stood to shake his hand. "Thank you for taking the time to talk with me," I said. "You've given me something to think about."

"I hope this helped. And I do hope you find his wife," he said, standing and following me to the door. "The man is incomplete without her."

CHAPTER TWELVE

Movies always portray the work I do as exciting. The lone detective, embittered by life, struggles to right the wrongs of the world. It makes for good entertainment, but that's all. Leads don't drop out of the sky. They usually come by way of boring and painstaking work. I had spent the past couple of days going over receipts and bank statements and talking to people who, in truth, weren't all that exciting. But the effort paid off. I did have a lead. In fact, I had a couple.

Claudia had run out on her husband. The police and I were in agreement on that. But that left me with two unanswered questions. The first was why? The second was where? I couldn't answer the why. Not yet. But Claudia had charged travel arrangements just a few days prior to leaving Lester. With a little bit of luck, I would soon be able to answer the where. Which, of course, might lead me to the why.

Lester had enemies, and right now, Wrang was at the top of my list. If harm had come to Claudia, the architect seemed to be the most likely suspect.

Claudia, on the other hand, had no enemies and seemed to enjoy everyone's favor. To be fair, she had the fun job. Working the charities, participating in social events, and sitting on civic boards will tend to endear you to everyone. Lester, on the other hand, was making decisions that affected other people's lives. I expected him to have enemies. By his own account, he had been on the outs with society for years. Since childhood in fact. And a lifetime of torment could make anyone see the world as an enemy. But things are rarely the way they seem, and until I found differently, I was going to have to keep an open mind. But that was becoming harder to do as I met the people on Lester's list.

I stopped at a Shell station to top off the tank and buy a Coke before getting back on the road.

I had exhausted Lester's list of enemies with varied results. But perception can be reality. If Lester perceived someone as his enemy, then he would react to him in that fashion. In a sense, he would become one for all practical purposes. But after years of being pushed aside and harassed, it was easy to see why Lester saw the world as his nemesis.

Still, it was far too early in the investigation to start formulating opinions, and I needed to check out the travel agency on Claudia's bank statements. If a rich woman were going to leave her husband, a travel agency would be a good place to start. I had a knack for picking up on the obvious leads.

Easy Travel ("We make it *easy* for you") was housed in a brick building on West Rockville Road in what had probably once been a bank. Inside were the usual racks of brochures touting a lifetime of fulfillment after just seven days on the beaches of St. Thomas, a cruise to the Bahamas, or a trip to Europe. For the moment, I was finding all the fulfillment I needed in the building's air conditioning.

"Can I help you?" a middle-aged woman asked. She had thinning hair and sat behind a metal desk that had been painted pink. A pair of glasses hung about her neck on a pink chain, overlying a pink blouse. Her manicured nails were painted with a glossy pink, and a pair of pink stones dangled from each ear. I glanced at the nameplate on the desk. Sharon Twiddle—Travel Consultant.

"My name's Colton Parker," I said, "and I was wondering if you have sold any travel to—"

"We don't sell travel, Mr. Parker. We sell dreams." She smiled on "dreams," almost singing the word.

"Sure," I said. "I was wondering if you have sold any dreams to this lady." I showed her the picture of Claudia that Lester had given me.

"Oh, yes, of course. Mrs. Seymour."

I've been told by the group of friends that I play poker with on occasion that I don't have much of a poker face. My expression must have given me away. The pink lady gave me a "Did I say something wrong?" look. I flipped the picture over, looked at it again, and then re-displayed it to Sharon.

"This lady is who?"

"Mrs. Seymour?" she said, this time as a question rather than a statement.

"Are you sure?" I asked.

"Well, I'm pretty sure." She turned to the other woman who was sitting at a desk in the back. This woman—and desk—seemed more subdued.

"Betty, do you remember this lady? Purchased a travel voucher here about a week ago."

Betty came over to where the pink lady and I were talking. She was wearing a smoke gray suit with a white blouse and had a pair of glasses perched on the end of her nose that was anchored by a gold chain. She gave me the once over before looking at the picture.

"Of course," she said. "This is Mrs. Seymour. Frances Seymour, I believe. Why? Who are you?"

"Mrs. Seymour is missing," I said.

"Oh my," Sharon said.

"And I'm trying to find her."

Betty continued to look at me. "Can I see some ID?" she asked.

I showed her what she wanted to see and asked, "What is a travel voucher?"

She sighed and gave me the once-over again before answering, "Clients may want to take a trip or vacation but not yet know where they would like to go. So they can purchase a voucher for an amount of money that is equal to their choice of travel options, and then cash that voucher in later when they have made their decision."

"And sometimes," Sharon added, "they can give them as gifts."

"What we're talking about here," I said, "is a gift certificate."

Both women nodded.

"Do the certificates have expirations dates?" I asked.

"They will often need to be redeemed within a prescribed time frame," Betty said. "That is typically one year from the date of purchase."

"So these are used most often as a sort of prepaid trip."

"Yes," Betty said.

"And that would make them excellent for someone who needed to leave sometime soon but who didn't know for sure where they were going to go."

"That is correct," Betty said.

"Has Mrs. Seymour redeemed her certificate?" I asked.

She studied me for a few moments with the same stern look she had given me since I entered the building. Then, turning to Sharon she said, "May I use your computer?"

Sharon stood up, giving Betty access. After a few keystrokes, she said, "No. She has not used the voucher. The computer says she hasn't redeemed it at any of our affiliated agencies."

Since she had just purchased it, I felt I could safely assume the certificate had not yet expired.

"Do you have an address for Mrs. Seymour?" I asked.

Her concern for her client overruled her obvious distrust of me.

She gave me the address. It was Lester's.

"Did she express any interest in any particular place? Did she seem like she knew where she wanted to go?"

Stern Betty and pink Sharon glanced at each other before looking at me and shaking their heads.

"This lady is missing," I said. "Her husband is desperate to find her. If you know anything that could be helpful, now would be the time to tell me."

They looked at each other again. This time, the two had joint expressions of confusion. It was Betty who spoke. "Did you say that her husband is looking for her?"

"Yes."

"He came in with her to buy the voucher," Sharon said.

Something didn't feel right. I had asked Lester if Claudia had mentioned any travel plans. If he came with her to purchase a travel voucher, even if it was for use at a later date, why didn't he say so?

"What did this man look like?" I asked.

The women looked at each other again.

"Tall and thin, with a scowl. Like Clint Eastwood," Betty said.

"But thinner," Sharon said. Then, turning to Betty, she said, "Clint Eastwood? I thought he looked more like John Carradine."

CHAPTER THIRTEEN

I didn't need to check with Lester. The description the two travel agents had given of Claudia's "husband" did not match the husband she had at home.

Despite Carne's statement that Wrang could be a threat, it was certainly starting to look like another man was involved. If that was the case, I was going to have to break the news to Lester. He was suspecting it, of course, and would find out soon enough when Claudia's attorneys began their predatory march toward his assets. But I felt like he ought to hear it from me first, from someone who didn't see his pain as an opportunity to make a buck. Unless my view of him changed, I felt that he deserved that much.

I was heading out of the parking lot of Easy Travel when my cell phone rang. It was Mary.

"Just wanted to let you know that nothing has turned up on your Jag yet. If it was sold or has had new tags issued, it has to have happened within the last hour or so. At least there is nothing as of noon today."

I thanked her and asked if she had eaten yet. She hadn't, so we made a date to meet at Armatzio's in half an hour.

Armatzio's was a popular Italian restaurant on the very near south side of Indianapolis, run by Tony and Francesca Armatzio, whose old-country personae added to the ambience. It was a longtime favorite of the Indianapolis law enforcement community too, and it wasn't uncommon to see local cops, federal agents, or federal judges discussing the latest investigation or constitutional issue over a plate of pasta or Armatzio's signature Chicken Parmesan. Mary was already in a booth, chatting with Tony Armatzio, when I arrived.

Tony extended a hand. "He-ey, Colton."

I shook his hand. "Tony."

"The usual, no?"

"The usual," I said, sliding into the booth opposite Mary.

He turned to her. "And you, Mizz Police Woman. What will you be having this fine day?"

"What's his usual?" she said, nodding toward me.

"Linguini with clam sauce and a hint—" Tony made an *O* with his thumb and forefinger—"just a tiny hint of oregano."

She paused to think. "Sure," she said. "That sounds good. Make it two usuals."

As Tony moved away I said, "What's with him?"

"He hit it big," she said.

"How much?"

"I don't know for sure, but he said it was more than a year of car payments."

Tony Armatzio was a gambling man. The ponies to be exact. Although his wife pretended to not know, we all suspected that she probably did and chose to ignore it. It was one of the few pleasures in life that Tony had. The other was his car. He always had a penchant for the imported kind. Big, flashy, and fully equipped. He leased a new one every year. When combining that fact with his knack for understatement, "more than a year's car payments" meant that he had done very well indeed.

"So, how have you spent your day?" Mary asked, pulling apart a bread stick.

I told her about Claudia, about the travel arrangements and the withdrawal of the money. I told her about Chatham and his grudge against

Lester. She nodded thoughtfully as I talked, and she waited until I had finished before offering her wisdom and insight, finely tuned after ten years as an FBI Special Agent.

"Are you that desperate for business? She left him for another man. Come on, Colton, get some real cases."

"I was hoping you could offer some insight," I said. "Some kernel that would indicate I was moving in the right direction. And just for the record, if any real cases would happen to come through the door, I would be all too happy to take them."

She shook her head. "Nope. Sorry. I think you're all washed up on this one big guy. She ran out on him—took him for a bundle. He'll be hearing from some expensive divorce lawyer soon who'll clean him out of the rest."

"You're hard," I said. "A hard, hard, woman."

She smiled, and I couldn't help but smile back. Mary was attractive. She was athletic, tall, and tanned, with thick black hair that cascaded around her shoulders and bounced with every move. I was attracted to her. Who wouldn't be? But then Anna would come to mind, and my heart would burn. It was too soon after her death, making any attraction I felt for Mary a useless exercise in cardiac gymnastics.

"What I am is grounded in reality," she said. "A realist. I've seen it too often before. And so have you."

She was right, of course. Claudia *had* run out on Lester and probably would soon send word that she had filed for divorce. But why the phony name? What was the point?

"So," Mary said, "what are you going to do about Callie?"

I took a bread stick from the basket. "I don't know. I'm stuck. No matter what I do she doesn't respond. Since her incident, she's totally shut me out."

"But she did want to come and live with you, right?"

"Right."

"And she hasn't asked to move back in with Anna's parents, right?"

"Right."

"So it sounds like she really does want a relationship with you. She just doesn't know how to get past the anger yet."

"I don't blame her," I said. "But—"

"You're not responsible for Anna's death. That whole idea is just absurd."

"Anna and I fought that night, Mary," I said. "She stormed out of the house and went for a drive and never came back. Callie saw us arguing."

"Just because Callie sees it as your fault doesn't mean it is."

The restaurant was beginning to fill up. I leaned forward and lowered my voice. "Mary, I see it as my fault. I messed up on the job and got fired. I messed up by arguing that night and Anna got killed. I was the one who was supposed to be a father to Callie but was always too busy with the job. That was my responsibility and I blew it."

Mary dipped a piece of bread stick into the marinara sauce. "How old is Callie?"

I had been on a roll, chugging down the tracks with my pity party when her question derailed my train. I settled back in my seat. "Thirteen," I said. "Why?"

"Thirteen? And you think you blew it? Let me tell you, Colton, you haven't blown it until that girl is out from under your roof—from under your influence. You haven't blown it until she shuts the door for good. That hasn't happened yet. But it will if you don't quit beating up on yourself and instead start beating up on the demons that girl is wrestling with."

"I've never been good at relationships—"

"Hooey! You can blame the fact that your mother abandoned you," she said, "or that you were shuttled from home to home, or that you are bitter toward God, society, or yourself. But at some point, you're going to have to come to grips with the situation and deal with it from whatever position you find yourself in."

"Here we go," Tony said, setting two plates of linguine on the table. "Anything else?"

I looked at Mary. She shook her head.

"Nope. That'll be all, Tony," I said.

"You enjoy. Is on the house." He spun away.

"He must've hit it a lot bigger than he's willing to admit," I said.

"Don't change the subject, Colton."

"I'm not. I was just making an observation."

"I know life has thrown you a curve. I know Anna's death and Callie's accident are formidable obstacles. I know you lost your mother as a baby. I lost a mother too, remember?"

"Your mother died, Mary. She didn't abandon you. She didn't leave you on the steps of the hospital ER with a note pinned to your clothing. You didn't grow up wondering how come your mother didn't love you enough to be in your life."

"No, but I—"

"You didn't watch the other mothers organize parties for your third-grade class and wonder what it would be like if you had a mother too. It leaves you with some serious self-esteem problems." I was beginning to feel sorry for myself again.

"No, Colton, I didn't. You're right. I haven't had those experiences. But we're not talking about you. We're talking about Callie. And I have been where she is. I did lose a mother and live the rest of my life with a part-time father. And I know that if you don't overcome whatever issues you're dealing with, that girl will slip away. And then, it *will* be too late."

CHAPTER FOURTEEN

No one likes to be told they're wrong, that they're going down the wrong path. But every once in a while, it's a necessary thing to hear. I didn't like what Mary had had to say. I didn't like the idea that she had such an accurate grasp of the situation. It made me feel exposed— spiritually and emotionally naked. Her words had struck their target somewhere deep within me. And I had kept it deep within me precisely because I didn't want anyone discovering it. But she had, and she had been right.

I knew that I had issues to resolve. Most of them had been created as a result of my need to right the wrongs. I had been abandoned by my mother and never knew my father. Most of my life had been spent in a series of foster homes, dreaming of the day when I could become a man and take control of my life. Now, forty years into it, I was trying to do just that and was making a mess of it.

I spent much of the night lying awake, thinking about what Mary had said and trying to find a solution to a difficult problem. But as the night wore on, the twin shadows of fear and doubt refused to surrender to even the tiniest ray of hope.

The next morning, I rose with the sun and checked on Callie. She was still asleep, so I closed the bedroom door and went into the kitchen.

I turned on the television, a nine-inch black-and-white that I kept on the counter near the stove, and started the coffee.

Until I met Anna, I had never been much of a breakfast eater. My years of law enforcement with its stakeouts, late-night arrests, and raids had quelled my need to eat first thing in the morning. Sleep was what I wanted the most. And the few times that I did have breakfast, it was the stereotypical cop-eating-a-donut kind.

But Anna had changed all of that, making sure that Callie and I left the house each day with a nutritionally sound meal. I wanted to continue that for Callie's sake. I wanted to keep as many of her routines in place as possible. Especially mealtime, and especially in light of my conversation with Sebastian.

The problem is that I don't cook. Except for breakfast, I'm strictly a thaw-it-out-and-heat-it-up kind of guy. But by the time the coffee was finished, I had scrambled some eggs, made some toast, and had a few strips of bacon going. Within a few minutes, I had Cally's place set and was putting a glass of milk on the table when I heard the local news update followed by the weather report that predicted another day of record heat.

"That's just great," I said, as I poured a cup of coffee.

I sat at the table with the morning paper and had just started the sports section when I heard Callie's alarm. She came to the table a few minutes later.

"Rise and shine," I said, spooning the eggs and bacon onto her plate. It was clear from her bleary expression that while she had indeed risen, she was not shining.

"Grandpa called the other night," I said. "He said that some of your friends from church are getting together this weekend to see a movie. They wanted to know if you could come along."

She forked the eggs over a couple times before trying them. "Yeah."

"Good. I'll find out from Grandpa what time you need to be there."

For most of the rest of breakfast she was quiet. That in itself wasn't unusual. What was unusual was that she agreed to attend the movie. A ray of hope between the fear and doubt.

After she ate, showered, and dressed for school, I saw her off on the bus and then washed the dishes and set them in the rack to dry. My interview with Sharon and Betty had tended to support the notion that Claudia was involved with another man and that she was planning on leaving with him soon. That meant I was going to have to eventually tell Lester of my suspicions that his wife had left him and that no evil had befallen her. I had wanted to wait until I found Claudia and talked to her. I didn't want Lester hearing half-truths. But I was convinced that the pain of his not knowing was the greater evil.

I changed my clothes and worked out with the free weights I had stockpiled in the basement. I finished off with a three-mile run around the periphery of Garfield Park, showered, shaved, and got ready to tell Lester the bad news.

I called him and asked if we could meet at his home. I didn't know how he was going to react, so if he didn't handle it well, I thought he might do it better there than on the sales floor.

I was halfway to his house when Mary called.

"What's up?" I said as I flipped the phone open.

"We found your car."

"The Jag? Where?"

"The state police found it in a ditch south of Terre Haute, along US 41."

"A ditch?"

"Colton, they said there's blood in the car."

I took the exit that I would have taken to get to Lester's house, but then I circled around and got back onto the interstate, heading the direction I had just come from.

"Where is it now?" I asked.

"Still there. Troopers are going over it now. I got wind of it a few minutes ago. I talked to the trooper in charge at the scene. I told him of your interest, and he said if you showed up before they left, he would talk with you. I don't think he's too keen on it though."

"I'll charm him," I said and hung up.

I called Lester, told him that there had been some developments, and promised that I would talk with him as soon as I checked them out. He said he would wait for me at his home.

It took a little more than an hour to reach the area where the police found Claudia's car, and by the time I got there, the Jag was hanging off the end of a tow truck.

I parked a few yards behind the suspended car and approached a gaggle of Indiana state troopers. Some of them were in uniform and some weren't. As I approached, all heads turned toward me. I displayed my ID to the highest-ranking uniform, a lieutenant who was taking notes, and asked to see the trooper in charge.

"That's me," one of the plainclothes troopers said. I approached him and extended a hand.

"I'm Colton Parker. I believe you spoke with Special Agent Christopher about me."

"Yeah." He sized me up as he shook my hand. "I'm David Chang."

Chang was about five nine or ten with a lean build and a clean-cut appearance. He was a mix of Caucasian and Asian and was immaculately dressed in a smoke gray pinstriped suit, a dark subdued tie, and black wing tips that gleamed like polished shale. A badge was clipped to the breast pocket of his coat.

I told him about Claudia, that I suspected she had run out on Lester, and that I had been on my way to meet with him and give him the bad news when Mary had called.

"Well, I think I would be less inclined to say she ran out on him if I were you. There is a considerable amount of blood inside the trunk."

"Could I take a look?"

His heavy sigh, hanging head, and full minute of total silence served to tell me he wasn't excited about the idea.

"Pop the trunk," he finally said to one of the troopers as he moved to the rear of the Jag.

I followed him as one of the uniforms reached through the open driver's window and pushed the trunk release button.

"Don't touch anything," Chang said.

I had a witty response but held it in check. Discipline is the mother of fortune.

I leaned over the open trunk that was nearly knee height as the front end of the car hung from the tow truck. Inside, the once plush carpeting was saturated with blood. It was beginning to smell like soured milk.

"Do you think the murder was done in the car, or was the body transported?"

Chang shrugged. "Don't know for sure that it was a murder. We don't have a body or a weapon."

"But you have a strong suspicion."

"That we do."

"And you have a name. Claudia Cheek."

"We have an APB on her."

"And you have her bloody and abandoned car."

"I said we have an APB on her." Chang slammed the trunk lid closed.

"Sure," I said. "Was the registration in the car?"

"Registered to a Claudia Cheek." He gave me Lester's address.

"Prints?" I asked.

He took a step back and looked at me as if I had suddenly turned into a banana.

"Why yes. You know, I believe we did dust for those. Much obliged to you for asking."

I thought it was best to ignore the remark and move on. "Any idea how long it's been here?" I asked, nodding toward the car.

"Well now, you know, we sometimes forget high-end police technology like fingerprints, but we do pride ourselves on good old standbys like observation."

"So when did you observe the car in the ditch?"

Chang turned to the lieutenant, who was still taking notes. "Jackson, when did you see the car here?"

"This morning, 'bout six. Why?"

"Private investigator Parker wants to know how long the car sat here before you noticed it." Chang was taking on a southern sheriff drawl. He was starting to sound a lot like Jackie Gleason's character in *Smokey and the Bandit*. The impression I had gotten earlier, that they didn't want me at their crime scene, was getting stronger.

"Is that so?" Jackson said, flipping his notebook closed and moving to where Chang and I were standing. He stopped less than a foot from my face.

"Yes, Virginia," I said. "It's so."

"You see," Chang said, "Jackson, here, patrols this stretch of highway all night long. And if he had seen this car in the ditch, he would have done something about it."

"Which doesn't include notifying you," Jackson said.

"Which brings us to another pivotal point," Chang said, dropping the drawl. "This is now a police investigation. Stay out of our way."

"Sure," I said, turning to go back to my car.

"We mean it," Chang yelled after me.

"Gee," I said. "In that case, I really care."

CHAPTER FIFTEEN

By the time I reached Lester's house, it was apparent that he had already heard about the discovery of Claudia's car. He greeted me at the door, disheveled and in obvious distress. He led me to the room where we had had our first conversation. I sat in the same chair I had before as he slouched in his. His eyes were red-rimmed, and he had that vacant stare that seems to define the hopeless.

"You've heard," I said.

He nodded his head.

"Who told you?"

"A state trooper. He said they found Claudia's car in a ditch just outside Terre Haute." His voice was mechanical. "They wanted to know where I was last night."

"It's routine, Lester. They need to check all the possibilities."

"Do they think I killed Claudia?"

"They have to check out all the possibilities," I said again. "It's routine."

He sighed, and nodded.

"Lester, is there any reason why Claudia would need to drive to Terre Haute?"

He shook his head. "No."

"She have any family or friends there?"

He shook his head.

"Any MAC commitments there?"

"No."

"Had she discussed any desire to travel recently?" I asked again to see if I got a different answer.

He shook his head.

I told him about my trip to Easy Travel and about the travel voucher she had purchased. I did not tell him about the alias she had used or about Clint Eastwood.

"I don't know about any travel plans," he said, "I don't know about any of this." His eyes began to refill. "I just know that something bad has happened to Claudia."

I tried to be reassuring. "We don't really know anything yet. All we know for sure is that her car has been found."

"In a ditch," he said. "With blood in it. *Her* blood."

I was a little annoyed that the police had told him about the blood in the car. It wouldn't have been standard procedure. They generally like to save that stuff and use it as leverage when interrogating a person of interest, which Lester now was, of course. But if Lester had asked about signs of foul play, maybe a rookie cop could have said something he shouldn't have said.

"We don't know it was her blood."

"Who else's would it be?"

It was a good question. But if Claudia had been murdered, why the travel arrangements? Why leave with her luggage and personal affects? And who was the man with her at Easy Travel? "The car could have been stolen," I said for need of something to say.

It was obvious from the subtle change in his expression that he hadn't considered anything but the worst.

"Maybe the thief was in an accident and left the car." I was trying to offer him something to hang on to.

"You think that could've happened?"

"Sure," I lied. "Why not?"

He shrugged. "I don't know. Maybe it could have."

"The important thing," I said, "is to not give up. We don't really know anything for sure. Not yet."

"We know Claudia is missing. We know that for sure."

He was teetering again.

"Yes, we do. And we'll find her."

He looked at me with ever-reddening eyes. "When, Mr. Parker? When?"

Chapter Sixteen

I called Mary and told her I wanted to know as soon as possible about any evidence the state police uncovered from the car.

"Well, I wouldn't expect a call from Chang," she said. "It doesn't sound like the two of you hit if off too well."

"You've talked to him?"

"Oh yeah. He wanted to make it clear that you're to stay out of what is now an official police investigation."

"Yeah," I said. "He told me the same thing."

"He said he didn't think you were going to listen too well."

"I told him that I cared."

"Just like that? Just the way you said it to me?"

"No."

She sighed a heavy sigh.

"From what you told me earlier, it didn't sound like he wanted to hit it off well anyway," I said.

"True," she said. "He knew who you were."

Knew who you were. My career with the FBI had been marked with a series of headstrong maneuvers, characteristic of my desire to avoid bureaucracy—which was not especially desirable when one worked for the Federal *Bureau* of Investigation. The result was that I had beaten a confession from a suspect who had buried a young girl alive. We found her in time to save her life, but he got off, and I got fired. I was viewed as unprofessional by many in Indiana's law enforcement community and, as such, a bit of a renegade.

"How do you know that?" I asked.

"Nothing specific. Just an 'Oh yeah. Colton Parker,' when I told him your name."

"So can you do that for me?" I asked.

"You mean find out what the Indiana State Police have developed as the result of a confidential police investigation and then pass it on to an unofficial party?"

"Yeah."

"Sure. I still have a few friends there."

There was a pause in the conversation.

"Lester knew about the blood in the trunk," I said.

"Do you think he slipped up?"

The thought that Lester may have killed Claudia or, at the very least, had her killed, did not escape me. As much as I felt for the guy, I had to keep an open mind.

"Maybe," I said. "But I don't think so. His despair seems genuine. And when he talks of Claudia, it's always in the present tense. Never, 'Claudia liked.' It's always, 'Claudia likes.'" I was recalling what he had told me about her love of art.

"He could be a convincing actor," she said. "We've seen it before."

"Yes, but we haven't seen it often. It's possible, but I don't think it's probable. I'm going on gut here. You know?"

"I know," she said. Both of us had been in law enforcement too long to ignore intuition.

"Could you find out which trooper broke the news to him?"

"An Indiana state trooper would not be likely to make a mistake like that," Mary said.

"I know. But everyone makes mistakes, even the police. Besides," I said, "Lester knew about the blood. Either he's responsible or someone told him."

Another pause.

"I'll see what I can find out," she said. "Listen, why don't you and Callie come over for dinner tonight?"

"Oh, I don't know, Mary, I—"

"Sure you do. I can cook pretty well."

She was right. She could cook.

"What time?" I asked.

"Seven?"

After agreeing to dinner, I drove to Wrang and Associates. Claudia's bloody car had been found, abandoned in a ditch seventy miles from home. Terre Haute to be exact. The same town where Wrang had said he was designing a new series of homes. When I considered those facts, along with what Carne had said, I had enough to justify another visit with the embittered architect.

I went into the office and found the reception area empty, but I could hear Wrang's voice coming from the rear of the building. I went down the hall, paused at the door the sound was coming from, and listened. The only voice I heard was Randall's, interspaced with moments of silence.

After I heard him set the receiver in its cradle, I knocked on the door frame and entered the office. Wrang had been sitting with his back to the door and his arm thrown lackadaisically over his head as he talked on the phone. After I knocked, he spun around in his chair.

"Sorry to trouble you," I said, "but do you mind if I ask you a few more questions?"

"About Lester and his wife?"

I nodded. "Just a couple more."

"You know, I think I saw this episode on Columbo once."

I went into the office and sat in a vinyl chair in front of his desk. "If wearing a rain coat would bring us some rain, I'd be wearing one," I said.

"What's the question?"

"Claudia's car was found in Terre Haute this morning."

"She okay?"

I shrugged. "Don't know. She wasn't with the car and the trunk was bloodstained."

His expression changed. "Why are you telling me this?"

"Because you've been in Terre Haute recently."

His face darkened. "So I'm a suspect now?"

"Just being thorough," I said. "Mind telling me where you've been the last couple of days?"

His eyes narrowed as he got out of the chair and came around the desk. His breathing was becoming labored.

"Don't," I said. "I do this for a living. You've spent too much time behind the drawing board."

He raised his finger. "I'm going to say this just once. I did not hurt Lester or his wife."

The man's anger was justified if he was innocent. On the other hand, he hadn't answered my question.

"Where have you been the last couple of days?" I asked again.

"Out."

"Someone can vouch for that?"

He picked up the phone and dialed. His breathing was still heavy and he kept his narrowed eyes on me.

"Chief Littleton, please. Tell him it's Randall Wrang."

Chief?

"Clarke? I have a private investigator here named Colton Parker. He wants to know where I've been the last few days. Care to speak with him?" There was a pause before he handed me the phone.

"Mr. Parker," the voice on the other end of the line said, "this is Clarke Littleton, chief of police with the Terre Haute PD. You have questions regarding Randall Wrang?"

"At the moment, Mr. Wrang may be a person of interest in the disappearance of Claudia Cheek. Her car was—"

"I'm aware of the circumstances, Mr. Parker. As I said, I'm the chief of police here."

"Sure. But that doesn't answer my question regarding your friend's whereabouts."

"This might," Littleton said. "Mr. Wrang has been with me the past three days. We were fishing." He gave me the location of the lake as well as the cabin where the two had been staying. "Check it out if you like. We just got back this morning."

It wasn't until I had talked with Littleton that I noticed a rod and reel standing in the corner of Wrang's office.

"That won't be necessary, Chief," I said, handing the phone back to Wrang.

"Satisfied?" he asked, setting the receiver down on the cradle.

Just my luck. A suspect who fishes with police chiefs.

"I'm satisfied," I said, feeling less like Columbo and more like Bozo.

Chapter SEVENTEEN

Prior to Anna's death, Callie had been an avid and accomplished soccer player with dreams of a scholarship to Florida State. When Mary had told her that she too had played soccer and had won the same scholarship, the two of them hit it off. While not exactly close friends, Mary and Callie were developing a bond that was helping to ease Callie's pain. When we arrived at Mary's apartment a few minutes before seven, Callie was as animated as I had seen her in months. And I was grateful.

It had been a dark time. Callie had been living with Anna's parents as I struggled to begin a new business and establish myself as a private investigator. But I also had concerns that were more personal. Concerns that I had not developed as a father. Like a lot of men I knew, my focus had always been on the job. The result was that I had left most of the child rearing to Anna. In Callie's thirteen years, I had never attended a parent-teacher meeting or a school open house, and I had missed most of her soccer games. The consequence was that when Anna died, I suddenly found myself responsible for someone else and ill-equipped to handle it. That fact had been underscored when Callie tried to harm herself. My skills as a parent were in the developmental stages, and it showed. I was an insecure father. But a determined one nonetheless.

"Hey, guys, come on in," Mary said, smiling and holding the door open wide.

The apartment was typical Mary. Brightly decorated and brightly lit, the place was nearly glowing. Pictures of Disney characters, paintings, posters, and some original frames from popular Disney cartoons hung on the walls. The sofa was dark leather with a matching recliner. A bean-bag chair sat to one side with an open DVD case of *Snow White* sitting next to it on the floor. The disc was still running.

"I brought dessert," I said, handing her an apple pie, compliments of the bakery at Kroger's.

Mary smiled and shook her head. "Did you think I wouldn't have dessert?"

"Do you?"

"Only if Baked Alaska is okay."

It was. "Keep the pie anyway," I said, following her into the living room and closing the door behind me.

"How are you, Callie?" Mary asked, stopping the DVD and ejecting it from the player.

"I'm okay," she said, with a shrug and her hands thrust deep into the pockets of her jeans.

"Do you remember when I told you I had some old movies of some of my games?"

Callie's eyes brightened. "Yes!"

Mary moved to a shelving unit and pulled videotape from the top shelf. "*Voila!*"

"Wow!" Callie said, smiling.

I was taken aback. It was the first sign of any exuberance I had seen in quite a while.

For the next hour, Mary and Callie went over the footage of Mary's old games—not for bragging rights, but as one soccer player to another. A sort of sorority, complete with its own lingo. I spent the next hour smelling the food in the kitchen while listening to terms like one touch, two-on-one break, AR, and chaining. At one point, Mary got caught up in the moment as she watched her game with the same enthusiasm of someone seeing it for the first time.

"Did you see that, Callie? That's called a Beckenbauer sweeper."

"What's that?" Callie asked.

"It was named after Franz Beckenbauer. He played for the New York Cosmos in the late sixties. He could use the sweeper for offense or defense."

Callie looked puzzled.

"Listen, honey," Mary said, "what you take for granted now was quite revolutionary back then. Beckenbauer was a fabulous player."

Callie smiled. "You were too, Mary." The way my daughter looked at my former partner was not lost on me.

"So are you," Mary said.

Callie's familiar expression of defeat returned.

Mary placed a hand on Callie's knee. "You can do this. You've done it before."

Callie nodded in agreement. "I know."

Mary glanced at me and then back at Callie. "Take time, honey," she told her. "You've been through a lot. Take time to heal. When the time is right, you'll step back onto the field, and you'll dazzle them with your ability." Callie looked at Mary and smiled as Mary replaced the tape with another.

"Mary?" I asked.

She redirected her attention from Callie to me.

"What smells so good?"

She frowned and pointed the remote toward the VCR as she started the tape. "Here we go," she said to Callie. "Notice how we…"

I sighed and flipped up the footrest on the recliner as I settled in for a long night and a dinner that would be late.

CHAPTER EIGHTEEN

The evening at Mary's motivated Callie. By the time we arrived home, she was showing some glimpses of her old self. The one that had existed before the tragic chain of events.

After Callie showered and readied herself for bed, I went into her room to say good night. She was in bed, lying facedown with her folded hands tucked under her pillow.

"Dad?"

"Yes?" I sat next to her on the bed and began rubbing her back.

"Do you think I should play again?"

"Yes," I said. "When you're ready."

"That's what Mary said—when I'm ready."

Mary had become a surrogate mother for Callie. It was a relationship I had neither encouraged nor prohibited. The two of them had a lot in common, and the relationship they were building was clearly beneficial to both. But life in the FBI can be harsh. Transfers are frequent and without warning. I didn't want Callie to lose another mother. Especially not this soon.

"Dad?"

"Uh-huh?" I continued rubbing her back.

"What if I don't get better?"

I stopped and looked at her. "Why would you ask that?"

She shrugged. "I don't know. Just...you know...what if?"

"You're fine right now," I said. "But you went through a lot. When Mom died, it changed life for all of us. And that includes you. When you're ready to play again, you'll know it."

"How?"

"You just will."

She smiled. "I hope so."

We were quiet for the next few moments as I continued to massage her back.

"Do you think that I could be an FBI agent?" she asked.

I stopped. "What?" I asked with a chuckle. "Where did that come from?"

She rolled to one side and propped her head up on one hand. "It isn't funny. I want to be an FBI agent. Like Mary. Do you think I could do that?"

She was right. The question wasn't funny, it was just something I hadn't been prepared for. "I wasn't laughing because I think it's funny. I was laughing because you caught me off guard. Yes, I suppose you could. I don't see any reason why not. When did you decide you might like to become an FBI agent?"

"I don't know," she said, rolling back into position and allowing me to continue working her back. "But Mary and I are a lot alike. Don't you think?"

"Yes. I think you are."

"I mean, we both like soccer."

"Yes."

"And we're both good at it."

"Yes, you are."

"And I will win a scholarship to Florida State too, right?"

I stopped massaging. "Honey, roll over for a minute. Okay?"

She rolled over onto her side and propped herself up again on the same hand as before.

"Mary is a very athletic, intelligent, federal agent, and there's no reason why you couldn't do the same thing. It would be nice if the whole world was full of Mary Christophers. Except if it were, then there would be no Callie Parkers. Mary is Mary, and you are you. You are the only one of you in the world."

"I know," she said. "But didn't you want to be like somebody when you were a kid?"

I thought for a moment and shook my head. "No. I didn't have a mom or a dad or a brother or anyone. I just wanted to grow up."

"Me too," she said. "I just want to grow up."

After she was asleep, I made coffee and reached for the Bible. It had been Anna's.

I wasn't used to reading it. In fact, I couldn't remember the last time I had opened it. But at that moment, I felt almost compelled to read it.

Callie's statement concerned me. Not because she wanted to grow up—most kids do. But because she was showing a side of me that I didn't want her to carry. A side that spoke of loneliness. A heartrending loneliness. It was the type that created a hardened shell and shut out meaningful relationships. Better to stand at a distance and not get hurt than to get in the game and feel the pain.

I didn't want that for Callie. I didn't want her to be like me—or Lester. But I felt powerless to stop it. I didn't know what to do.

Anna had become a born-again Christian a few months prior to her death. Anna's parents had been overjoyed with their daughter's conversion. But to me, Christianity had always seemed to be a crutch for the weak. A tool for those who could not face the difficulties of life. Much easier to cop out and say "God is in control" than to ask where He was in a time of crisis.

It wasn't that I didn't believe in God. I did. I certainly could accept that there had to be a higher power—a force that sat above us. But to believe that He would reach down and interject Himself into someone's personal affairs was ludicrous. I had seen too much and lived through too much to believe in that kind of a God.

I opened the Bible and found a passage that Anna had marked with the ribbon that was attached to the book. It was in Psalms, and a verse had been highlighted in yellow.

> Hear my cry, O God;
>   listen to my prayer.
> From the ends of the earth I call to you,
>   I call as my heart grows faint;
>   lead me to the rock that is higher than I.
> For you have been my refuge,
>   a strong tower against the foe.

I closed the Bible. *A crutch for the weak,* I thought. Right.

Chapter Nineteen

Callie was quiet during breakfast the next morning, more like her pre-Mary self. Withdrawn and sullen. I had tried oatmeal and thought I had done a pretty good job. But she spent most of the time with her head propped on her hand, spooning it out and watching as it plopped back into the bowl. By the time she needed to get ready for school, less than a third of the cereal was gone.

After she left, I spent the morning cleaning up. I started the laundry in the basement and then ran back upstairs to dust, vacuum, and put away the dishes from breakfast. By noon, I'd had enough of domestic bliss and called Dale Millikin.

Dale had been Anna's pastor. After her conversion, his frequent visits and sermonizing had been a constant source of irritation. But the man's concern during Callie's incident had been genuine, and my view of him had changed. Events like that can alter a man's perspective.

Millikin had stuck with me during Callie's crisis, when she seemed to teeter over the abyss. The feelings of anger I had toward him, the view of him as an interloper in issues that did not concern him, had changed. I no longer viewed him as a problem but as a potential resource. An annoying one, perhaps, but a resource nonetheless. He was someone who may be able to help. And who may be able to connect with Callie in a way that I could not, if for no other reason than because of his connection to Anna.

We met at Armatzio's for lunch. Dale arrived a few minutes late, wearing a blue knit shirt, khaki slacks, and brown loafers. He looked around the room before spotting me and then smiled as he approached.

"Colton, how are you?"

"Fine, Pastor," I said, shaking his hand. "How are you?"

"Look," he said, sliding into the booth, "could we drop the 'pastor' thing? It makes our friendship a little too formal, don't you think? Dale will do just fine."

"Sure," I said.

Tony came to the table. "He-ey, Colton," he said, with a friendly slap on the back. Then, glancing at Millikin with a polite hello, he said, "Mary tell you I hit it?" He looked over his shoulder then leaned down closer to the table and said, "Big?"

"She mentioned something about it the other day," I said.

"I would have told you myself but…" He glanced toward the kitchen. "Mama was around then."

"And she isn't around now?" I asked.

"Sure, sure. But is not so obvious now. She is in the kitchen."

I looked at Millikin. "This is Tony Armatzio, Dale. He owns and operates this establishment."

Millikin stuck out a hand. "How are you?"

Tony shook the minister's hand. "Fine," he said, smiling. "Nice to meet you." He turned back to me. "Scoot over," he said. "Is seldom I get to talk to you anymore."

I slid over and Tony joined me in the seat.

"So, how much?" I asked.

He glanced again over his shoulder. "Ten."

"Ten? Dollars?"

"No, no, of course not ten dollars." He smiled. "Ten *thousand* dollars."

I let out a low whistle as Tony smiled, gratified with his gambling prowess.

"That's a load, Tony. What're you going to do with it?"

He sat back in the seat, a thoughtful expression on his face. "Don't know. Maybe I will take a trip. Go back to Sicily for a while."

"Maybe you'll play the ponies again too, huh?" I said.

He smiled. "Maybe."

"Or you could give it to the church," I said.

Tony's smile faded as he slowly turned to look at me.

"Tony, I failed to introduce my friend here. This is Dale Millikin. *Pastor* Dale Millikin."

Like a kaleidoscope, Tony's face crossed a spectrum of vibrant colors before he rose, shook Dale's hand again, and offered to send a waiter "right over."

"That wasn't fair, Colton," Dale said, chuckling as Tony strode away. "That guy will never speak to me again."

"It's okay. I've known Tony for years," I said. "He'll think about it, and then I'll have to pay for it one way or another. No one gets anything over on Tony."

The waiter approached, a nice young man of Italian descent who looked a lot like he could be one of Tony's relatives. He exchanged pleasantries with us and took our orders. After he left, Dale said, "How's Callie?"

"Better, I think. It's hard to tell. She doesn't talk to me much."

His expression told me he knew there was more. He knew I hadn't called him for the first time in almost four months just to chat.

"I'm not sure how to address this thing about Anna," I said.

"What do you mean?"

"I think Callie's bitter toward me because of the fight Anna and I had on the night she died. I think she blames me for Anna's death. The problem is that I wonder if she isn't right."

"Maybe she is," he said.

"I beg your pardon?"

He leaned forward and was about to open up when the kid brought our drinks. "Lunch will be right out," he said.

After he moved to another table, Millikin continued. "I know that you've talked to Mary about this, and she's concerned."

Mary had talked to Millikin about my conversation with her, but I didn't see it as a violation of my trust. Since meeting Millikin at Anna's funeral, Mary had begun attending church. On a spiritual quest of her own, she was spending a great deal of time with the minister outside of services, and I suspected that I was often the topic of conversation.

"And I don't want to betray her confidence," he continued, "but I think you should know that she and I are not in agreement about the situation. Her statement to you that you're not responsible for Anna's death, and that, in effect, you should face that and move on, isn't going to help your situation with Callie."

"Do you think I'm responsible for my wife's death?" I asked, squeezing the lemon into my iced tea.

He shrugged. "Maybe."

Millikin was frank. His answer wasn't what I had expected.

"Let me ask you this," he said. "What do you want?"

"I want my life back."

"The way it was before Anna died," he said. It wasn't a question.

"Yes."

"Sorry. You can't have it. Anna's gone, Colton. Gone from this earth, anyway, and she isn't coming back. Ever."

Anna's death, along with all the pain and family upheaval that it had wrought, was too recent. This tack he was taking was beginning to agitate me.

"And the fact remains," he said, "that she died in a car accident after fighting with you. And that she would not have been in that car, trying to clear her head and get away from you, if you hadn't been fighting."

"Just a minute," I said.

"What? You're going to tell me this isn't true?"

"Of course it is. I had just lost my job."

"Of course," Millikin said.

"We were arguing."

"Sure," he said again, stirring sugar into his tea.

"And things were said that shouldn't have been said, and she stormed out."

"I understand, Colton, I really do."

"But that doesn't mean I'm responsible for her death." My agitation had turned to heat.

"Then why are you carrying that burden?"

"Excuse me?"

"I asked, why are you carrying that burden?"

"Well, I...it's just that Callie thinks that—"

"Have you asked her? Have you asked if she thinks you killed her mother?"

"I don't have to," I said, raising my voice. "I can sense it."

"How?"

"Her isolation. The look in her eye."

"Then you may be right. She might blame you for the death of her mother."

"Exactly," I said before looking around the room and seeing other patrons looking in our direction. "Why else," I said, lowering my voice, "would she be hostile to me?"

"Here we are, guys," the young waiter said, setting our lunch on the table. "Will there be anything else?"

I managed a smile and told him we were fine. We waited until he moved away before we resumed our conversation.

"A lot of reasons," Millikin said. "You weren't involved in her life all that much, even *before* Anna died, right?"

I had to admit that I wasn't.

"And then, after Anna died, you sent Callie to live with Anna's parents, right?"

"That was because I didn't have a source of income and I felt that—"

"Maybe."

"Maybe?"

"Maybe you just couldn't handle the responsibility of raising a child on your own," he said, rolling his fork through the linguini to cool the steaming pasta.

"I seem to be doing fine now."

"Really?"

"Really."

He nodded, thoughtfully, as he ate. Then he said, "So why are we here?"

"I came to get your opinion. To see what—"

"No you didn't. You came to get affirmation of something you have already decided. You wanted me to tell you what Mary has told you. That you aren't responsible for Anna's death and that Callie's needs can be met as soon as you recognize that fact. You want absolution for something you feel guilty about and for which Callie holds you responsible."

Millikin had pushed all the right buttons again. I could feel myself tightening up the way I used to when I was a Chicago beat cop and was facing an inevitable confrontation.

"You want Callie to forgive you because you can't forgive yourself until *she* does. So you tell yourself you're not responsible, which means whether she forgives you or not, you're off the hook. Except that it leaves her *on* the hook. She blames you, and she can't get past that until you ask for her to forgive you. Colton, you've got yourself on a ride that you can't escape. Not until you ask for Callie's forgiveness."

I was having a difficult time controlling myself.

"Here," he said, writing on a paper napkin. "Look this up and tell me what you think." He slid the napkin toward me. He had written Matthew 18:21-35. "Give her a chance to do what this Scripture says. It will free her—and you."

"I think I better leave, Dale. This was a mistake." I stood and dropped enough money on the table to pay the bill.

"Go cool off. When you're ready to talk, call me," he said.

I jammed the napkin into my pocket and stepped into the steam-laden August air, which only seemed to further kindle my brewing anger. My phone began to vibrate, and I flipped it open. "Yeah?"

"Geesh, what's up with you?" It was Mary.

"Nothing," I said, struggling to subdue my temper. "What's up?"

"I just heard from the state police on your client's car."

"Yeah?"

"There are two sets of prints. One is from your friend Lester. No surprise there."

"Yeah. And the other is from Claudia?"

"No. We don't have prints for a Claudia Cheek. Not in the car, and not on file. Not anywhere."

"Then she hasn't served in the military or has a record. So what?"

"We do have prints for a Beverly Graves."

I suddenly stood frozen in the boiling humidity of an August day. "What did you say the name was?"

"Beverly Graves," she repeated.

I hadn't heard that name for a long time. I hadn't heard from Beverly for even longer. As I stood transfixed in the parking lot, my mind raced to an earlier time, and all thoughts of Millikin vanished. Beverly was back. Lucky me.

Mary continued. "Got a lengthy criminal record attached to her. Arrested ten times for prostitution, five times for running a 'house of ill repute,' and twice for shoplifting."

"Any current warrants?" I asked.

I must have sounded mechanical. Mary asked, "Are you okay?"

I told her I was.

"Well, let's see...no. Nothing outstanding."

"Have a last known?"

"Yes, as a matter of fact I do," she said. "It's 1441 Chestnut Lane."

CHAPTER TWENTY

I drove back to the office and picked up my picture of Claudia, a city map, and my Taurus .38 snub-nose. I slipped the gun into my waistband, and within two minutes, I was out the door and in the car, heading toward the west end of town.

I picked up I-465, the highway that encircled the Circle City, and drove west and then north as I headed toward Thirty-eighth Street. Traffic was unusually slow for early afternoon. By the time I exited and was heading east, my Escort—which had seen better days—was showing signs of having reached the boiling point.

I pulled into the parking lot of a mini-mart and flipped open the map. Chestnut Lane was off of Hinsdale Road, which intersected with Thirty-eighth just two blocks west of the intersection with Georgetown Road. That intersection, Thirty-eighth and Georgetown, was one of the busiest in the city with a nearby indoor shopping mall, several strip malls, and the resultant traffic. According to the map, Chestnut was a residential street that dead-ended on either side of Hinsdale.

I folded the map, started the car, and slipped back into the flow of traffic, keeping an eye on the heat gauge as the needle toyed with the red zone. By the time I reached Hinsdale, I was driving on borrowed time.

I turned south, drove two blocks, and found Chestnut. I turned right and crept down the street, searching for 1441. I found it on my left, sitting as the second-to-last house at the end of the street.

I parked in front of the house and got out of the car, flipping my shirt-tail over my belt to hide the gun. Three young kids playing in a wading pool either didn't notice or didn't care that I was there. A young woman in her mid-twenties, wearing a Day-Glo pink tank top and cut-offs, sat on the porch in a rocking chair as she watched the kids. She was smoking and blew smoke through both nostrils as I approached the front steps of the house.

"He ain't here," she said.

"He ain't?"

She shook her head. "Nope." Her legs were crossed, and she swung one foot as she held the cigarette between the first two fingers of one hand.

"Do you know where he is?" I asked.

She took a long drag and looked past me at the kids. "April, you leave her alone. You hear? Just leave her alone." She blew the smoke out again and turned her attention back to me. "Nope. I don't know where he's at. And I don't care, neither."

"Well, that makes two of us," I said, placing one foot on the lower step and sliding my hands into my back pockets.

She was about to inhale, but paused with a puzzled look. "Who are you?"

I pulled my identification from my hip pocket and showed it to her. "Colton Parker. I'm a private investigator. I want to ask you a couple of questions."

She frowned. "You ain't looking for Terry?"

I shook my head. "No. Sorry to disappoint you."

She took a long drag and exhaled, studying me through the haze. "Thought you was a cop," she said.

I turned to look at my rusted fourteen-year-old Escort. "In that?"

She shrugged. "So what questions?"

I showed her the picture of Claudia. "Know her?"

"Sure, I know her."

"How?"

"Why? She in some kind of trouble?"

"Maybe."

She took another long drag and exhaled. "We bought this house from her."

"We?"

"Me and Terry. Until he ran off with..." She let the words trail, as she inhaled again on the cigarette.

"How long ago was that?"

"When we bought the house, or when he ran off?"

"When you bought the house," I said.

"Six, seven years ago."

"Do you know where she went?"

"You mean the woman in the picture?"

"Yes."

She shrugged. "Ain't none of my business."

"Do you remember who listed the house?"

"Sure. It was Green Leaf. I remember because they always wear those green jackets."

"Would you happen to remember the agent's name?"

She shook her head as she took another long drag. "Uh-uh." She tilted her head back as she let out a long plume of smoke. "Don't remember that one."

I slipped the picture into my back pocket. "Okay, thanks."

"Sure."

I turned and moved down the steps. The kids were just as oblivious to me then as when I had arrived a few minutes before.

"Hey!"

I turned back toward the porch in time to see the woman flick the cigarette butt to the ground.

"If she's in trouble, I hope you find her. She was really nice to me."

You don't know her, I thought.

CHAPTER TWENTY-ONE

"What was the address?"

"It's 1441 Chestnut Lane," I said. "It sold about six or seven years ago."

The man typed into the computer as I gave him the address. His fingers were long and bony, like the rest of him, but nimble as they flew across the keyboard. He wore a plaid shirt, white trousers, a toupee that was probably designed for a man thirty years younger, and the green jacket. The gold nameplate on the coat identified him as Chuck.

"Let's see," he said, moving his finger down the spreadsheet on the monitor. "I have a listing for 1441 Chestnut Lane that sold six years ago." He looked at me as his nervous jaw worked over a wad of gum. "Do you need to know how much?"

I shook my head. "No. I need to know who sold it and who owned it at the time of the sale."

He licked his fingers, reached for a piece of paper with the Green Leaf Real Estate logo printed across the top of it, and copied down the information from the screen. He read from it before sliding the note toward me. "The owner was Beverly Graves," he said. "Lynnette Martin sold it." He looked from the paper to me. "We call her Lynny around here."

I took the paper and slipped it into my pocket. "Is Lynny here?" I asked.

He pointed to a middle-aged woman with big hair, a big bust, and bright lipstick, who was working at a desk near the corner of the room. Her green jacket was hanging on a coatrack near her chair. "That'd be her. Hey, Lynny!"

The woman looked up at Chuck.

"This gentlemen would like to speak with you."

In obvious hopes of making a sale, she smiled and invited me to have a seat. I thanked Chuck for his help and moved to the other side of the room, where I took a seat by the side of Lynny's desk.

"And how can I help you?" she asked.

I told her my name and asked, "Do you remember a sale you made, about six years ago for Beverly Graves? The house was on Chestnut Lane near Thirty-eighth Street."

She smiled and shook her head. "No, I'm afraid I don't."

I showed her the picture of Claudia. "Do you remember this face?"

She took the picture and smiled almost immediately. "Sure, I remember her. Is this Beverly?"

"How do you remember her?"

"I sold a house for her."

"Do you remember where you—"

She held up a hand. "Honey, I sell a lot of homes. I don't always remember names or listings, but I *always* remember a face." She had that high-voltage smile only sales people can muster.

"Sure," I said. "Would you happen to have any information on Beverly Graves that could help me locate her?"

Her smile faded. "Is she in trouble?"

"She's missing." I didn't want to tell Lynny that Beverly might be dead. If that high voltage smile swung the other way, she could be in for a near meltdown.

A genuine look of concern overshadowed her previous expression of joviality. "Are you the police?"

I told her that I was a private investigator, hired to find her former client.

"Is she in danger?"

"Possibly." I wasn't lying. Beverly's bloodstained car had been found in a ditch, an hour from home.

Lynny turned toward her computer and began to type. A series of spreadsheets flashed across the monitor. When she finally landed on one of them, she reached for a piece of paper just like the one that Chuck had given me and copied some of the information from the spreadsheet. When she was done, she handed me the note.

"Beverly was employed at the Honey Basket. A bar on west Sixteenth Street. Her Social Security and driver's license numbers are on that paper."

I slipped the note and the picture into my hip pocket. "Thank you for your, help," I said.

"I hope you find her," she said. "She's a real gem."

Gem? Fool's gold would be more like it.

CHAPTER TWENTY-TWO

I had about an hour before Callie got home from school, which wasn't enough time to race across town, conduct an interview, and get over to the south side before she got off the bus. I opted to head for home, knowing that if I was going to make any headway as a private investigator and small business owner, I was going to have to become more comfortable leaving Callie by herself. Given her recent history, I knew that wouldn't come easy.

I stopped on the way home, picked up a two-liter bottle of Coke and two sausage and pepperoni pizzas, and rented a movie. It was Friday night, and I wanted to spend it with Callie. A lot of what Millikin had asked was already beginning to take root. Maybe I did want someone to affirm that I wasn't responsible for Anna's death. But hadn't Mary already done that? And if I wasn't responsible, then why did I feel so deeply that I was?

I made it home less than ten minutes before the bus arrived. I watched again from the window as Callie moved forward in the bus and then down the steps.

"In here, honey," I said.

She came into the kitchen with her book bag still on her back. "What are we having?"

"Pizza," I said. "And a movie."

"Okay." She turned and began to move across the living room and down the hall toward her room.

"Any homework?" I asked.

I was answered by the closing of her bedroom door.

That evening we ate two frozen pizzas and watched one of the *Vacation* movies that used to make Callie laugh. It didn't tonight. For the most part, she seemed to be somewhere else.

"You okay?" I asked.

"Yes."

"You don't seem like it," I said, as the credits were rolling.

"I'm fine."

I turned on the lamp and flicked off the TV. "I need to ask you something." I adjusted my position on the sofa, to face her. "Callie, are you angry with me? You know, for Mom's accident?"

After more than ninety minutes of raucous comedy, the silence hung heavy in the air.

"I need to know, Callie."

"Why?"

"Why what?" I asked.

"Why do you need to know what I think?"

"Because you're my daughter and I love you. If you're hurting, if you blame me for Mom's accident, I need to know."

She paused to gather her thoughts. "I heard you and Mom arguing."

"Yes, you did. But it didn't mean we didn't love each other. Sometimes, people fight. Even people who love each other."

"But people who love each other don't fight until one of them is dead."

"Do you think I caused Mom's accident?"

"She wouldn't have been out that night if you hadn't told her to."

"Told her to what?"

"You told her that if she didn't like the way you were doing things, she should leave."

The words stung. I hadn't remembered saying them, but it was obvious that Callie had remembered hearing them. I didn't like having them played back to me. Not now. Not like this.

"I didn't mean that I wanted Mom to leave."

"Then why did you say it?"

"I...don't know."

Callie stood. "But you did, Dad. And now Mom is dead."

CHAPTER TWENTY-THREE

The remainder of the weekend had been tedious, so when Monday rolled around, I was glad to be back on familiar territory. The Friday night discussion with Callie had not proven to be a hit, and by the time I drove her to the Shapiros, to meet up with her church friends, I was convinced that she would never speak to me again. She spent the rest of the weekend with the Shapiros, who would take her to school, so I had not yet heard how the event with her friends had gone. If Sebastian was right, it was something she needed. Me too, for that matter.

My concern for myself centered around my ability to help Callie out of her lethargy. If I failed, she was heading for trouble. I was in unfamiliar territory, and the tension was building.

When stressed, I've always found that working myself to near exhaustion seems to help. And, at the moment, I needed to be exhausted. So I went downstairs early Monday morning and laid siege to the weights.

My usual bench press is two hundred fifty for my sets. I'll usually do three sets of ten reps before moving on to curls or lat work or some other exercise. I try to vary the workout to avoid boredom and to give the muscles the shock that they need. But that morning the adrenalin kicked in, and I found myself doing two seventy-five on the bench. By the time I was finished lifting two hours later, I had the exhaustion that I wanted.

After showering and shaving, I put away the dishes from breakfast and drove to Armatzio's to spend a couple of hours with Tony. I was marking time mostly, waiting for the Honey Basket to open at noon.

Tony's place, like the bar, didn't open until twelve, so Tony and I sat at a table reading the morning paper. I had already finished with most of the news and was waiting for Tony to work his way through the sports section so I could take a look. He was a slow reader, and as he read, I noticed that his lips moved.

"How 'bout them Indians?" I asked.

Tony grunted and continued reading.

I let a minute pass. "Reds are doing well."

Nothing.

"Of course, anything can happen," I said.

He lowered the paper and looked at me over its edge. "You want more coffee?"

"Sure." I held out my cup.

"Then go get some and leave me be."

I got up and went to the coffeepot that Tony kept on a shelf behind the cash register. I poured another cup and sat back down.

"You sore?" I asked.

"Sore about what?" He kept reading.

"About the preacher. I was just kidding with you," I said.

"Is okay," he said, without taking his eyes off the paper. "I will just be kidding with you too someday soon."

I drank some coffee and let another minute go by.

"Think the Red Sox will go to the World Series again?" I asked.

Tony sighed and handed me the sports section.

"Thanks," I said.

I read the paper until it was time for Tony to open. When he did, I phoned Mary and asked her to run the Social Security number and driver's license number for Beverly Graves. I wanted her to see if any credit cards or licenses had been issued to those numbers and to cross-check them with the names Beverly Graves, Claudia Cheek, and Frances Seymour.

"You think they're the same person?" she asked.

"Yes."

"A con?"

"Yes." *Of the worst type,* I thought.

"Okay. I'll let you know as soon as I hear something. Shouldn't be long."

I thanked her and glanced at my watch. It was 12:01.

I thanked Tony for the coffee and the use of his newspaper and drove to the Honey Basket. By the time I reached the bar it was nearly 12:45.

Except for a couple of pickup trucks and a rusting station wagon with a St. Louis Cardinals bumper sticker, the lot was vacant. When I went in, I was forced to squint as I tried to adjust to the dark interior.

I counted three patrons and one bartender—a woman who looked like a cross between ugly and mean.

"Can I help you?" she asked in a throaty voice as she wiped at an imaginary spill on the bar.

"I'm looking for Beverly Graves. She working today?" Beverly had once worked here. If she had left Lester, she might have run home to Mama.

"I don't know no Beverly Graves. You got the right place?"

"This the Honey Basket?" I asked.

"Yep. You got the right place, I guess. But there ain't no Beverly Graves workin' here."

I turned to face the patrons. "Anybody here know Beverly Graves?"

A late-middle-aged man in a tank top and St. Louis Cardinals ball cap said, "Yeah, I know her."

I moved to where he was sitting and pulled up a chair. "How do you know her?"

"The same way everyone else does." He chuckled and took a long swig from his beer.

"And how would that be?" I asked.

"In the sack, man. You know?"

From what I knew of Beverly, I wasn't surprised by his answer. "When did you see her last?"

"Been a while." He pushed the Cards ball cap back on his head. "Five years. Maybe longer."

"And you remember her after all that time?" I asked.

"You would too if you knew her like I did. That was one hot little woman." He took another long swig.

"Any idea where I might find her?"

He laughed "Probably with some rich guy. Was always telling me how she wanted to hook up and be a 'kept woman'. I used to say, 'Ain't no rich man gonna want a woman like you, Bev. You belong right here, doing what you do best.'"

"Sure," I said. If what he said was true, it was clear that she wasn't going to maintain a relationship with the man that I was talking to for very long. At least, not judging by the station wagon in the lot. "Do you know if she hooked up?"

"Hooked up?" He laughed. "That's a good one." He shook his head. "Naw. Never did see her again after that. Went over to her house one night, and there was a For Sale sign with a Sold sticker stuck on it. She was done gone."

I pulled out the picture of Claudia and showed it to him. "This the same woman?" I asked.

"Oowhee! That's her alright. It's been a long time though. She's older now. And different. It looks like she cleaned herself up. Looks like a respectable woman."

"Okay," I said, standing. "I appreciate your help."

"Sure thing, man," he said. "Hope you find her. An old bed bug like her needs to stick to what she knows best."

I stepped outside and squinted against the noonday sun. As I got into the car, my phone began to vibrate.

"I have a couple of things for you," Mary said.

"Shoot," I said, pulling out of the lot of the Honey Basket. I was heading east on Sixteenth Street.

"First, I talked to the trooper who spilled the beans to Lester."

"About the blood in the trunk?"

"Yes. And you were right. He was a rookie and made a mistake."

"That makes it better for Lester," I said. "Moves him off my suspect list."

"Never was on it, was he?" Mary said.

"No."

"The second thing I've got is that the Social Security number comes back to Beverly Graves. The driver's license number comes back to Claudia Cheek. But the date of birth tied to the Social Security number comes back to all three. They are all the same person."

I wasn't surprised. Searching for any one of the identifying numbers would not produce conclusive proof. But when both numbers were together, I had to go with the evidence.

"I've got more," Mary said. "Frances Seymour opened a charge account two days ago."

"Do you have an address?"

"As a matter of fact, I do." She read the address to me. It was an apartment complex on the west side, about fifteen minutes from Beverly's old address on Chestnut Lane.

"She's a creature of habit," I said as I turned north on Tibbs Avenue and headed for Lafayette Road.

"Most cons are," Mary said. "They use the same DOB or Social number or last name, or they return to the same area. It makes it easier. Less to remember when you're living a life of lies."

Mary had no idea. Beverly Graves was far more than a liar and a con. And I was looking forward to seeing her again.

It had been a long time.

Chapter Twenty-Four

The complex was upscale. Nicely paved lanes wound through a picturesque setting that seemed to belie the caustic noise of the busy city streets. A pool, bedecked with chaise lounges and scantily clad young women, sat just over a rise from the office, on grounds that were well maintained with azaleas and lamp-lit sidewalks dotting the landscape. The Cheshire Court was a long way up from my position in life, but it was lot farther down from where Beverly had been when she was with Lester.

I parked in front of her building and tucked the snub-nose .38 into my waistband as I pulled a set of lock picks from my glove box.

I had not seen Beverly for a long time. The thought of seeing her now brought a curious mix of anger and elation, like the blending of vivid color and subtle understatement of an Andy Warhol painting.

I went into the building and found a row of mailboxes with the corresponding apartment numbers. Seymour was in apartment F on the second floor. I buzzed apartment K on the third floor and I got lucky.

"Yes?"

"Mr. Provost, I'm supposed to check your cable today. We've had reports that some of the lines are giving out. If the line is okay, I'll check

108

it and be out of your hair. If not, it will only take a couple of minutes to fix."

Provost didn't answer, but he did buzz me into the building.

I didn't expect Beverly to answer her buzzer. She had no reason to expect visitors and every reason to anticipate that Lester would try to find her. But a knock on the door is harder to resist, particularly when it could be a neighbor in need—someone who would have already had access through the main security door downstairs.

I approached apartment F and paused to listen at the door. It was quiet. No guarantee that she wasn't home, but a good bet.

I examined the lock. It was a standard dead bolt. They are the most common types of locks in houses and apartments and relatively simple to pick. The key turns the cylinder that's attached to a mechanism called a cam. The cam will pull back the bolt, unlocking the door. I didn't have the key, but that wasn't going to be an obstacle.

I inserted my tension wrench into the lock and slipped a pick in over it. After a few minutes I had the pins in line and the door opened. I slipped the picks back into my pocket and pulled the gun from my waistband.

When I entered, it was clear that she wasn't at home. The place was quiet except for the steady drone of the air-conditioning fan. The drapes were pulled tight.

I closed the door. I hadn't wanted to find an empty apartment. I wanted to find Beverly. But home is where the heart is, or at least in her case, where it is for a while. She would be back, and I would be here when she came.

I slid the gun into my waistband in the small of my back and moved through the apartment. I found a few books, romance novels mostly, and a few magazines—*People, Us,* and *Time*—and a day-old copy of the *Indianapolis Star.*

I noted that the refrigerator was partially stocked, and when I sifted through a stack of bills that were in a hanging basket on the side of the kitchen cabinets, I found that she had paid her cable bill through the end of the month. One minute in the apartment had already told me she had been here as recently as yesterday and would probably be back soon to eat her food and watch her cable. It also told me she wasn't dead. That meant that all I had to do now was wait. And make arrangements for Callie.

I used my cell phone to call Anna's parents. Frank answered.

"Frank, it's Colton. Listen, I'm in a bit of a jam right now."

"What's wrong?" His tone was cautionary, revealing his concern that I had gotten myself involved in some type of legal situation.

"I'm on the job and I have to…" I paused searching for the right phrase. It wasn't always wise to tell your former father-in-law that you were in the process of committing a felony. "I have to stake out a place. I don't know how long I'm going to be here. Could you possibly—"

"Sure. That's no problem. What time does she get home?"

"You'll need to be there by three," I said.

He assured me that wouldn't be a problem. I hung up and continued my search through the apartment. I went through her trash and found nothing useful. I worked my way through her closets and found nothing there either. Then I entered the bedroom and found an answering machine. An odd item to have if you're on the run.

I pushed the Play button.

"It's me again. See, there's no point in running—I've got your number." There was a cough. *"So how about it? I won't wait forever. You want the geek?"* Another cough. *"Then you know what you've got to do."*

A beep indicated a second message. *"I'm not waiting forever. I want that information—now."* Cough. *"And I want something else too, right? It's not like we haven't done it before."* Another cough, and the line went dead.

I ejected the tape and slipped it into my pocket. I was on my way back into the living room when I heard a key turning the lock.

CHAPTER TWENTY-FIVE

I went into the darkened living room and took a seat in a recliner that faced the door. I watched as the thumb latch on the dead bolt turned and the door opened.

A woman entered, carrying a small bag of groceries. It appeared that she had been shopping for perishables, judging by the load of bread and carton of eggs that protruded over the top of the bag. They obscured her view of me.

I watched silently as she moved toward the dining table. From her profile, I could see that she fit the photo of Claudia that Lester had given me. She was tall and graceful—almost elegant, but I knew that was where the illusion ended. This woman was anything but elegant. She was a snake in lamb's clothing.

She walked to the dining table and set the bag down, along with her purse, before flipping on the light switch. She removed the eggs from the carton as she kicked off her shoes. When she turned to move into the kitchen, her eyes fell on me as the eggs fell from her hand.

"Who are you?" Her expression, along with the tone of her voice, told me she had been caught off guard and was genuinely scared.

"Have a seat, Claudia," I said, gesturing to a recliner that was opposite where I sat.

"I don't have any money," she said.

"Sure you do," I said. "You've been cleaning out Lester for the past several months."

Some of the fear seemed to recede from her face. "Who are you?" This time, the tone was different. More demanding.

"Sit down."

She hesitated as her eyes flickered toward the end table next to the sofa where I was sitting.

I opened the drawer and found a snub nose .38. It was like mine, only blue steel. I removed the gun, opened the cylinder, and ejected the five cartridges onto the floor. I flipped the cylinder shut and tossed the gun back into the drawer.

"I'm not going to tell you again," I said. "Sit down."

She inched her way to the recliner, refusing to take her eyes off me. This woman was no amateur. She had lived too long on the wrong side of life to turn her back on an intruder in her home, even if he had just emptied her gun onto the floor instead of into her.

"Who are you?" she asked again, though less demanding this time.

"We'll get to that in a moment. What I want to know is why?"

"Why what?"

"For starters, why you left Lester."

"Is he okay?"

"If you mean physically, yes. Otherwise, he's torn apart."

She put her face in her hands and sighed heavily. "I didn't want to hurt him. That's the last thing I wanted to do."

"Is that so?"

"Yes." She uncovered her face.

"What exactly did you think was going to happen to him when he found out his wife had left? No note, no phone call, no reason given, just gone."

"It isn't that simple," she said.

"Sure it is, lady. You married a man. You took vows—'Till death do us part.' But then, when your personal agenda gets in the way, you up and leave. Tell me again how this is all that complicated."

"He's better off without me."

"I can agree with that. But the problem is that he doesn't see it that way."

Tears filled her eyes. Her lips began to quiver. "He doesn't now, but he will."

"Is that how you rationalize all of this? That doing whatever you want, whatever floats your boat, will be better in the long run for the others in your life?"

She didn't say anything. The tears, real or contrived, were lost on me.

I waited a moment, giving her time to absorb all that had happened. I wanted to have a solid anvil for the hammer I was about to use. The hammer that would drive home the answer to her question about who I was. The answer that would leave her with the ringing truth she had ignored forty years ago.

"Is that how you justified running out on me?"

It took a moment for her to realize what I had said, for the impact to take root and reach full maturity.

I had thought about this moment for most of my life in the Children's Guardian Home and in a series of foster homes. I daydreamed about it in school. I dreamed about having parents on Christmas morning and Mother's Day. I thought about it at school functions, like Christmas plays, when the other kids' parents would brag on them or applaud their efforts. I wondered what it would be like to crawl into my mother's lap when I wanted her to read a story to me, or have her put her hand on my forehead when I was sick. I thought about this moment a lot. As a child, I dreamed that she had come back for me. But as an adult, I had dreamed about going after her.

And now I was here. And the expectations had given way to the reality.

"Is it?" I asked again. "Is that how you justified running out on me... *Mom?*"

Chapter Twenty-Six

The woman in front of me was my mother. It was the first time I had seen her in forty years. I wasn't impressed.

"Colton?"

"Yeah, that's me. Colton. Colton Parker."

She studied me like someone who had been lost but was now found—however reluctantly.

She put her face back into her hands. "Oh, God," she said. "I'm so sorry."

"Of course you are. Getting caught and having to deal with the consequences of your actions will always make you feel sorry for yourself."

She raised her face from her hands. She had grown pale and was perspiring. "Can I have a glass of water?"

I wanted to say no, to deny her the basics of life the way she had denied me. I hated the woman, and doing anything for her, however trivial, went against the grain of that hatred. But I gave in to some basilar instinct, went into the kitchen anyway, and rinsed a washcloth under the tap. I came back into the living room with the cold rag and a glass of water.

"Thank you," she said, placing the cloth on her forehead and drinking the water.

"So tell me—what could have been so bad that you would walk out on a three-month-old child. Then tell me about Lester. Tell me how Lester could have been so bad that you would stick it to him too."

She leaned her head back, keeping the cold rag on her forehead. "Colton, I'm ... " She paused, as she searched for a smooth way of telling me.

"A hooker?"

She swallowed hard. "Yes."

"And my dad?"

Another hard swallow. "I don't know."

"A john?"

"I don't know."

"Do I have any brothers or sisters?"

She shook her head.

"So this whole thing with MAC was because of me?"

She nodded.

"What happened? How come you didn't love me?"

"I did love you, Colton."

A string of uncontrollable expletives bellowed from me.

"I don't blame you," she said.

"You don't have any right to blame anyone," I said.

"I know," she said, following a significant pause. "But at the time, I couldn't care for you. I was trying to work, tending bar, and ... I had no family. I had no one to watch you while I worked."

She paused, waiting for some reaction. I didn't have any. None that would lead to a discovery of the truth, anyway.

"So I did the next best thing," she said. "I took you to work with me. Freddie—the owner of the bar—was okay with it. But when he sold the bar, the new owner fired me." She drank more water and swallowed hard. "I had to do what I knew best."

"And it wasn't tending bar."

"No, it wasn't."

"So you unloaded me," I said.

"I couldn't take care of you. So I took you to the hospital and—"

"Left me."

She nodded and drank from the glass.

"On the sidewalk in front of the emergency room. And then you went on with your life, never looking back."

"I couldn't, Colton. I had to let you have the best home possible."

"Didn't the idea of adoption ever enter your mind?"

"I was young, just nineteen. It seemed…easier to do what I did."

"For you, maybe. But it wasn't so easy for me." I told her about the string of homes I had been raised in, some abusive and some not. But none of them loving. I told her about the pain and about the anger it instilled. I told her about how her selfishness had left me to fend for myself without the nurturing guidance of a mother.

"I'm sorry," was all she could seem to say.

"When I joined the Chicago Police Department, I ran your name through the NCIC," I said. "Beverly Parker. But nothing ever seemed to come up. Until one day, an arrest record came along."

"How did you know it was me? Who told you?" she asked.

I stood and moved to the windows. The apartment was dark, which seemed to overload the setting. I opened the drapes and allowed the sunshine to enter.

"Leaving a helpless child outside the doors of an emergency room isn't a natural act. When it happens, the authorities tend to get involved."

I looked down on the courtyard that lay behind the building. A young mother was teaching her toddler how to ride a tricycle.

"So," I continued, "they printed me and ran it against the hospital records, and the rest was easy. I've always known your name. When I saw your arrest record, I knew it was you. Later, when you changed your name to Graves and began to develop a record with the police, I was able to pin you down by matching your DOB and photos. But by that time, I had lost interest in trying to find you."

"I'm sorry," she said.

"Sure," I said, sitting again. "Let's get something straight before we move on. You didn't want me as a child. You ran out on your obligations and broke the most natural bond in the world. You are nothing to me now. From this point on, our temporary relationship is centered on the business at hand."

She nodded.

"Lester hired me to find you, and I've done that. I have an obligation to tell him that I have found you but, beyond that I—"

"Please don't do that."

"Why not?"

"It would hurt him."

"Look around you, lady," I said. "Everyone who gets near you gets hurt. It goes with the territory."

"No, you don't understand," she said.

"You have a knack for the obvious. You're right. I don't understand."

She shook her head. "No, I mean, if I go back, he's going to know... going to find out."

"Find out what? What could be worse than what he already knows?"

"He doesn't know about me. Not the way you do. To him, I'm Claudia Cheek. Outgoing socialite who came into his life and filled the void. He doesn't know about my past." She put her head in her hands. "He doesn't know that I'm nothing more than a..."

I had dealt with a variety of people in my life. Killers, thieves, cheats, prostitutes, and scam artists. I could usually feel some level of pity for them. I felt nothing for Beverly.

"He'll get over it," I said. "He's a big boy. He knows the score. But you owe him an explanation. First, why you ran out on him. Second, why you bilked him out of thousands of dollars. He deserves to know why."

She nodded. "I know he does, but wouldn't it be better if I just disappeared?"

"For you, maybe. It seems to have worked for you before. The problem is that you just keep leaving people in your wake. People you've hurt. But not this time. This time you're going to face those people, starting with me and ending with Lester. Besides," I said, "what do you care? He's just another john."

She shook her head as tears welled in her eyes again. "No, you're wrong. I fell in love with him. He treated me like I was something special. He didn't know about my past, so it was a new start."

I laughed. "You're one for the books. You fell in love with him? You fell in love with his money."

She shook her head. "No. If it were the money, I would've stayed."

"Then what was it? Why did you leave? Why did you run out on a man you claim to love?" I could feel my outrage growing as I sensed the irony of my question. A woman who could abandon her child was capable of deserting anyone. Even a man she claimed to love.

"Because I was being blackmailed."

"By whom?"

"Someone who doesn't like Lester."

"Name?"

She dabbed at her face with the washcloth. "His name is Douglas Chatham. He's an attorney. The managing partner of Chatham, Kern, and Brubaker.

"What's his beef with your husband?" I asked, already aware of the animosity.

She drank some more water. "There was a piece of land. They both wanted it, but Lester was able to get it zoned for…oh, I don't know. Some land deal. Douglas lost a bundle and he blames Lester."

"Chatham's not hurting," I said. "He owns half of Indianapolis."

She shook her head. "It's not the money. It's his pride."

"And what are you to this guy?"

She looked at me. "I was a hooker, Colton."

"And he remembered you?" I asked.

"Yes."

"You've been with him recently?"

She shook her head. "No, I haven't…lived that way since I met Lester."

"But he still recognized you after all that time?"

She nodded again. "He saw me in an interview that I did on the news. I was doing it for MAC. He saw it, recognized me, and began calling me at the office. He threatened to tell Lester. Even take it public."

"And you were able to buy him off with a few thousand? That doesn't make sense. The guy has to be worth several million. Why would a—"

"No," she said, softly. "He doesn't want money. He wants revenge. He wants Lester."

"Lester? What do you mean?"

She took another long drink of water before answering. "Lester and Chatham are at odds. But you probably already know that."

"What I know is irrelevant. It's what you know that matters now, isn't it?"

She paused to drink more water. After setting the glass down, she looked at me with admiration. The look made me angry.

"I've been following you," she said, changing the subject.

"Following me?"

"I read in the paper about the kidnapping you investigated. About how you found the little girl but got fired because of it. When I saw your name in the paper I just...I just knew you were my son."

"And?"

"And I followed you. Your career, I mean. I saw your ad in the paper when you opened your business, and I knew you would probably need help getting it started." She paused to reach for the glass and take another drink. "I decided to call Lester's attorney. I told him we would appreciate any business that he could throw your way."

"Why would you do that?"

"Because you're my son."

"So?"

"Colton, you don't have to believe me. But you asked, so I'm telling."

"You're telling me that Lester hired me because of you?"

She nodded. "Yes, in a way. Lester doesn't make a move unless he asks his lawyer. If you came recommended by him, that would've been good enough."

I remembered Lester telling me that he had gotten my name from his attorney.

"But I didn't think you would be involved in this," she said. "I had no way of knowing at the time that something like this would ever come up."

"But it has," I said.

Tears formed in her eyes. "I just assumed that when I left, Lester would be angry. Hurt at first, maybe, but then angry. Angry enough that he would leave me alone. I guess I judged wrong."

"That's an understatement," I said.

"You have to understand, Colton. I didn't leave Lester because I wanted to, I left because I *had* to."

"Had to?" I could hear the sound of my voice rising in a way that made me feel detached. Like an observer, listening to someone else. "Had to? Why? Because some lawyer recognized you after all these years and was blackmailing you for a one night stand?"

"No, there was—"

"And an old hooker like you wasn't about to do something like that? Right?"

"No, I wasn't." She maintained her poise. "I can't help what I was. I can only help what I become."

I knew that I had stepped over the line, and if it had been anyone else, I would have felt remorse.

"So you didn't sleep with him, but you took Lester for a ride instead? Do you consider that to be the moral high ground?"

"I'm not taking Lester for a ride, Colton; Chatham is. That's why I left. Chatham is setting Lester up for a federal investigation."

"What kind of investigation?"

"His employees. Chatham wanted me to give him information on Lester's stores. Employee complaints, violations, anything that he could use to force the Department of Labor or OSHA or…anyone to go after Lester."

"He's looking for inside stuff?"

She nodded. "More than that. Chatham is agitating. Trying to find a way to poke a hole in Lester's business. He wants me to give him data from the stores."

"You could have gone to the law," I said.

"Chatham threatened to tell Lester about me, Colton. So I left. It seemed the best way. I couldn't live seeing the pain on Lester's face when he found out about me. I couldn't live with hurting him like that."

"But you can live with hurting him like this?"

She stood and went to the window. "I love Lester, Colton. And whether you believe me or not doesn't matter. I want to go back. I want to make things right. But I can't. Chatham has ruined all of that. So I am going to fix the problem—for good."

"And taking Lester for over a hundred grand is going to fix the problem?"

"Yes." She turned to face me. Her expression of despair and shame was replaced by one of harshness. "It will. I've hired someone to kill Douglas Chatham."

CHAPTER TWENTY-SEVEN

"You did what?"

"I hired someone to kill Chatham," she repeated.

I stood and began to pace the room. "Do you realize you're guilty of conspiracy to commit murder?"

"Yes."

"And that you've implicated me?"

She looked puzzled. "How have I implicated you?"

"Because I know. You've just told me that you've set a murder in motion. If Chatham dies, you're going to jail. What happens to your life with Lester then?"

"Thanks to Chatham, I don't have a life with Lester."

She had all the features of someone who is desperate. Someone who had given up hope and would do anything necessary to find it and restore some semblance of happiness. That made her a very dangerous person.

"Who did you hire?"

"I don't know," she said, moving from the window to the chair where she had been sitting previously. "I hired him through someone I know." She sank into the seat.

"Who?"

She was hesitant.

"Look," I said, "let me spell this out for you. If we don't get to this man and stop him from killing Chatham, you are going down. Do you understand that? No life. No Lester. Nothing."

"I don't have Lester anyway, Colton. If Chatham dies, I might have a shot at rebuilding my marriage."

"You may have a shot even if Chatham doesn't die. Lester seems to truly love you. The man hired me to find you. He wouldn't have done that if he didn't want to try to work it out."

She paused to think. "Do you think he might take me back? Do you think my past wouldn't matter?"

"I don't know. All I know for sure is that if Chatham dies, so does any chance that you and Lester might have had."

It was clear that in her anger and desperation, she hadn't thought about the implications of her actions.

"If there is a chance that Lester will have me back..."

"Who connected you with the hit man?"

She opened her mouth to tell me, hesitated, and finally said, "His name is Vincent Gagliardi. He said to call him Vinny."

"Where can I find him?"

"I don't know. My circle isn't made up of the best, Colton. I had a number. A PO box. I left him a coded message, and he called."

"What's the box?"

She gave me the number.

"The message?"

"I was supposed to send a post card. It was to read: ALL PACKED. READY TO MOVE. It was to be typed and in all capital letters."

"Was he the man who went to Easy Travel with you?"

"Yes."

"Why did you buy a voucher?"

"It's for him. He said he was feeling some heat and wanted to get away for a while. I bought it under an assumed name."

"But you used your own card."

"I'm not a professional at this, Colton. I've never contracted to kill someone before."

"What was the price of the hit?"

"Seventy-five for the hit and twenty-five as a 'finder's fee.' The rest was for me to get away."

"People kill for a lot less than seventy-five thousand. You were either taken for a ride, or you bought yourself some quality talent. What happened to your car?"

"I don't know for sure. He said that if I was to stay clear of this, I would have to vanish. He said the car would lead the police to me."

"So that's why the new identity?"

"Yes." That could explain the blood in the car—to make it look like she was murdered. It was a stupid move. The police had assumed Claudia was leaving Lester of her own accord. Now, with her bloody car, they would be looking for her. I was beginning to get the impression that no matter how much talent seventy-five thousand can buy, the go-between didn't seem all that bright.

I stood and went into the kitchen. "Where do you keep the coffee?" I asked.

She told me, and I filled the basket with a filter and coffee. After I had poured water into the reservoir, I flipped the switch and came back into the living room. I didn't sit. I needed to think, and moving about seemed to help oil the process.

"Lester was alone his entire life," I said, "until you came into it. Whether that was for better or for worse is up to him. If he wants to work it out with you, he must know the whole truth. That means you have to tell him everything."

"If I tell him everything, he won't want me back."

"That may very well be the case," I said, turning to her. "But he's going to know."

She reluctantly agreed.

"But if you tell him about the…the deal you've made, you'll implicate him as well."

"So what do I do?"

I paced as I thought. The apartment was quiet. The only sounds were coming from the coffeemaker and the air-conditioning fan.

"If we can find the hit man you've hired and stop him before the hit goes down, we might be able to piece all of this together. That would leave the conspiracy charge, but maybe we can get past that if no harm was done."

"I don't know how to find the man I've hired. I don't even know who it is," she said.

"No, but you do know the contact."

"He told me that our business was finished and not to contact him again."

I shook my head. "We won't. At least, not the way you did. It would take days to move through the mail, and we may not have days."

I went into the kitchen and pulled two cups from the cup tree on the counter.

Coffee?" I asked. "It may be a long night."

After I cleaned up the eggs Beverly had dropped earlier, I found a package of Danish in the cupboard over the sink and brought those into the dining area with two cups. "There's creamer and sugar here too," I said as I set the packets of both on the table. I was struck by the fact that I didn't know how she took her coffee. Just one of the many things that I didn't know about my mother.

She joined me at the table, and for a few minutes, we drank coffee and ate rolls. Neither of us said anything.

"If we can't find the man in time," she said, breaking the awkward silence, "I'm not going back. I can't face Lester. He's the best thing that ever happened to me."

"If the hit goes down, you won't need to worry about facing Lester. The police will find you, and you can pretty much write off the whole thing."

So could I. I would have known, in advance, about a planned murder, even the name of the victim, without reporting it. But I understood Lester's position. I too was alone and had been most of my life. If there was a chance I could prevent the hit and help him restore his marriage, it was a chance I felt compelled to take. Not for her sake, but for his.

"This thing can go down two ways," I said, thinking out loud. "First, if the hit is made, Chatham dies. You and I go to jail, and Lester loses his marriage. The second way, if we can stop the hit, reason with the killer, and let him keep the fee, we might be able to move ahead. Chatham lives, none the wiser, and you and Lester have a chance to save your marriage."

"You're taking a lot of risk for me," she said.

"I'm not taking anything for you," I said. "I'm trying to help out a client. What I do, I do for him."

She nodded her understanding.

"What were your plans after the hit?" I asked.

She shrugged. "Who knows? I haven't thought that far ahead." She sighed. "I'll think of something."

"Sure," I said. "Always another Lester around the corner."

She lowered her eyes.

"This is the deal. You will stay here. You will not leave the building until I put this thing to bed. I will check on you periodically. Understand?"

She nodded again.

"So help me, if you are not here when I call, I will turn you over to the police and walk away from the whole thing."

"I'll be here," she said.

"You are to have no contact with Lester until this thing is cleared up. You are not to have contact with *anyone* who might know Lester. You are to make no attempt to reach him for any reason. I don't want him mixed up in your sordid affair any more than he already is."

"Okay."

I stood to leave. "One more thing. When this is over, you are never to attempt to enter my life. Understood?"

She nodded.

Chapter Twenty-Eight

Callie had spent the night with the Shapiros, who had taken her to school the next morning, so I had invited Mary out for a run. When she arrived, we jogged around the park and through the winding pathways that took us around the bandstand and back along the periphery. We talked about the bureau, people we knew, and cases we had worked on together. She was in excellent shape, conversing while running as easily as if we were sitting in a booth at Armatzio's. We finished up back at my house.

"Want something to drink?" I asked, turning on the window-unit air-conditioner.

"Water would be great," she said, falling into a chair at the kitchen table.

I pulled two bottles of water from the refrigerator as I collapsed into a chair across from hers, chugging the water in a way that was not medically sound.

"What's going on?" Mary asked as I rubbed the cold bottle across my face.

"I found Claudia," I said.

"Uh-uh. You didn't call me for that." She uncapped the bottle, and took a long drink.

I smiled. "Vigilant as always."

She waited for the rest.

"Claudia is my mother."

"Your *mother?*"

"Yep."

"Have you talked to her?"

I drank from the bottle. "Yep."

"What did she have to say?"

Another drink. "Nothing that mattered," I said.

"Did you know that she was your mother when you took this case?"

I shook my head.

"I'm sorry," she said. "I don't know what to say."

I shrugged. "There's nothing you can say. What she did, she did. It can't be undone. I've hated her for so long I can't go back, and I'm not motivated to go forward."

"Hate won't help, Colton."

"Not now, Mary," I said.

Mary had recently become a Christian, the result of extensive conversations with Millikin as she pursued a deeper knowledge of God. The conversion was now causing her to see things in spiritual terms, things she had once seen in legal terms. I didn't want to have that discussion today. I swigged the water again as neither of us said a word. It was the type of quiet that would have been uncomfortable if it weren't between friends.

"At any rate," I said, breaking the silence, "that isn't why I called."

She arched her eyebrows in an "Oh really?" fashion.

"What I have to tell you, I can't officially tell you. It would compromise you, and I don't want to do that."

"Tell me what you can. I can put the rest together."

"You'd still be compromised," I said. "You would still know."

"Let me worry about that. Nothing says I have to act on every bit of information I receive, legitimate or otherwise."

"Okay," I said. "It seems my mother has gotten herself into a bit of a bind, and I need to try to extricate her from it. That is, if she and Lester are going to have any chance to get back together."

"What kind of a bind?"

"A very tight one. Involves an unknown hit man and a go-between. I have a description of the go-between."

"Colton," Mary said in her official tone, "there was blood in Claudia's Jag. If a hit went down, you'd better tell me now."

"If I knew that a hit had already gone down, I would tell you."

"But you think that one might be about to go down."

"People die every day," I said, making it clear to her that I didn't want to compromise her any more than I already had.

"And the mark?"

I didn't want to reveal Chatham's name to Mary. She would be morally and legally obligated to tell him, which would drag the entire judicial system into the whole mess, ending Lester's chances with Claudia. I had also never lied to Mary, and I didn't want to start now.

"I don't know where he is," I said. It was technically true. I did not know where Chatham was at the moment.

"But you do know it's a man," she said. "If I'm not mistaken, you did say *he*."

She wanted a response. I didn't give her any.

"You're risking a lot for a woman who abandoned you."

I shook my head. "No. I'm risking a lot for a man who has never had it easy. A man who's had a lot of money, maybe, but who's never had anyone else in his life who cares. For some unknown reason, he loves my mother. And I believe she loves him—at least as much as she's capable of loving anyone. If I can pull this off, they'll be fine."

"And if you can't," she said, "a man will be dead, your mother will go to jail, Lester will lose what he probably never really had to start with, and your career, such as it is, will be in the can."

"Gee," I said, "you're putting a damper on things."

Mary sighed. "Tell me what you have," she said.

I told her about Vincent Gagliardi. I gave her a description and the fact that he and Claudia had purchased a travel voucher from Easy Travel under the name of Frances Seymour with her credit card.

"She used her credit card?"

I smiled.

"You want to know about this guy, right?"

"Anything and everything," I said.

Chapter Twenty-Nine

I had asked the Shapiros to pick Callie up from school again, which left me with a little more time to do some legwork. Time was a factor, and waiting for Mary to come up with some information on a go-between could take time that I didn't have.

I filled a plastic travel mug with coffee and left for the east side of Indianapolis.

During my time with the FBI, I often found myself working alongside some of the worst of society's offerings. Men who would beat an old lady's head in for the change in her purse might be useful in catching a foreign spy. The consequence was that we often overlooked one wrong in exchange for information on another. The courts often did the same thing and called it plea bargaining. Not all of these people were as horrible as it may sound, and some of them were caught up in lifestyles from which they were trying to escape. I knew one of these people. His name was Sean O'Toole.

I drove past the downtown area, parked outside a two-story brick building on the near east side, and went up the steps that ran alongside the building. When I reached the second story, I pulled the .38 snub from my waistband and knocked on the door. It took a few minutes before a tall, solidly built, redheaded man in his mid-thirties answered the door.

He was wearing gym shorts and an Indiana University T-shirt. I had obviously awakened him.

"Agent Parker?" he asked, rubbing his close-cropped hair with one hand.

"Hi, Sean. Can I come in?"

He looked past me and down to the street below before stepping aside and letting me enter.

The screen door slammed shut behind me as I stood in the kitchen. It was cool and dark, with linoleum flooring that was yellowing, a dripping faucet, and a refrigerator that hummed. There was no table.

His eyes focused on the gun. "What's wrong?"

"Precaution," I said as I tucked the gun back into my belt.

I could tell from his puzzled look that this was going to take some explaining. Sean had been too ingrained in the IRA to not know when someone was lying to him.

"I'm no longer with the bureau."

"What happened?"

I told him about my dismissal. About the kidnapper. How I had felt compelled to force the girl's location from him. How I had found the girl but lost my job.

"Did you mess him up bad?"

"Yes."

"Good for you." He went to the refrigerator and pulled out a beer. He held one out to me.

"No, thanks."

"Come on in here and sit down," he said, uncapping the bottle.

I followed him into the living room.

Equally as dingy as the kitchen, it was more elaborately furnished with a sofa that sat balanced on some phone books, two wingback chairs (one sitting directly on the floor), a recliner, and a large-screen television that was wired to an expensive-looking home theater system. A DVD player and a VCR were sitting on top of the TV. Two floor lamps finished the decor.

"Like TV, Sean?"

He swigged the long-necked beer and nodded as he looked at the television. "I do," he said. "I really do. Big screen like that," he gestured toward the TV with the beer bottle, "I can follow I.U. basketball like I was sitting right there."

We both looked at the blank screen for a few seconds before Sean got around to the heart of the matter.

"I'm straight, Agent Parker."

"It's Colton. I'm not with the bureau anymore, Sean."

"That's right, you're not. Sorry," he said, holding up the beer. "I forgot." He took another swig.

In Ireland, Sean had been involved in the planning of an IRA attack on a busload of British soldiers. But the information Sean was given had been wrong. The bus had been carrying school children. Disillusioned, Sean left the IRA shortly after that.

It wasn't that Sean had a problem with killing. He didn't. In fact, he had a penchant for it. A true one-of-a-kind talent. The kind of talent that could command a high fee. But the death of innocent children had left him shaken. And questioning.

His former comrades didn't take his decision lightly and dispatched two assassins to take care of the problem. It was a plan that would leave two would-be assassins dead and Sean on a plane bound for the United States.

Sean had come to my attention during my tenure with the FBI when he was questioned for a series of hits in the Indianapolis area. There had been a gang war, and the local bosses had brought in some out-of-town talent. Sean hadn't been involved in the gang war, but he had known the men responsible. The fact that we had interviewed him had caused some concern for those men. A contract was put out on Sean, and two men showed up at his door one evening. Two men who, like the assassins in Ireland, left in body bags. It was then that Sean did what so many in his line of work do: He sought the help of the FBI.

His testimony yielded a lot of convictions. In exchange, he was offered protection in the Federal Witness Protection Program administered by the United States Marshal. He declined. Living a life on the run was the only life Sean knew. After his testimony, most of those who wanted him dead were either dead themselves or locked up, helping Sean to sleep easier at night. Still, he was on edge, which made him just as deadly as ever.

"I'm looking for a go-between. Name's Vincent Gagliardi."

Sean nodded as he swilled the beer around in his mouth before swallowing. "I know him," he said in his thick Irish brogue. "You've got yourself one bad fella there."

"Who does he work with?"

He drank from the bottle again, studying me over the rim. "Why do you want to know?"

"It's business."

He nodded. "Aye, it is. Yours—not mine."

I looked around the room.

"Need money?"

"Can always use more money."

I opened my wallet and found two twenties. I gave them to him.

He nodded his thanks.

"So," I said, "who does he work with?"

"Why do you want to know?" he repeated.

I was getting a little peeved. "Sean, I just gave you forty dollars. It's all I have."

"And I thank you for it. But I didn't say anything was for sale."

I sighed. "No, Sean, you didn't."

"Why do you want to know?" he asked again, swigging the beer.

"I'm trying to stop several lives from getting destroyed. I can't do that unless I stop a hit. Vinny knows the gunman. I don't."

Sean smiled. "Well, why didn't you say so?"

As I drove south, I pondered the list of potential hitters Sean had given me. Like Sean had been, they were all freelancers. They were all

Italian except for one Irishman and one Russian, and all of them worked through Gagliardi.

Despite Sean's help, I was as lost as before. I knew most of the suspected hitters in the Midwest, but I didn't know any of the names Sean had given me. That fact pointed toward out-of-state talent, which was going to make my job a lot more difficult.

Chapter Thirty

I went back to the office and reexamined the phone records Lester had given me. I had made note earlier of a number that had been recorded on Claudia's cell bill but that hadn't been recorded in her address book.

The number had a north-side prefix, and the person using it had called Claudia's phone on three occasions, all of them preceding the time she left Lester.

I wrote down the dates. The first was February third, the second was April sixteenth, and the final call was on August tenth. I called Beverly.

"Yes?"

"It's Colton. You told me you didn't know how to contact Vinny."

"I made contact through a PO box."

"Right. Did he ever contact you?"

"Yes." A pause. "He called me on my cell. The number might—"

"What did he want?"

"He called in February, right after I sent the postcard, and told me his fee. He said I was to send it, and then he would initiate the transaction with the professional."

"He called two more times."

"He called again in..." She paused to think. "April, I believe. That was when the final payment to him was made. After that, he told me the amount for the contract. When it was paid in full, he called again with instructions to meet him at the Lafayette Square Mall in the parking lot. He got in the car and told me he needed to leave town, and we drove to the travel agency. We drove back to the mall, and he told me to leave the car with the keys under the floor mat in one week. I haven't seen or heard from him since."

I would have had a hard time believing her story if it hadn't been for Sean's knowledge of Vincent Gagliardi. Still, I wondered how Beverly could have been so gullible as to hand over a hundred grand and her car to a total stranger.

"You acted on a lot of faith," I said. "How did you know you weren't being taken for a ride?"

"I told you. I know people who know people. He came recommended by people who should know."

"Who?"

The phone line was silent.

"Tell me and save me the trouble of finding him myself."

"His name is Juan Cortez."

"And where can I find Mr. Cortez?"

She hesitated for a second. "He owns a dry cleaners on Thirty-fourth Street."

"A dry cleaner who knows a go-between?"

"He launders more than clothes," she said.

"I'm going to have to talk with him."

"If he knows that I—"

"He won't."

Another pause. "Be careful," she said.

"Why, Mother," I said, "I didn't know you cared."

CHAPTER THIRTY-ONE

Cortez Dry Cleaners was positioned in the middle of a strip mall that had seen better days. It also housed a pawnshop, a bar, and an auto parts store, but half of the real estate was vacant.

I parked a few feet down from the entrance to the dry cleaners on an asphalt lot that had weeds growing through it here and there. I wanted to watch and see the type of clientele that Cortez serviced. It didn't take long to get a handle on his chief trade.

For every man or woman who went in or out of the building with clothing, I saw ten who didn't. Most of them were young and dressed in gang paraphernalia. Some of them occasionally flashed gang symbols to each other as they entered and left the building. The steady flow told me that Cortez was probably in—and available.

I eased out of the car and tried to look like I fit in as much as possible. It was a stretch. I had no clothing to dry clean and nothing that identified me as a gang member or even a wannabe.

The shop was a two-story operation with racks of bagged jackets, blouses, pants, and shirts hanging in every available inch of space. Near the center of the room was a staircase that led to the upper floor, where an electrically operated rack fed the clothing to the downstairs area and back up again.

I saw two young men sitting on the counter near the cash register, flirting with the young woman who was operating it. One of the men was Hispanic, about twenty, with a thin build. He was wearing a red T-shirt, black jeans and boots, and a black fedora. A mass of gold hung around his neck, and he wore gloves with the fingers missing. The other was Caucasian, about twenty-five, with a shaven head and a muscular build. He was wearing a tank top, jeans, and tennis shoes. Tattoos extended from his shoulders to his wrists, and he wore a ring in his nose. The girl at the register was Hispanic, pretty with long dark hair and a thousand-watt smile. She was dressed in a white buttoned blouse with Cortez Dry Cleaners stenciled across the front. She seemed enthralled at the attention the men were giving her. All heads turned to me when I entered.

"Can we help you, bro?" the Hispanic man asked. Nose Ring chuckled.

The girl giggled and swatted at his arm. I heard her mutter, "I'm supposed to ask that." Then turning to me, she said, "Can we help you?"

"I hope so," I said, realizing that except for the three in front of me, I was the only one in the shop. "I'm looking for Cortez."

The girl glanced at the two men as her smile faded. "He's not in. Can I help you?"

I shook my head. "No, I don't think so." I turned to nod toward the parking lot. "When I was sitting out there, I saw a lot of people coming in and out of here. But now, I don't see anyone. Where is everybody?"

The Hispanic man slid off of the counter. "If Charlene say Cortez is not in, then he is not in."

"Sure," I said. "But where is everyone else?"

The guy flashed a fake smile and said, "That ain't none of your business, bro."

Time was running out. I had to find that hit man before the hit went down. Cortez was my best link to the go-between, and I wasn't about to let this kid become a get-between.

I grabbed the chains that hung around his neck with my left hand

and punched him in the forehead with my right, just above the eyes. He went down with a groan.

The larger man jumped off the counter and swung at me. I ducked the punch and hit him in the right kidney, followed by a right to his mid-section. The two blows seemed to take some of the zip out of him and he went down. Before the girl could say anything, I had the .38 in my right hand and had grabbed the Caucasian by the nose ring with my left.

"Now," I said, "where is Cortez?"

She pointed to a staircase behind a rack of clothing.

"Is there an office up there?"

She nodded, keeping an eye on the gun in my hand.

I yanked Nose Ring, by the nose ring, to his feet.

"Hey!" he yelled.

"I'm going up there to talk to your boss," I said to the girl. "If you call him and tell him I'm coming, I'm going to kill your friend here. Understand?"

She nodded. The smile was gone.

The Hispanic man was starting to push himself up. I pushed him back down with a foot on his back and led Nose Ring up the staircase. I kept the .38 in my hand and an eye on the steps above me.

When we reached the top of the stairs, I saw a room that had been hidden from my view by the conveyor belt of clothing. A plywood door that led into the room was closed, but I could hear people talking on the other side.

I turned to Nose Ring and held one finger to my lips with my gun hand. He nodded his understanding that I wanted no noise.

I kicked in the door and shoved Nose Ring in first. He fell to the floor yelling in pain. I still had the ring in my hand.

"Sorry," I said as I leveled the gun at the ten or so men in the room. "Well, well, what have we got here?"

CHAPTER THIRTY-TWO

There were half a dozen tables scattered around the room. Several men were cutting the cocaine at a couple of them, while at a couple of others, it was being packaged and weighed. There were several large stacks of cash on the other tables.

The room was silent. I had caught them by surprise, but I didn't expect it to stay that way for long. I focused on a large Hispanic man near the corner of the room wearing a long-barreled revolver on his hip. I figured him for security. I pointed the snub at him.

"You, Pancho, drop the gun belt."

He looked at the men in the room and then back to me before I heard someone say something to him in Spanish. The man glared at me and slowly undid the buckle of his gun belt. He let it slide to the floor.

"My friend does not understand English," said a Hispanic man approaching from the middle of the room.

"You Cortez?"

He smiled. "Who wants to know?"

My battle wasn't with Cortez. I had to find a hit man. Still, I was standing in the middle of his illicit operation with a gun in my hand. Telling him my name now was like asking for a bullet between the eyes.

"It doesn't matter who I am," I said.

He smiled again. "Oh, but it does, senor. It matters very much to me."

I kept a wary eye on everyone in the room. There were too many to watch, and I was standing in the open doorway with a .38 in one hand and a nose ring in the other. It was beginning to occur to me that I hadn't spent enough time thinking this thing through.

"Can we talk?" I asked.

He kept his eyes on me and the smile on his face as he gestured to the group of men behind him. "They are all friends," he said.

I pointed the barrel of the gun toward Cortez' midsection. If any of the men in the room was to pull a hidden gun, I wanted them to know that I wouldn't hesitate to kill Cortez.

"Someplace private," I said.

"And where would that be, senor? As you see," he gestured about the room again. "You have invaded my space. I have nowhere else to go."

I backed out of the doorway. "Outside," I said. "Let's go outside and talk." I motioned to him with the gun. As I moved back, several of the men stood. Cortez held up a hand but kept his eyes on me.

We moved down the staircase backward. I kept an eye out behind me while trying to keep my attention on Cortez and the room above.

As we inched our way down the staircase, I heard the young Hispanic man say something to Cortez in Spanish. Cortez responded.

"What did he say?" I asked, as we moved down the steps.

"He wanted to know if I wanted him to kill you."

"And?"

Cortez smiled. "Not yet."

It was getting difficult to watch my back, the room above, and the girl at the cash register. I needed to close the space, so I grabbed Cortez by the shirtfront and put the barrel of the gun in his belly. He quit smiling for the first time.

"You are making a very bad mistake, senor," he said.

"It wouldn't be the first time," I said.

"Perhaps it will be the last time," he said.

I backed up, steering Cortez toward the entrance. As I approached the door, I said to the young Hispanic man, "Come over here and open the door."

He didn't move.

"Do as he says," Cortez said.

The young man kept a glaring eye on me as he pushed the door open, allowing us to pass.

I steered Cortez to a point on the sidewalk that was about thirty feet from either the door or windows of his shop but still under the overhang, where I wouldn't be vulnerable to a shot from above. I glanced around the nearly isolated parking lot and did a quick pat down of Cortez. He was unarmed, so I slid the snub into my waistband.

"I don't want any trouble," I said.

He smiled again. "Unfortunately, senor, you now have it."

I nodded. "Probably." I gestured toward the building. "Now that I know, so do you. Maybe we can make a deal."

"A deal? In exchange for your life?"

"In exchange for both of our lives," I said.

He slipped a hand toward his back pocket. I grabbed him by the wrist.

"Mind if I smoke?" he asked.

I reached into his pocket and pulled out a pack of cigarettes. I had felt them during my pat down, but the chance always exists for missing something.

He shook a cigarette from the pack, stuck it between his lips, and lit it with a match. After shaking the match out and exhaling, he slipped the cigarettes and matches back into his pocket.

"To come into my place of business like this," he paused to inhale deeply, "you are either a very hard case or a very stupid one." He exhaled slowly.

"Maybe a little of both," I said.

He smiled again. "Maybe." He studied me for a moment. "So, what is this deal you are offering for both of our lives?"

Chapter Thirty-Three

"I have no interest in your operation," I said.

"But I do," he said. "And, unfortunately for you, you are now a liability for me."

I shook my head. "No, I'm not. Not if we can both get what we want."

He inhaled again and let the smoke out through his nostrils. "And what do you want?"

"I'm looking to hire someone."

"Hire someone?"

I nodded.

"I am not an employment agency."

"Maybe not. But for this type of job, I have heard that you might know where such an agency exists."

He continued to study me. "You are not the police." It wasn't a question.

"No."

"Where did you hear this about me?"

"Around."

He laughed as he shook his head. "No, senor, not around. You do not hear of these things around."

"I'm told that the best outside talent can be found through a go-between named Vinny."

He exhaled and nodded as he flipped the cigarette to the sidewalk and crushed it underfoot. "Yes, I know of such a man."

"I need to meet with him. I need his connections for some business I need to have done."

He smiled and shook his head. "No, senor. You are too accomplished at what you do, even if you are stupid for doing it. You do not want him for the purposes that you have described."

I nodded toward the dry cleaners. "This…business that you own, is it yours?"

He smiled again. "Mostly."

"And the part that isn't yours?"

He shrugged as he glanced around the parking lot with what I was quickly learning was more of a perpetual sneer than a smile. "There are other parties."

"Parties that hold you responsible for its well-being," I said.

The sneer began to fade.

"Parties that would take it very personally if it went up in smoke."

The sneer had been replaced with an embryonic look of vendetta. "It would be best to not threaten me, senor."

"Sure," I said. "And it would have been best to not raid a cocaine operation with maybe five million of the stuff just lying around. And it probably would have been best to not haul your sorry tail out here in the public square to make a deal. But…" I shrugged.

The sneer returned and then morphed into a broad, gregarious smile. "You are a very dead man, senor."

"Well then, it seems I don't have anything to lose."

He glanced over his shoulder at the cleaners and then turned back to me. "Okay. He is of no consequence to me, so I will tell you how you can find him," he said.

"Thank you," I said. "And I would appreciate it if you wouldn't tell him that I'm coming."

"I have no need for such a thing," he said. "You belong to me now. And no one will tell you when I am coming, senor."

CHAPTER THIRTY-FOUR

I had a bead on Vinny now and had made a new enemy in the process. All in all, just another day.

I glanced at my watch as I pulled out of the parking lot. Callie was probably already home, and the Shapiros had filled in for me once again by being there when she arrived.

Callie was thirteen and certainly able to fend for herself. But at fifteen months, the pain from Anna's death was still acute, and any semblance of normalcy was welcomed. An empty house was not normal for Callie, and I didn't want anything happening that could stoke the fires of her kindling anger.

I zipped across town and arrived home just before the evening rush hour reached full swing. By the time I got into the house, Corrin was already making dinner, and Frank was trying to help Callie with homework. He looked up at me when I came through the door.

"Am I glad to see you," he said. "How do you figure out 2X minus 3X divided by—"

"Stop, Frank. You've already lost me," I said, sliding onto the sofa. "Let me take a look, Callie."

She penciled something onto her paper. "No, that's okay. I've got it now. Thanks, Grandpa." She gathered her books together and called to Corrin in the kitchen. "When is dinner, Grandma?"

Corrin told her it would be a while, and Callie announced that she would be in her room doing her homework.

"Did you see that?" I asked Frank.

He nodded.

"Tell me I'm wrong. Tell me she doesn't have hard feelings toward me." I was feeling sorry for myself again.

"No, I can't say you're wrong," he said. "She certainly seems to resent you." Then he reached out to put a hand on my knee. "But I wouldn't sweat this too much. She'll come around."

"I'm not so sure," I said.

"Then you'll have to do all that you can to assure that she does."

"How do I do that, Frank?"

Corrin stood in the doorway of the kitchen. "By giving her time."

"What does that mean, Corrin? Do I sit idly by and just wait for the weeks and months to pass?"

Frank shook his head. "No. It means you need to understand the makeup of a young girl. Particularly one who has suffered such a major loss."

"I think I do. I had those losses too."

A frown unfolded across Frank's face. "No, you haven't. You lost a wife. But…" He glanced at Corrin. "As hard as it is for me to say this, you may find a new wife someday."

"No one could replace Anna."

"No, Anna cannot be replaced. She was our daughter. Our only child. But the fact remains that you are young and can marry again. But Callie cannot get another mother."

Corrin returned to the kitchen.

"She has also lost her self-image," Frank said.

"But she has always had good self-esteem, Frank. She—"

He shook his head. "No. Not self-esteem. *Self-image*. She has lost the way she views herself."

I had heard this before. "Are you a psychologist, Frank?" It was an attempt at levity. He wasn't amused.

"She's lost her self-image," he repeated, slower this time, in case I didn't understand.

"I know," I said. "Because of Anna, and—"

He nodded. "Yes, partly. But also because of the suicide attempt." He called it what it was, avoiding the term "cry for help." "Then," he said, "there's the move and the loss of her social status. In one year, she went from an honor roll student with the potential of an athletic scholarship and a mother who adored her, to a motherless child whose grades are barely passing. And on top of that, she's living with the knowledge that she attempted to harm herself. Add to that the loss of her previous economic status, and… " He stopped as a flash of regret crossed his face.

"I know, Frank."

He squeezed my knee. "It's okay, Colton. You provide for her. You are a good father. But all of this will take time. Not time in the sense of minutes or days that pass, but patience on your part. A willingness to do what needs doing and then allowing God to do what only He can."

"I have no problem with patience, Frank. But how much longer? How much longer before she begins to come around and understand that I love her? I'm not the enemy."

He shook his head. "She doesn't see you as the enemy. She sees her circumstances as the enemy. You just happen to be available." He put a hand on my shoulder. "I know you've never been one for the things of God. But He can make a difference."

"Sure," I said, more to pacify Frank than from true belief. After all, if God would or could intervene in the problem, wouldn't it have been better for Him to have not allowed the problem in the first place?

CHAPTER THIRTY-FIVE

I drove Callie to school the next morning, hoping we could talk. But my hopes fizzled when she slipped the earpieces of a Walkman over her head as soon as we pulled away from the house.

When we arrived at the school, she asked me to let her out about twenty yards from the main entrance. I did and watched as she struggled with her book bag, moving along the sidewalk toward the gathering crowd of students who were inching their way into the school.

Callie had been popular at her old school. But now, I didn't see a single student—girl or boy—acknowledge her presence.

After she had moved into the building, I pulled away from the curb and headed toward Nashville, Indiana, an hour south of Indianapolis. Cortez had given me Vinny's address on the outskirts of town and a promise to not notify the go-between that I was coming. Of course the promise came from a cocaine dealer who had made it clear that my life wasn't worth the paper that packaged his product. So I wanted to arrive early and stake out the place before I made a grand entrance.

During the drive to Nashville, I thought about Callie, the recent events in her life, and what Millikin had said about Anna.

Maybe I *was* responsible for Anna's death. Was I? Millikin was right, of course. I had been arguing with my wife the night she stormed out of the house and died. But I had long since forgotten what was said. That is, until Callie reminded me. Did Anna storm out of the house? Or was she simply doing what I had asked her to do?

For an hour, I ran these questions through the filter of the past days' events. I ran them through my conversations with Mary. I compared the differing viewpoints between her and Millikin. I measured against my last words to Anna. Words that I had forgotten saying but that Callie had vividly recalled hearing.

The thoughts didn't produce an answer but helped the time to pass. When I arrived in Nashville, I began to follow the directions Cortez had given me. I inched my way through the downtown district, past the many log cabins that housed candy shops, craft stores, and restaurants; past the ambling throngs of people who were looking for bargains or a pleasant way to spend a day.

I was soon clear of the foot traffic and making my way along a hilly gravel road that wound its way through fields and streams and over bridges—some that were solid as well as some that weren't.

As I neared the top of a hill, I noticed a red cabin that sat nearly a hundred yards off the berm of the road just as it began to curve and roll into another gully. Twenty yards past the cabin, I pulled over, parked behind a cluster of bushes, and killed the engine.

The map that Cortez had given me didn't show an open field on all sides of Gagliardi's cabin. But it made sense. Someone like Gagliardi, who dealt as a merchant of death, who played with snakes, was going to anticipate the day when he would get bitten. He could forestall that day if he could see the snake approaching.

I eased out of the car, pulling my pump shotgun from behind the front seat. I had three shells in the magazine and five more in my pocket. With any luck, I wouldn't need any of them. After all, I hadn't come to butt heads with Gagliardi; I just wanted to know whom he had hired on Beverly's behalf.

But I also couldn't ignore the fact that this was a business transaction that had made Gagliardi a lot of money and that depended on his ability to keep the identity of others a secret. Killers of the type that Gagliardi could secure on behalf of a client were not apt to become involved in messy affairs. That meant that no matter how nice of a guy I was, or how politely I asked, he probably wouldn't just hand over a name.

I knelt behind the bushes to study the layout of the property. I didn't see any way to approach the cabin without being seen. That was going to eliminate the element of surprise. Assuming, of course, that Cortez had not already eliminated that for me.

I flipped open my phone and called Mary. When she came on the line I asked, "You doing anything tonight?"

"No, why?"

"I've got a bit of a problem. I need to stake out a place and I won't be home before midnight."

The line was quiet for a moment. "Where are you?"

"It would be better for you if you didn't know. Can you get to my house and keep an eye on Callie?"

"It sounds like you're the one who needs looking after."

"I'll be okay. I just have to run down a lead, and I don't like leaving Callie alone."

Another moment of silence. "Okay. I'll be there. By the way, I've got some info for you on your go-between."

That was just like Mary. Timely as ever. "Shoot," I said.

"The bureau has been watching this guy for a long time. We haven't been able to pin anything on him yet, but he's long been suspected of ties to organized crime."

"Surprise, surprise," I said.

"There's more. Do you remember those two gangland style slayings that happened on the south side about a year ago?"

"The ones where they were nearly cut in half?"

"Those are the ones. Your go-between had been seen at the location moments before any shots were fired. He was picked up and interrogated, but nothing came of it."

"So you're telling me that he's a very combative individual."

"Slightly. I would say vicious is a better description. If he was the hitter, he's probably responsible for a number of them. We have a lot of shotgun slayings to account for, most of them gang related, and he's probably good for plenty."

I thanked her for her help, flipped the phone closed, and got back into the car. If I was going to approach the house of a man like Gagliardi, who was not just a go-between but a killer in his own right, I wanted to do it under the cover of darkness. That wasn't going to be for several hours, so I had a lot of waiting to do.

Chapter
Thirty-Six

By the time the sun had gone down enough for me to approach the cabin, I had been cramped in the car for almost ten hours. I hadn't seen any activity in or around the cabin during that time. In fact, I didn't see much activity in the area that surrounded the cabin. Occasionally a car would pass or a plane would fly overhead, but all in all, this area of Brown County seemed quiet.

I got out of the car, stretched the kinks out of my legs, grabbed the shotgun, and climbed over the barbed wire fence. Except for crickets and the occasional mooing of a cow, the evening was quiet. From where I now stood, I could see a light on in the cabin, but I saw no other signs of life as I began to creep along the edge of the property.

As I moved closer, I noticed two entrances to the building. One was the front door, which had a screen in front of it. The other was on the west side of the cabin. That door did not have a screen, making a sudden entrance into the cabin more feasible. I didn't think I was going to be able to knock and ask if I could come in.

I had fifty yards to clear from the west side of the cabin to the door. I chambered a round in the shotgun, glanced around, and made a dash across the field. When I reached the small stoop next to the door an automatic motion-sensitive light came on, flooding this area of the building. Whatever chance I had for a surprise entrance was now lost.

I jumped onto the stoop next to the door and kicked it in, leveling the shotgun as I did.

The cabin was small with one large central room that seemed to serve as the core. To one side was a grouping of chairs, a television, a stereo, and a coffee table with two end tables and lamps. On the other side was a small kitchen. Neither the television nor the stereo was on, and the kitchen was quiet.

To the right of where I stood was a staircase and a door that was slightly ajar. I kept the shotgun level, first glancing up the staircase and then at the nearly open door. Chances were high that Cortez had warned Vinny that I was coming. He could have left the door partially open as bait and be waiting to blast me from the staircase above. If Mary was correct, and a shotgun was his instrument of choice, I could be in deep trouble.

I moved along the wall, keeping my eyes moving from the door to the top of the stairs. The cabin was quiet except for my chest, which felt as if Gene Krupa were drumming on my heart.

When I had positioned myself alongside the door, I looked through the open area for any signs that the door was armed. If Vinny knew that I was coming, wiring the door to blow when I opened it would be as easy as shooting me from above. But I considered that possibility less likely because it would cost him the cabin. On the other hand, from the looks of the door, losing it would be no great loss.

I didn't see any evidence of a trap on the door, but of course, not all traps can be seen. I transferred the shotgun to my left hand and braced myself against the wall. Keeping an eye out on the stairs above, I pushed the door open with the heel of my right hand.

Nothing. No bang, no fire, no pieces of Colton Parker spread over Nashville. I let out a breath and moved through the doorway with the shotgun at waist height. Gene Krupa was going full tilt.

The room had a queen-sized bed, a chest of drawers, a mirror that stood on four legs, and a closet. I closed the bedroom door behind me to prevent easy access from anyone who might be upstairs, and I opened the closet door by standing to one side. Except for a few articles of clothing, it was empty. I searched the chest of drawers and came up with the same.

I left the bedroom and began to methodically climb my way upstairs. The creak of each step was loud in the otherwise quiet cabin, trumpeting to anyone who might care to listen that I was moving upstairs.

The staircase had a tight spiral, so I kept the barrel of the shotgun pointed straight up with my right hand as I held on to the rail with my left. When I reached the top of the stairs, I eased my head up, looking to each side cautiously.

The upper area appeared to be a loft that Vinny was using as an office. No one was there.

I moved up the last step and into the loft. A long desk along one wall held a computer and a phone. A file cabinet stood to one side.

I sat at the desk and turned on the computer. After it booted up, I checked Vinny's recent history. From what I could see, he had a penchant for exotic travel. That fit with his visit to the travel agency.

I opened the desk drawers, one at a time, and found the usual office supplies: a stapler, paper clips, printer paper, and toner.

I stood and went to the file cabinet. It was locked, so I went back to the desk and fashioned a pick from one of the large paper clips. Within a few seconds I had the drawers open.

The top drawer had a brown accordion-style folder that was held shut with a large rubber band. I tossed it on the desk and continued my search.

The second drawer held two phone books. The third was empty.

"Let's see what you've got here, Vinny," I said as I opened the accordion file.

I shook the contents onto the top of the desk and began to sort through them.

I found several bank statements, phone records going back several months, and five keys bundled together by a twist tie.

I examined the phone records. Several calls had been made to various parts of the country. A large number of these were to Florida and had been made in the past several months. If I was right, the Florida phone number belonged to the hitter hired by Beverly.

I picked up Vinny's phone and dialed the Florida number. It had been disconnected.

I examined the bank statements. Large deposits corresponded to the dates that Beverly had taken the money from Lester's accounts. Some of it had been withheld—the amounts deposited added up to far less than the seventy-five thousand that Beverly said she had paid for the hit. Either this register wasn't complete, or Vinny was holding out on whomever he had hired.

I slipped the register and other paperwork back into the folder and tucked it under my arm. I examined the keys. They belonged to the US Postal service, and Vinny had placed a numbered piece of tape around each of them. Most likely, he had several PO boxes and was trying to keep track. At any rate, I now had access to them and a lead that I didn't have just a few hours before.

I sat back down and checked the computer for any other items of interest. There were none.

I had expected Vinny to be home. I had expected a confrontation, and I had expected to come out on top. There was an overall sense of letdown as Gene Krupa toned down and began to work the skins with brushes instead of sticks.

Before I left the cabin, I wiped down the areas I had touched and turned off the security light that could reveal me to anyone who might be waiting in the surrounding field.

I didn't know Vinny personally, but the FBI did. If he was as bad as Mary said, I would run into him soon enough.

CHAPTER THIRTY-SEVEN

By the time I arrived home that night, Callie was asleep, and Mary was channel surfing.

"Thanks for taking care of Callie," I said as I set the accordion file onto the coffee table and sank into my recliner.

"Problems?"

I shook my head. "No."

"Did your suspect show?"

"No."

"So was the night productive?"

I nodded. "Yeah, I think so."

She glanced at the folder on the table. "So was ours."

"Oh?"

Mary nodded. "I think I've been wrong, Colton."

"About what?"

"You. And Callie."

I shifted uncomfortably in the chair. "Why?"

"Callie and I had a long talk tonight about you. She told me some of the details about your arg…your discussion with Anna on the night of her death."

"She tell you that I told Anna if she didn't like it here, she could leave?"

"Yes."

"I didn't mean it."

"I know. And I think Anna knew also."

"But Callie saw her leave," I said.

"Yes."

"Saw her mother leave because her father told her to."

"Yes."

"And she never came back."

"Yes."

"Mary," I said, sighing as I rubbed the fatigue from my eyes, "this is old news. Callie has already told me that she blames me for Anna's death."

"I'm not so sure she's wrong."

I continued to rub my eyes with both hands. The day had been long, and I was very tired. My body ached from hours in the car, my eyes burned, and my mind was numb from the methodical search of Vinny's cabin. I wasn't in the mood for an introspective discussion about my failings as a husband and father.

"Mary can we do this another night?"

She stood. "Sure," she said. "But don't wait too long. Callie has bitterness toward you that I didn't see before." She paused at the door. "And, Colton?"

"Yes?"

"It's taking root."

CHAPTER THIRTY-EIGHT

Callie was quiet during breakfast. When I asked if her homework was done, I got a yes. When I asked if she enjoyed having Mary over last night, I got a yes. When I asked her if she was going to ditch school and join the circus, I got a yes.

She boarded the school bus as she always did—with an overloaded book bag and without a goodbye for me. After the bus pulled away, I went into her room and began my search.

Her recent attempt at a drug overdose, combined with her sulkiness and flat demeanor, concerned me about the possibility of another attempt. If she had a stash of drugs put away, I needed to find them and eliminate them before she eliminated herself.

I opened her closet and went through her clothing, one pocket at a time. Nothing.

I went through the chest of drawers. Nothing.

I looked in the drawers of the desk and behind the desk. Nothing.

I looked under the desk, the bed, and the mattress. Each time, I came up with nothing.

I sat on the edge of her bed, half-ashamed and half-proud. Ashamed that I had assumed drugs were at the root and proud that they weren't. Then I saw it. The edge of a piece of tape protruding over the back of the headboard. I pulled the bed away from the wall and saw a box in a plastic ziplock bag taped to the bed.

I opened the bag and the box. I didn't find drugs. I found a diary.

Thirty minutes later, I was sitting with Tony Armatzio, drinking coffee. The post office didn't open for another hour, so I had a little time to kill. I also needed to talk with Tony.

"Coffee's too strong," I said.

He licked one thumb and turned the page of the sports section as he glanced over his bifocals at me. "Make it yourself then."

We were silent for a minute as Tony read the sports page and I drank his too-strong coffee. He was still mad over the incident with Millikin. Tony didn't take lightly to being put upon, and he wanted me to know.

"Tony, I didn't mean to embarrass you the other day. Sorry."

He looked at me again over his bifocals. "I won't mean to embarrass you too, when time comes." A faint, almost imperceptible flicker of his upper lip told me he was okay. His anger was his way of saying, "Got you."

"How are you and Nick doing?" I asked. Nick was Tony's son. The two had barely spoken since Nick had told Tony that he had no desire to take over the restaurant when Tony retired.

Tony made a back-and-forth wiggle of his hand. "So-so."

"See him much?"

"Some," he said, engaged in the paper.

I got up from the table, went to the counter, and poured myself another cup before returning to my seat. "Do you hold his decision against him?"

Tony set the paper down, removed his bifocals, and leaned back in his chair with a frown on his face. "Why you ask me these questions?"

"Callie blames me for Anna's death. I'm afraid she's withdrawing, and I don't know what to do." It was the first time I had ever heard myself admit it out loud.

"Why ask me? I don't know either. I am not even talking to Nick."

"Is it all because of his decision not to run the restaurant? Or is there something else?"

Tony put the bifocals back in place and flipped the paper open again. "No, that is pretty much it," he said.

"Does he call?"

"He talks to his mother," Tony said, scanning the page for any sports trivia that could bring him a few bucks.

"What's he going to do?"

Tony shrugged. "Not my problem," he said. "He doesn't want to stay in restaurant, doesn't want to follow in father and grandfather's footsteps, that is his problem. He can do whatever he like."

"That's what concerns me, Tony. I'm afraid Callie will do just that."

I thanked Tony for the coffee and drove the two miles to the post office. It had just opened, and most of the traffic was from people who were opening their boxes. I would have fit right in if I hadn't had five boxes to open.

I scanned the wall of PO boxes, looking for the ones that fit the keys I had in my hand. They were all at this branch but scattered around the wall. I already knew which one Beverly had used to contact Vinny. But as long as I had all of his keys...

I slid the key in place and unlocked the first box. It was empty.

I tried the next two and found the same thing. On the fourth one, the one that corresponded to the number Beverly had given me, I got lucky.

Inside was an envelope that had no return address but did have a postmark from Destin, Florida.

I closed and locked the box and tried the fifth box just to be thorough. It was empty.

I went out to the car and opened the envelope. A typed note contained only two lines:

PACKAGE RECEIVED—WILL ARRIVE 8-29.

ISOLATE MARK—COMPLETE CONTRACT 9-04.

I studied the letter. No watermarks, no smudges. Nothing unusual.

All indications were that the writer of the letter had arrived in town yesterday and would make the hit within the next five days. That is, if I was interpreting it correctly. If so, Vinny had hired out-of-state talent as I had suspected. That would explain the large fee Beverly had paid. But it didn't identify the hitter. Only Vinny could do that, and with only five days to go, I needed to find him—and soon.

Chapter THIRTY-NINE

I was heading back to the office to go over the paperwork from Vinny's cabin when my phone rang. It was Millikin.

"Colton," he said. "Glad I found you. I didn't like the way we left things the other day. Could I come over for a while?"

I didn't like the way things had been left either, but I was also very busy trying to stop a murder and rehab several lives in the process. My own included.

"Sure," I said against my better judgment. "Meet me at my office in half an hour."

"I'll be there," he said. "And I'll bring the donuts."

Forty minutes later, Millikin and I were sitting in my office with the fan going, eating chocolate long johns and drinking coffee. Hot coffee may not be the right thing to drink on a hot day, especially when you're sitting in a third-floor office with no air conditioning, but having donuts without it was like buying a suit without the coat.

"These are really good," I said. "Where did you get them?"

He licked the chocolate off one finger. "A little place not far from the church."

We were silent for a minute or two as we worked our way through the bag.

———

"Listen, Colton, I really am sorry if I upset you the other day. It wasn't my intention."

"I know," I said, "and it's okay. But I know you well enough to know that you always have intent behind everything you say."

"Yes. That's true. I just wanted to make you think a little bit. I want you to see that the possibility exists that you *are* responsible for your wife's death."

I fished in the bag for another donut but they were gone. Millikin held his out to me. I shook my head.

"I have thought about it," I said. "I've thought a lot about it since we talked."

"And?"

"I know that Callie believes I'm responsible for killing her mother."

"Then you are." He bit into the donut.

I shook my head. "Sorry, but I don't see how."

"Yes you do. You've been carrying this with you since Anna died. You want absolution. You want someone to tell you you're not responsible. And Mary has been doing that, yet that isn't enough. Why do you think that is?"

I shrugged. "Guilty conscience?"

He smiled as he tore off a piece of the donut. "Could be. But a guilty conscience usually means you are guilty of something." He popped the piece of donut into his mouth.

"Wait a minute," I said. "Anna told me what you told her. That Satan will use the past to make people feel guilty but that they shouldn't worry about it. Just ignore it."

He shook his head. "That isn't exactly what I said. After a person comes to Christ, and I mean truly comes to Christ, his sins are forgiven." He paused to study my reaction. He must have seen a blank slate because he continued. "The Bible tells us that once we confess our sins before Him and repent of them—that means we turn away from our old life and our old perception of things—He is just and will forgive us of those sins. But that doesn't mean we weren't guilty. But since we're still human and still have human hearts, and will as long as we are on this side of heaven, Satan will use our past transgressions against us to make us doubt our faith in God's forgiveness."

"So he uses our guilt as a wedge in our relationship with God?"

He smiled a broad smile. "Exactly." Then, leaning forward across the desk, "You do believe that there is a Satan, don't you, Colton?"

"I believe that there is evil in the world," I said. "I've seen too much of it to doubt its existence."

"Evil does indeed exist," Millikin said as he finished off the last piece of the last donut. "And so does Satan."

"So, help me to understand," I said. "What does all of this have to do with Callie and me?"

"You just said it. Satan uses our guilt as a wedge between God and us."

I thought for a minute. "So my guilt over Anna's death is a wedge between Callie and myself?"

He nodded. "At least she certainly seems to see it that way. You must admit, since Anna's death your relationship with your daughter has not improved, has it?"

"No. But I didn't have much of one to start with."

He nodded. "I know. We talked about that before."

We were both silent for a moment. I wanted to tell him about what I had read in Callie's diary but decided I didn't need more psychobabble at the moment.

"This isn't psychobabble, Colton," Millikin said as if he had just climbed out of my head. "It's biblical."

"So where do I go from here?" I asked. "Callie hates me and—"

"She doesn't hate you. On the contrary, she loves you. And that love is your ticket out of this situation."

"How do you figure?"

"The Bible tells us that love covers a multitude of sins. In other words, she *wants* to forgive you. Her forgiveness will also free her from the anger she's carrying." He leaned back in his seat. "It's been said, Colton, that forgiveness is a gift we give ourselves."

"If I thought my daughter felt a need to forgive me so she could stand to be near me, that alone would make me feel guiltier than ever."

"In that case, you take it to God."

I mulled this over as I drank some coffee. It had gone cold.

"God gave His son to die in our place. It was a horrible death that included insults, public humiliation, and eventually a severe beating that led to death by dehydration and suffocation on a cross. That tells us that God is both just, which means He cannot tolerate sin, and loving, because He does not want to inflict that punishment on any of us." He paused to allow what he said to sink in and take effect. "In other words, love covers a multitude of sins."

"So?"

"When Callie tried to commit suicide, did you feel alone?"

"Yes."

"But you weren't. God was right there with you. You could've turned to Him then, and you can turn to Him now. He wants to help. He wants to restore everything to the way it was meant to be."

"And I should ask Callie to forgive me for killing her mother?"

He sighed. "Ask her to forgive you for driving Anna out of the house that night. But be prepared."

"For what?"

"For her to forgive you. It may take time, but when it comes, it will highlight your sin against her."

"I'll feel guiltier than ever."

"Yes, you will. But she can't forgive you for something that didn't happen. At least in your mind, it didn't. If she can hear you ask her to forgive you, she can do that and move on, as can you. But as long as this guilt exists, it will be a wedge."

He waited for a response. I had none.

"Ever read the story about the prodigal son?"

I shook my head.

He wrote the reference down on a piece of paper and slid it across the desk to me. "Read this," he said. "It's the perfect illustration of how God wants to forgive us."

I took the paper and put it in my pocket.

"But understand this, Colton. Forgiveness is a two-way street. We are also to forgive others."

"That's a little hard to do sometimes," I said.

He nodded. "Yes, it is. Did you read the other Scripture passage I gave you?"

"Yes."

"Jesus tells Peter that we are to forgive others not just seven times, but seventy times seven."

"I read the passage, Dale."

"And Jesus goes on to illustrate how we are to forgive others as we want to be forgiven."

"I read the passage, Dale," I said again.

He smiled.

I turned up the speed on the fan. The morning had started out hot and was now getting hotter.

"You see," Millikin said, pausing to drain his cup, "Callie wants her life back too. But she feels like she would be letting her mother down if she doesn't hold you to the fire for Anna's death. If you ask for her to forgive you, you acknowledge that she's correct, you admit your own guilt, and you free her to make the choice to forgive without being disloyal to Anna."

I eased back in my chair. "And that's when things really get dicey."

He nodded. "For a while. Her anger toward you may even grow as you admit what she has suspected all along. But forgiving you is what she needs. It will help to tear down the wall of separation that Anna's death has created. And she won't do that until you ask." He tossed the empty donut bag into the trash can and stood to leave. "And, Colton?"

"Yeah?"

"Don't wait too long. Bitterness takes root."

"I know," I said. "I know."

Chapter FORTY

"He's what?" I asked.

Mary said, "They found his body about an hour ago. And I'm willing to bet that was his blood in Claudia's Jag."

We were sitting in my office, an hour after Millikin left, drinking iced tea. I had just bought an iced tea maker, and when Mary came by to tell me the news, it looked like a good time to give it a whirl.

She had come with a surprise, something that I had never liked in an investigation. They always come at the wrong time and always seem to put just enough bends in the road to make you realize you had perceived the situation entirely wrong.

"Where?" I asked.

"In a junkyard west of town. The body was in the trunk of a 1999 Pontiac Grand Am that was partially compacted."

"Why didn't the body get compacted?" I asked.

"Whoever did it bungled the job," she said. "The magnet had been released too soon, and the car fell into the bin, nose first. Since the body was in the trunk—"

"The part that got compacted was insufficient to hide the evidence," I said.

"Right."

Mary had just told me that Vinny was dead. Which meant that my best chance of finding the hitter was also dead. "I wonder why the killer didn't dispose of the body."

Mary shook her head. "I don't know. Scared off?"

"Maybe."

"Maybe he left once he dropped the car and never bothered to check and see if his plan worked."

"Maybe" I said. I leaned back in my chair. "I'm going to need to know what happened."

"Of course. But if you march in there now, you're going to rile a lot of state troopers. One in particular."

Mary was right. Chang had told me to stay out of what was now a police investigation. Now that a body had been found, that warning would be in force.

"I'm going to have to talk with whoever found the body."

Mary smiled. "I might be able to help with that one. Our guys got called because the body was found in the trunk of a car that still had plates on it. Out-of-state, *stolen* plates."

That made it an inter-state crime. Time to call the FBI.

"Who's working it?" I asked.

"Goetz and King."

Danny Goetz was a good guy. Knew all the rules and knew when they should be applied. But he also knew when the human element needed to be considered too. Jimmy King, on the other hand, had been Hooverized years after Hoover was gone. Impeccably dressed in a white shirt, dark suit, and dark tie, he wore a haircut from the nineteen thirties and spoke in the crisp and curt tones of Jack Webb. He followed the rules so tightly that many of us had begun to suspect that he was coming unwound.

"Please tell me that Goetz got there first."

She nodded. "It's how I found out."

"You talked to him?"

She smiled again. "Putz. Of course I did."

"Were you going to make me pry it out of you?"

"A little sweating will do you good." She stood to refill her tea and drop a packet of Splenda into it before sliding back onto the chair I kept in front of my desk.

"Is this thing going to drag on all day or are you going to tell me what you know?" I asked.

She stirred her tea. "Goetz told me that the manager came in this morning at about seven. He always comes in early to drink coffee and read the paper. He's retired from his day job and runs the junkyard for something to do. Three days a week he has two cronies come in, and they talk politics and smoke cigars or whatever until opening time at nine. Then he walks the grounds before opening the gates. Does it for exercise every day. He's got the yard's inventory memorized."

"And that's when he found the body?"

She shook her head. "No, that's when he noticed that the magnet they use to hoist the cars wasn't where he left it when he closed the day before. When he found it, it was poised over the compactor."

"He examined the compacter and found the body," I said.

"Then when he found that the chain on the rear gate had been cut, he called the police."

"Who called the FBI to cover their bases when the out-of-state tags were found." I drank a large gulp of tea. "And we *know* it's Vinny Gagliardi?"

"Not yet, but the description matches the one you gave me. Prints will be run."

I was ready to suggest that Mary contact the travel agents at Easy Travel for confirmation that the body was the man who came in with Claudia. But that would lead to Claudia, which would lead to me, which would cause the whole plan to unravel. I closed my mouth.

"You were going to say something?" Mary asked.

"Just that I know you'll call me as soon as you hear anything."

"Of course," she said. "What else do I have to do?"

CHAPTER FORTY-ONE

After Mary left, I drove back out to Sean's. It was nearly noon, but he answered the door with the same disheveled look and was wearing the same Indiana University T-shirt.

He had the standard O'Toole breakfast—a bottle of Guinness and a piece of dry toast. He looked down to the street below as he had done the last time I was there and then held open the screen door.

I went in as he closed the door behind me. We stood in the kitchen as he bit into the toast and swigged the beer, patiently waiting for me to state my reason for being there again.

"Vinny's dead."

"That's bloody bad for you now, isn't it?"

"Yes."

"And you want help?"

"Yes."

"You know that I'm out of it for good. Right?"

"Sure," I said. "Just like I am."

He smiled and swigged the beer again to wash down the last bit of toast. "I'm not sorry to hear about Vinny," he said. "He's had it coming for a long time."

"Me either. I'm not particularly crazy about the guy myself. But it does complicate what I'm trying to do."

Sean finished the beer and tossed it into the trash can. From the sound of its landing, I was betting the bottle had found companions.

He leaned against the counter. "Did you do him?"

"Would I be here if I had?"

Anyone who wants to stay in this game must learn to read people. To look beyond the words. Sean was no novice.

"No. I know you didn't," he said.

"If I don't stop this hit, innocent lives are going to be ruined," I said.

"Yours?"

"For starters."

He continued to lean against the counter studying me. He needed to know if I was who I said I was. Our previous encounters had been brief, and in Sean's world, an unknown entity was a known danger.

"Innocent lives get taken all the time," he said.

"Yes. But when there's a chance to stop it, shouldn't we?"

He lowered his head. "Do you know the mark?"

"Yes."

"Does he deserve it?"

"We all deserve it, Sean."

He nodded. "Aye."

I waited while he mulled over the possibilities. He could help me, or he could refuse. But he couldn't stay neutral. I knew that, and he knew that I knew.

"You put me in a bit of a bind," he said.

I nodded.

"I have enough blood on my hands as it is. I don't want any more."

I didn't say anything. He was going to have to think this one out for himself.

"If I say no, you say innocent people will die. And I will have to live with the knowledge that I could have helped you stop it. If I say yes, you will kill the shooter, and I will have had a role in someone else's death. And maybe exposed myself as well."

I shook my head. "No. I won't kill him, and no one will know of you."

He grinned. "Be careful what you promise. He may make you kill him."

Sean was right, of course. My *intention* was to not kill the man.

Sean crossed his arms and sighed. "What do you need from me?"

I pulled the list from my back pocket and handed it to Sean. "Which one of these names is from Florida?"

He glanced at the list and then pulled open one of the kitchen cabinet drawers and took out a pen. He circled the Russian's name—Ivan Rulenska—and handed the list back to me.

"How well do you know him?" I asked.

"We did some work together once," he said. "He doesn't take his work personally. Even when it is." Sean opened the refrigerator and pulled out another Guinness. He held it out to me.

I shook my head.

"Oh, that's right," he said, keeping the bottle for himself and closing the refrigerator. He popped the top of the beer and took a long, slow drink. "After our job was over, he got word that a friend had been killed. A drug deal that went sour." He resumed his leaning position at the kitchen sink. "He found the shooter and marked his movements for almost six weeks while he staged the kill. When it was finally showtime, he cut the guy's throat and left. Never mentioned it again." Sean shook his head. "No malice. No anger. He didn't let his guard down—not for a minute. Just did the guy and let it be."

"Is that his preferred style?" I asked.

"Detached? Yeah. I'd say he—"

I shook my head. "No. I mean, does he do the job up close?"

Sean took a long swig of the beer. "Yeah. He's a hands-on kind of guy. Almost always takes a knife over a gun. He told me that it guarantees the kill. The accuracy of the act and the accuracy of ID. He told me he's never hit the wrong mark. And…" He swigged the beer again. "He's never left a job undone."

"What does he look like?"

"Tall, maybe six four, six five, with close-cut hair." He paused to think. "Last time I saw him was seven or eight years ago. Back then he had dark hair with gray eyes. And was very solid. Very strong." Sean set the bottle of Guinness down on the counter and held his hands about six inches apart. "He had big hands, like this."

"Where does he keep the knife?" I asked.

Sean shrugged. "When I worked with him, he kept one in his left sleeve and one in his right-hand pocket. But he has been known to do the job with a garrote."

If Rulenska had killed Vinny, which seemed a reasonable assumption since Vinny's records suggested that he was holding out on the hitter, he would have done it with a knife. That would explain the large blood stains in the Jag.

"Does he carry a gun?"

Sean nodded. "Absolutely. He prefers up close, but is not above using a gun if he has to."

"How can I find this guy?"

Sean shrugged. "That could be tough. He moves around a lot when he's on a job." He took another swig from the bottle and paused to think. "He likes women. Might try some local clubs, hooker hangouts, or escort services. Other than that…" He shrugged again.

There were quite a few of those types of places in Indianapolis. In fact, there were too many. Too many of them, and only four days to go.

Chapter Forty-Two

The first place on my list was a known mob-run establishment. DeNights was run by Antonio DiCenza, an up-and-coming wise guy who used the place as a part-time gambling operation and part-time escort service. I had had one run-in with him already and had been on the receiving end of one of his threats. It was a threat I didn't take lightly.

On the way to DeNights, I called Mary. "Can you check with the bureau in Florida? There's an Ivan Rulenska there, and I'd like to know if he's still in town. And I mean, at the moment."

"I assume that since you're asking about him, the bureau has a current interest in him."

"You have assumed correctly," I said.

"Okay, I'll let you know as soon as I can. But I do have a job, you know."

"Sure."

"By the way, your friend Vinny had his throat slit, and the blood in the trunk of Claudia's Jag matches his type."

"Wonderful," I said. The MO for the murder was a good indicator that I was on the right track in pursuing Rulenska. The letter had been sent from Florida to Gagliardi, but since Gagliardi was a known go-between, a contact man, Rulenska could have been talking about a target other than Chatham.

"*Wonderful?*"

"Nothing," I said. "I was just talking out loud. So, you know it was Vinny?"

"We do now. He's been busted before, mostly small stuff, and had a military record. Marines."

I thanked her for the information and for the help. I was nearing DeNights. If Sean was right and Rulenska had a penchant for night life and the women who came with it, this place could be on the menu.

DeNights was housed in a pink stucco building on the near north side of Indianapolis. Generally the parking lot was full, and music wafted through the walls to fill the night. Today, at mid-afternoon, the place was preparing to open, and the lot was mostly empty.

I went in and found a young woman that I guessed to be in her mid-twenties stocking the bar. The room was empty, and the stage was bare. Chairs remained in their inverted position on top of the tables that were scattered about the room.

"We ain't open yet," she said, hoisting a case of liquor onto the bar.

"I'm looking for DiCenza. He in?" I asked. I had the .38 in my waist-band.

"He expecting you?" she asked, using a box cutter to open the case.

"No."

"Then he ain't in."

I knew the way to his office, and I knew that there would be at least one of his associates with him. I also knew the girl would call back to the office and, by the time I went through the door, I would be facing a welcoming party.

"Call back. Tell him Colton Parker is here and would like to speak with him. Out here," I said.

She gave me a reluctant look, glanced toward DiCenza's office, and called. Within a few seconds, DiCenza came through the door, followed by a beefy-looking thug dressed in a black T-shirt with the DeNights logo in pink.

"You must be crazy coming in here," DiCenza said. "I still owe you for the last time."

I flipped a couple of chairs over and pushed one with my foot toward DiCenza.

"Have a seat," I said. "Your homey can stand."

I sat in one of the chairs and placed the .38 on the table within reach. DiCenza and the thug glanced at the gun.

"Insurance," I said. "I didn't come in here for trouble, Tony, but if it has to happen, I'll take as many with me as I can. Starting with you."

DiCenza smiled. "You're stupid, Parker. When we get it on, it won't be in here."

I crossed my leg. "I'm looking for someone."

"And how is that my problem?"

"He's Russian. A hitter out of Florida. His name is Rulenska, and he's in town."

DiCenza's eyes flickered. I had his attention. "Get us something to drink," he said over his shoulder to the girl. He looked at me.

"Just a Coke," I said.

"Coke and a whiskey sour," DiCenza said.

Neither of us said anything until the girl brought the drinks. As she was setting them onto the table, the whiskey sour slipped from her hands and onto DiCenza's lap. He recoiled.

"You stupid little—"

The girl began to take a step back. "I'm sorry, Mr. DiCenza. I just—"

The T-shirted thug grabbed her by the wrist.

I kicked him between the legs, and he doubled over, releasing the girl's arm. He tried to straighten up and make a run for me, but I had the .38 in my hand with the hammer cocked.

DiCenza looked at his lackey with disgust. "Go take care of yourself," he said. "I'm alright out here." Then, turning to the girl, he said, "You gonna just stand there? Get me a towel."

She ran back to the bar and came back with a towel. As DiCenza toweled off the drink, he said, "Get me another, will you? Do you think that you can handle that?"

She went back to the bar, stifling her tears.

"So what do you know about him?" I asked.

"Why should I help you?" DiCenza asked, sitting down again. "You need to give me a reason."

"Favors," I said. "The day will come when I can do you a favor. You'll call and I'll help you."

"You've been watching too many Godfather movies," he said.

"And you've been living in too many of them."

He nodded toward the office where the thug had just gone. "Besides, I can buy all the help I need."

"Business must be bad," I said, "if he's the best you can afford."

The girl brought the drink. DiCenza tossed the towel onto the table and glared at her as he took it. She went back to the bar without saying a word. He sipped the whiskey.

"What do you know about him?" I repeated.

"I know he'll kill you if you get in his way," DiCenza said.

"Has he been in here?"

DiCenza shook his head. "Not lately. A few times over the last couple of years."

"Have you heard anything about him being in town?"

"Like?"

"Like when he arrived. Where he might be staying?"

DiCenza studied me for a minute. "Why? What's he to you?"

"I need to find him."

"Why?"

"Personal," I said.

He laughed. "Always is, isn't it?"

"Where can I find him?" I asked.

DiCenza shook his head, smiling. "I don't know. I really don't. Even if I did, would you trust me to not sell you out?"

"No. But I would trust you to know that if he failed, I wouldn't."

The smile eroded. "I think our conversation here is done. And don't come back until it's time for me to collect." He stood, downed the whiskey, and went back into his office.

"Thanks for the Coke," I said, and left the bar. As I was unlocking my car, the girl came out the rear door of the bar.

"Thanks for what you did," she said.

"Sure," I said. "What's your name?"

"Kelly."

"You like working here?"

She shook her head.

"Why do you stay?"

She shrugged. "I ain't got nowhere else to go."

"Any family?"

She shook her head. "I never met my dad. Mom's dead. I tried college for a while but…" She smiled. "I heard you talking about a Russian. Is he…" She turned to look back at the bar. "Is he part of them?"

"Kind of," I said. "He's someone you don't want to know."

She crossed her arms like someone who is trying to ward off a winter's chill. "I have a friend who might know him."

"Who?"

She glanced over her shoulder again at the bar. "Promise you won't tell her I told you?"

"Yes."

She tightened the grip on herself. "Her name is Amy Compton. She used to work here but started sleeping with the customers. She used to talk about a guy she was doing. Some Russian. She said he used to come up from Florida and always made it a point to see her."

"How long ago was that?" I asked.

"Six months. Maybe a year."

"Have you talked to her lately?" I asked.

She shook her head. "I don't want her getting hurt or nothing. If you can help her…"

"Do you have an address?"

She gave it to me, and for a moment, our eyes locked. I saw a level of despair beyond her years.

"What will you do?" I asked.

She turned to glance back at the bar. "Go back to work, I guess."

"You can do better."

She lowered her eyes. "Not right now. Maybe someday."

I gave her my card and told her to call if she ever needed anything. She gave me a half smile and slid the card into the pocket of her jeans as she went back into the bar. I watched until she was inside and then got in my car.

As I pulled out of the lot and moved into the flow of traffic, I wondered how this young girl ended up working for a man like DiCenza and what would become of her if she didn't leave. But then I recalled Callie's diary, and wondered how I was going to keep her from following the same path.

CHAPTER FORTY-THREE

Amy Compton lived in a ratty duplex in a complex on the city's near southwest side, off of US 40. As I approached the door, I could hear her music, the head-banging kind, forging its way out of the open windows. Most of the rest of the apartments appeared to be vacant.

I knocked. No answer.

I knocked again. No answer.

I pounded on the door. It opened.

A young girl I guessed to be about the same age as Kelly stood in the open doorway. She was barefoot, dressed in an army green tank top and fatigue pants. She had a joint in her left hand as she leaned on the door with her right.

"Yeah?"

"Are you Amy Compton?"

"Yeah." Her eyes had a glassy look.

We are all something to someone else. A neighbor, a friend, a parent, a child. We have roles to fill. In this case, I felt the father in me welling up. I opened the screen door.

"Hey, what the—"

I pushed her back and shut the door behind me as I reached out and took the joint with one hand and crushed it into the carpet.

"What do you think you're—"

I led her by the arm to the stained sofa that sat near the door.

"Sit down," I said.

She was scared but too stoned to really show it. "Who are you, dude?" She was trying to focus.

"Who I am is not important. Who you have been doing, is."

She took a deep breath and let it out slowly as she blinked her eyes a few times. "I do a lot of guys," she said. "Is that what you want?"

"No. It's not what I want."

"Oh." She looked genuinely puzzled. "Then what do you want?"

"Who is the Russian?"

Her brow furrowed as she tried to muster deep thought. "Russian?"

"You have been with a Russian from Florida. Have you seen him recently?"

She put her hand to her forehead. "Oh, man, I've got a headache."

"Amy, I need for you to think. Have you seen a Russian from Florida? He's tall."

She sat back on the sofa and put both hands to her face. "Oh, sure. Igor."

"Igor? Could it have been Ivan?"

She blinked a couple of times. "Maybe…no, I think it was Igor."

"Was he here?"

"Uh-huh."

"When?"

She was trying hard. "Uh, yesterday? No, wait, it was…uh…yeah. It was yesterday."

"Is he coming back?"

She shook her head while keeping her hands on both sides of her face. "No."

"Did he say anything?"

"Say anything?" She shook her head again. "No. He…just said that he was tired."

"Tired?"

She nodded. "Uh-huh. He said the planes keep him up all night."

"The planes?"

"Yeah." She let both hands drop from her face.

"Do you have any more pot?" I asked.

"It's not for sale," she said, trying hard to focus.

"I don't want to buy it. I want to flush it. Where is it?"

She sat for a moment as she tried to focus on what I had asked her and then turned to lie on her side and curl up. "I'm sleepy," she said.

I stood and looked around the house. There wasn't much in the way of furniture. Not much in the way of hope, either. But if I could get guys like Rulenska out of her life, Amy would have a much better chance of having one. For that matter, so would a lot of people.

Chapter
FORTY-FOUR

My watch said that I had about an hour before Callie got home from school. After what I read in her diary, I definitely did not want her coming home to an empty house.

I drove west on US 40 and picked up I-465 southbound. As I drove, I called Millikin.

"Listen," I said, "Are you ready to talk some more?"

"Sure."

"Are you free for dinner?"

"Sure."

"Are sandwiches okay?"

"Sandwiches would be fine."

"See you at six."

Callie came home as her usual dour self. I was used to the silent treatment and went to the basement for a workout to burn off the stress of the day. By the time I showered, I had about thirty minutes before Millikin arrived. Callie was still in her room with the music blaring when I went in to check on her.

"Dinner will be ready at six," I said.

She was lying prone on the bed, looking at an open book, drumming her pencil to the music. She didn't say anything.

I went over to the stereo and turned it off. She looked up at me with anger in her eyes. Not as intense as before, but there none the less.

"I said, 'Dinner will be ready at six.'"

"I know. I heard you."

"Pastor Millikin will be coming over tonight."

She had always liked Millikin. As Anna's pastor, he was a pleasant memory, a favorable link to Anna.

"Okay," she said, turning back to her book.

I turned the music back on but turned the volume down as I left the room.

In the kitchen I sliced a tomato, a green pepper, and an onion and set out the meat, cheese, and hoagie buns. I had bought the fixings for submarine sandwiches and slid a frozen apple pie into the oven. My kitchen skills were lacking to be sure, but we wouldn't starve.

As I was finishing up, Millikin knocked, and I answered the door.

"Come on in, Dale," I said, using the familiar in an area where I was still uncomfortable.

"I brought some ice cream," he said, holding out a half gallon of vanilla. "If I remember correctly, Callie likes vanilla."

I thanked him and told him she was in her room and to feel free to go on in and say hello. He did, and I put the ice cream away. If I had any chance to save Callie, it seemed clear to me it was going to come through someone other than myself. Mary had been helpful. But the diary had made it clear that I was heading into spiritual waters that were too deep for me. I needed help. I needed Millikin's kind of help.

Before long, Callie and the minister came out of her room. She was still downcast, though less so, and Millikin had his arm around her.

"I was just telling Callie how much she is like her mother," he said.

"Absolutely," I said. "Everyone says that."

Callie smiled for the first time in a while. "When are we going to eat?" she asked.

After dinner we had apple pie a la mode and settled in the living room. Millikin told Callie stories about Anna, some that I didn't know, and how Anna had told him about the great hopes she had for her only daughter. Callie took it all in with some evidence that what Millikin told her mattered. But not much.

"You've got homework, don't you, honey?" I asked. "You'd better get on it."

She didn't say much, just said goodbye to Millikin and shuffled off to her room. After she left, Millikin turned to me.

"Something's wrong," he said. "The last time I saw her was a few weeks after she came home from the hospital. She's different."

"Tell me about it," I said.

"She's depressed, Colton. Clinically depressed."

"I think we surmised that from the attempt," I said.

He shook his head. "No. That was the result of loss. A moment of crisis. This, her change in personality, is a result of hopelessness. More than a momentary crisis."

"Hopelessness?" I said. "Try anger."

I told Millikin about my concern that drugs may be at the root of Callie's mood swings. I told him about my search for drugs and about finding the diary instead. I told him I'd been reading it.

"She wrote, and I'm quoting her, 'My mother is gone. She's gone, and my dad killed her. What do I do? Where do I go from here? Is there anybody who thinks I'm important?'"

"But she hasn't said that to you directly?"

"No." I stood. "Want some coffee?" I asked.

"Okay."

I left the room to get the coffee going and then came back into the living room, where I took a seat on the sofa next to Millikin. "She told me that if I hadn't been arguing with Anna that night, she wouldn't have died."

"She told you this?"

"Yes, and I can live with that."

"You can?" he seemed surprised.

"Yes. It's the rest of what she wrote that concerns me. She went on to say that she had lost everything that mattered. Her mother, faith in her father, and everything that mattered. She wrote that without those things in her life, she would rather get out of here as soon as possible. She wrote that she was 'living in a bubble' and that 'he is pumping out the air.' She said the sooner she gets out of here the better. That I had ruined her life. And that 'life is a hole of darkness, with no chance for light.' Her words," I said.

"She's lost those things that define her self-image," Millikin said. "And that loss, coupled with the sudden nature of it all, has further eroded her sense of well-being."

I had heard the same thing from Frank Shapiro. "So she feels like she's on shaky ground," I said, trying to rephrase what Millikin had said.

"Yes."

I could smell the coffee and tell from the gurgling sounds of the brewer that it was done. I went into the kitchen and poured two large cups.

"Black?" I asked as I came back into the living room.

He nodded.

"So," I said, handing him his cup and sitting again, "what's the bottom line? What do I do?"

"You do what we talked about this morning."

"Ask her to forgive me for driving Anna out of the house on the night she died?"

"Yes. Then you show her you love her. Be the best father you can be." He drank some coffee. "That doesn't mean you buy her everything she wants or give in to her demands. It does mean you spend time with her. Put her first on your list of priorities."

"That's not always so easy. My job often requires me to be out late at night, dealing with the lesser elements of society. By its very nature it's dangerous. The people I associate with don't keep regular business hours. I'm going to miss the occasional school function. How do I balance that— providing for her—with being both mother and father?"

"You can't. You're her father. You can't be her mother too. But you do the best you can do. You have a terrific support system. You have the Shapiros and Mary as well. You're not exactly alone."

"You sound like PBS," I said, recalling the ant documentary I had seen. Millikin seemed confused, but he had learned to let comments like that from me slide by.

I told him of my concern about Mary. How Callie was seeing her as a surrogate mother. I told him that Mary, who was childless and had often talked of her desire to have a child, may play into Callie's wishes. I also told him that the FBI can be an unforgiving taskmaster and that Mary could be transferred at any time, causing another loss in Callie's life. Or worse, Mary could die in the line of duty.

He shrugged. "It's a balancing act, Colton. Like I said, you do the best you can. I'm not sure Callie will respond to your efforts, but I know you will have done the best that any single parent can do."

"And if that's not good enough?"

"Then it isn't. But I believe that if you ask God for help and honestly face the situation as it is, you'll do fine."

"I hope so," I said. "For her sake."

CHAPTER FORTY-FIVE

I got up early the next morning to read the passage of Scripture that Millikin had given me. It was the story of the prodigal son. Familiar to most, but new to me.

I had never known my father and until very recently, not much about my mother. But the Scripture Millikin gave me highlighted the role of both. I understood the love the father had for his son. I felt the same for Callie. But it wasn't until I read the passage for the second time, that I was able to tie it in with the other Scriptures Millikin had asked me to read.

> *But while he was still a long way off, his father saw him and was filled with compassion for him; he ran to his son, threw his arms around him and kissed him.*

Millikin had said that love covers a multitude of sins and that Jesus had told us we are to forgive as we want to be forgiven. I had to admit, it moved me. Even though I could accept that there was a God, I had a hard time seeing Millikin's God as the only one. But if He could help Callie, I would read what I had to read and believe what I had to believe.

I was beginning a third go-round through the passage when Mary called.

"I was out on interviews all day yesterday," she said, "but I have some information on your friend in Florida."

"Shoot," I said, setting my coffee down and reaching for the pad and pen that I kept near the kitchen phone.

"Ivan Rulenska lives in Destin, Florida, and has for the past seven years. Before that, he lived in Washington. DC, and before that, the former Soviet Union. He has no arrest record, but the local field office suspects he's a player-for-hire in a variety of the crime families in New York, Chicago, and LA. Apparently, Interpol has an interest in him too."

"If they're interested, that makes him an international hitter, not some local yahoo."

"He's not a yahoo," Mary said. "According to a communique from them, he's six feet four, weighs two hundred and thirty pounds, and has dark hair and gray or blue eyes. No one knows if he's currently in Destin, but no airline tickets were purchased in his name. I also have a photo, although it may be a bit dated."

"Can you get it to me?"

"Do you have a fax?"

"No."

"Then you may have to come get it. I'm going to be gone, so I'll leave it in an envelope with the receptionist."

"Where did you get the photograph?"

"Interpol," she said. "It's a military picture. Probably at least ten or fifteen years old."

"I'll take what I can get," I said.

"There's more," she said. "When he lived in Washington, he was attached to the Embassy of the Soviet Union. When that country collapsed, he fell off the radar screen and surfaced again about six years ago when the bureau began to suspect him of organized crime involvement."

"Do you think he's KGB?"

"Maybe. Or GRU, most likely. At any rate, Colton, he's very dangerous."

"Of course," I said. "What else would you expect?"

After picking up the photograph, I drove to the Indianapolis

International Airport. Amy had said that Rulenska was tired because the planes kept him awake. That would make it reasonable to assume that he had a room at an airport hotel. All I had to do was to check with all of them. An easy task if you have several days. I didn't.

I parked in the short-term parking of Indianapolis International and began my trek around the hotels closest to the airports, working my way out into a wider circle. I now had three days to find Rulenska.

By the time I had reached the hotels along the I-465 corridor, I was beginning to tire of the methodical search. Then, an hour and a half after I began, I hit gold with a dump called the Rest and Eat.

"Yeah. I think that's him," the clerk said. He looked closer at the photograph. "Gee, he's a Rusky, huh?"

"Yeah," I said. "A Rusky." The photo showed Rulenska in the uniform of the army of the Soviet Union.

The clerk, a young man in his early twenties who was still fighting acne, said, "What's this country coming too, huh? Commies in our own backyard."

"Sure," I said, fighting off an urge to tell the kid the cold war was over. "Who could've guessed?"

He typed on the keyboard and scanned the monitor. "You know," he said, "my dad fought in Vietnam. Fought the communists up close. You know?" He took another look at the picture. "I knew he looked suspicious."

"How's that?" I said.

"You know. Just the way he carried himself. The accent. I knew right away that he didn't fit. You know?"

I assured him that I did.

"I'm glad you guys are on him."

I was guessing that by "you guys" he meant the police or FBI. I didn't dissuade him from believing what he wanted.

He scanned the monitor and reached for a piece of paper to take notes. "Can I ask you a question?"

"Shoot," I said.

"Do you think I could be a spy? I mean I'm not interested in the stuff you see on TV, you know? But I was wondering…do you think I have what it takes to catch spies in our own country. You know?"

"Sure," I said. I glanced at his nametag. "From what I'm seeing, Jamie, you're just what we're looking for."

He smiled as he slid the note across the counter to me. "Oh man, that is way too cool."

I looked at the slip. "This the room number?"

"Yep."

"He still here?"

"The computer shows that he didn't check out."

"Listen," I said, leaning forward and lowering my voice, "I don't want any gunplay here. You understand?"

His eyes widened as he nodded agreeably.

"So I'm going to need the key. And I don't want anyone else knowing that he's here. Better for you too if he doesn't know that I got this from you."

The kid seemed genuinely excited by the prospect of personal danger. "Sure," he said, handing me the key. "But don't worry. I have a brown belt in Tae Kwon Do. I know how to take care of myself."

"Great," I said. "Just stay here."

I went out of the lobby and around back. The room Rulenska was staying in was on the second level. I found two sets of stairs and took the one that would bring me closest to where Jamie had said the hitter was located.

As I came to his room, I drew the .38 and listened at the door. The television was on, and I could see the light of the screen flickering through an opening in the drapes.

There was no way to enter the room quietly and without fanfare. Regardless of what I did, I was going to be noticed.

I reached across with my left hand and slid the key into the lock. Once I had it in, I quickly forced my way into the room in a crouched position and lowered the .38. I wasn't prepared for what I found.

Chapter FORTY-SIX

Rulenska wasn't in the room. The television was playing, some clothing was still in the closet, and a packet of cigarettes and a folded three-day-old newspaper were lying on the nightstand. All these items suggested that Rulenska was here, but wasn't.

I opened the bathroom door. Deodorant, aftershave, and a packet of razor blades sat on the counter. The smell of hot water was fresh, and a coating of steam on the mirror was just starting to evaporate. Rulenska had just left.

I closed the room door and slid the .38 back into my waistband as I began to toss the room.

I went through the nightstand drawer and found the Holy Bible stamped with the Gideons' insignia. The spine of the book was stiff when I flipped through it, meaning that it had never been opened. *No surprise there,* I thought, admitting to myself that I had never opened a hotel room Bible.

The other drawers in the room were stocked with socks, underclothes, and a couple of oxford shirts. The wastebasket contained two adult magazines and an empty bag of Cheetos. The closet held a sport coat that had a tag safety-pinned onto the sleeve. It was a dry cleaning ticket from Cortez Dry Cleaners.

The rest of the search turned up nothing. Except for the dry cleaning ticket, which established a direct link to Cortez, I hadn't come up with anything.

I sat on the edge of the bed, picked up the phone, and dialed the front desk. Jamie answered.

"I'm in the commie's room right now, and he isn't here. Could you take a look at his bill and let me know what charges are on it?"

I waited a minute while Jamie searched the computer.

"I have it," he said.

A hotel notepad sat next to the phone. "Shoot," I said, pulling the pad closer.

"The bill shows that he called a local number."

He gave it to me. Judging from the prefix, it wasn't far from the hotel."

"Anything else?" I asked.

"No. I don't see any other charges."

"When did he check in?"

"Two days ago."

"Okay. Listen, Jamie," I said, "I think you have a great future in this business."

"Thank you, sir," he said. I could almost see the kid saluting.

"Keep this under your hat, okay?"

"Yes sir," he said, again. "You can count on me."

All indications were that Rulenska was coming back to the room. If he did, I wanted to be there. I positioned the chair to one side of the door, in the corner of the room by the side of the bed, and kept the .38 on my lap. I left everything else as it had been when I entered the room. The television was tuned to ESPN. The Cubs were playing, and the game was in the bottom of the eighth. The Cubs were down by four.

I waited and watched the game as the nightstand clock ticked the minutes away. Time was running out for the Cubs—and for me.

CHAPTER FORTY-SEVEN

After the Cubs lost, I watched a postgame wrap-up show where the overpaid talking heads spent an hour telling me about the game I had just seen. Bored, I looked at the newspaper I had seen when I tossed the room. When I opened it to find the comics, I noticed that the section I had in my hand had been folded lengthwise to the car ads. One was circled in blue:

> FOR SALE: 1999 Pontiac Grand Am
> 100k miles. Some rust but good condition.
> Runs great. $2500 obo.

A phone number at the bottom of the ad matched the other phone number on the room charge. The car matched the one found at the junkyard with Gagliardi's body in it.

I tried the number but didn't get an answer. I glanced at the clock on the nightstand. It was almost time for Callie to be home from school. After what I had read in her diary, and after my conversation with Millikin, I was more reluctant than ever to leave her home alone.

Still, the possibility existed that Rulenska might return. I dialed the front desk again and reached Jamie.

"Jamie, you know who this is?" I asked.

195

"Yes sir."

"I'm going to leave for a while. Is there any way you could let me know if our friend returns?"

"Sure," he said. "I get off in a couple of hours but I could stake out the place until classes start. I'm getting a degree in criminal justice," he said.

"Great. Stay as long as you can and call me if he returns." I gave him my cell number. "And Jamie?"

"Yes?"

"Under no circumstances are you to try and apprehend this person on your own."

"No sir," he said. "I won't."

After ending the call with Jamie I called the FBI. I wanted to ask Mary to check the phone number in the car ad against the Criss Cross directory. If the number was found, I'd have an address. But Mary wasn't in, so I asked for Tim Deckert, one of the clerks who I had befriended during my time with the FBI. Tim wanted to be an FBI agent as badly as Jamie, and had asked me for a reference when he applied for the position. Unfortunately, a pre-employment physical determined that he didn't meet the standards necessary for entrance into the academy at Quantico. His hopes had been dashed, giving rise to a level of resentment that threatened to derail his otherwise exemplary record.

When I asked for his help, he was more than willing despite my less-than-desirable status with his supervisors. I wasn't sure if he saw this favor more as a way to help me or as a way to "stick it to the man." At any rate, I soon had the address and was on my way home.

Callie arrived on time as usual and went directly to her room as usual. But I had different plans, making this something other than the usual night.

"Do you have much homework?" I asked, opening her door.

"Some."

"How soon can you have it done?"

She was lying prone with her back to me. She shrugged. "About a half hour," she said.

"I have tickets to the Indians game tonight. I thought maybe we could eat dinner out and see the game."

She rolled to one side so she could look at me. "Okay," she said flatly.

I checked the cell phone, and seeing no messages from Jamie, I showered and changed clothes. By the time I was ready, Callie was finished with her homework. I showed her the tickets.

"First base line," I said.

She looked at the tickets but didn't say anything.

"Okay if we eat at the park?" I asked.

She shrugged.

It was shaping up to be a long night.

We drove to Victory Field and took our seats twenty minutes before game time. Each of us had a hot dog, Coke, and fries. The sun was going down, so the weather was more warm than hot, and the crowd buzzed with the excitement that goes with a baseball game on a summer night.

Victory Field was new. Sort of. The original Victory Field, named in honor of the efforts of Hoosier veterans, was located a few miles away. The name was later changed to Bush Stadium and then back to Victory Field. The new stadium was built because the old one was deemed too old, too much in disrepair, and too expensive to restore. But the new stadium was also an integral part of the downtown Indianapolis revitalization project and fit well with the city's unofficial model of "amateur sports capital of the world." Not that the Indianapolis Indians were amateurs. Far from it. As a child, I had lived in more than one foster home where baseball—Indians baseball—was the focal point of a summer evening.

By the time the game started, we had devoured the hot dogs and fries and were watching as the Indians took their position in the field.

I looked at Callie as she watched with anticipation. Sports had always attracted her, and she had always been physically capable of playing any activity she chose. Softball, basketball, and volleyball had all come easy. But soccer was the crown jewel.

During the game she clapped, yelled, and cheered as the Indians went on to victory. By the time the evening was over, she was "up" for the first time in many weeks.

On the drive home I seized the capital and tried to open her up.

"You know," I said, "you've been a little down lately. We're all concerned."

She looked at me with a bit of surprise on her face. "Concerned?"

I didn't want to let her know that I had read her diary, but I needed to find where she was on the emotional road map.

"Sure," I said. "It's natural to be a bit down. Maybe even a lot down. Especially when a person has had to go through a period like you've gone through. But we want to be sure that—"

"Who's we?"

"Me, mostly. But Mary is concerned about you. Pastor Millikin is concerned. Grandma and Grandpa are concerned."

"How do you know?"

"Because they've asked about you," I said, maneuvering the car through the downtown foot traffic. "We want to be sure you're okay."

"Why wouldn't I be okay?"

"Well, with Mom…dying, and your accident"— I didn't know how else to refer to her attempt when speaking to her—"and moving to a new place and a new school…that's a lot for anyone to deal with." I wanted to tell her that having all of this fall on you when you're only thirteen years old doesn't help either, but I didn't want to take the chance of putting her on the defensive.

She turned to look out the window and was quiet for the next few blocks. She seemed contemplative—almost serene.

"I think about Mom a lot," she said, breaking the silence.

"Me too."

"I miss her. A lot."

"Me too."

"I wish things could go back to the way they were."

"Me too."

She sighed, glancing at the passersby as we moved south along Meridian Street. I didn't push. She was opening up a little, and I wanted to allow her the chance to do that on her own.

"Why did you get fired?"

It wasn't until she asked that I realized we had never told her the story of what happened. Anna died that night, and her death had taken precedence.

"There was a girl, about your age, who had been kidnapped by someone. And—"

"Why did he kidnap her?" she asked.

"Because she came from a wealthy family, and the kidnapper thought he could collect a big ransom."

"Did her family pay it?"

I shook my head. "No. They called us instead."

"So why did you get fired then?"

"Mary and I found the kidnapper and—"

"How?"

"We were able to find him when he called the girl's parents. He used a cell phone and we tracked him."

"The FBI can do that?"

"Yes."

"So what happened next?"

"Mary and I found him, and we took him in for questioning. We needed to find out where the girl was. He had buried her in—"

"Was she dead?"

I shook my head. "No. He put her in a wood box and buried her in a field."

"How did she breathe?"

"He put a metal pipe into the lid of the box and ran it up through the ground."

She was quiet for a moment. Then she said, "So what happened next?"

"We questioned him, and he wouldn't tell us what we needed to know."

"Why not? You had already captured him."

I nodded. "Yes, we had. But he thought if he didn't tell us where the girl was, we couldn't prove in court that he had kidnapped her. Do you understand?"

She nodded. "Yes. You needed evidence."

I smiled. "That's right. But see, we had enough evidence."

"You did?"

"Yes."

"Then why didn't he tell you where he buried her?"

"I don't know. We already had him and had enough to send him to jail. But we wanted to find the girl before something happened to her."

"Like what?"

"Well, if it rained, she could drown, or—"

"Oh. Okay. So, why did you get fired?"

"I saw a picture of the girl. She was just about your age, and I knew how her mom and dad must have felt. I know how I would have felt if you had been in that box." I paused. I wasn't proud of what I had done and didn't want to tell her the details. I didn't want her to know how her father could lose control.

"So," I said, continuing, "I asked Mary to take a break and get herself something to drink. When she left, I told him I was going to move him to the county jail for holding. When I got him in the car, I drove him out to the country. To a field."

Her eyes were focused on me like two dark brown lights. I didn't want her to know about the kind of man that I was, or what I was capable of doing. But she had asked, and she deserved to know what led to her mother's death.

"When we got to the field I got him out of the car and handcuffed him to a tree." I looked at her to see if she could fill in the blanks. To see if she could save me the shame of saying out loud what I was hoping she could figure out for herself. She kept her eyes focused on me without emotion.

"So, I began to beat him until he told me where the girl was buried."

"Did he eventually tell you where she was?"

"Yes."

"Was the girl alive when you found her?"

"Yes."

"And that's why you got fired?"

I nodded. "Yes. That's why."

She was quiet again. As we continued to work our way through the city and toward home, she turned to me. "Is that why you and mom were fighting that night?"

"Yes."

"She was mad because you got fired?"

"Yes."

"But you saved that girl."

I merged into the south flow of traffic. "Yes, I did, Callie. But your mom was mad at me for more than that." I didn't want Callie blaming Anna for the argument that lead to her death.

"What else?"

"I'm sometimes…not as responsible as I should be." It was hard to admit. Hard to say. "I had been in trouble at the FBI before. Sometimes I was a little overzealous in…" I paused and looked at her, "do you know what that means?"

"Overzealous? Sure. It means you're eager."

"That's right. Well, I was too eager sometimes to put bad guys in jail, and sometimes I did things I probably shouldn't have. So I was in trouble a lot, and when I got fired, Mom just kind of blew up."

She nodded. "Okay," she said.

"Do you understand?" I asked.

She nodded. "Yeah. I understand."

She was silent as we continued to work our way through the city toward home. With each intersection, the passing shadows crossed her face. Like the interchange of their light and dark, I hoped we were crossing the same threshold. I hoped we were exchanging the shadow of dark for the light of life.

CHAPTER FORTY-EIGHT

The game, and the conversation that came afterward, thawed some of the ice that had existed between Callie and me. Over the weekend, we talked about Anna, soccer, and the FBI. Callie's developing interest in the bureau was being fueled more by her developing bond with Mary than with me, but that was okay. Any point of common interest between the two of us might tear down a little more of the barrier that separated us. And for that, I was grateful. But I still had a job to do, and time wasn't my friend.

I made two phone calls to the hotel, and each time, I was told Rulenska had not returned. My two attempts to connect with the family who sold Rulenska the car were equally unsuccessful, and finally one of the neighbors told me the family was gone for the weekend. Two days had passed without progress, and by the time Monday rolled around, I was becoming increasingly edgy and trying to not let it show. The oppressive heat didn't help.

The morning dawned to a cloudless sky that, by all indications, was going to remain as hot and humid as it had been all month. By the time Callie came to breakfast, the temperature had already climbed to ninety.

"Look at you," I said, pouring milk over a bowl of cereal. "What's the occasion?"

She shrugged. "Just couldn't sleep."

I wondered whether her night had been as restless because of what she had learned about me or because of all the other issues that had been plaguing her. I decided not to ask. We had made progress over the weekend, and if we continued down the same path, she would tell me when she was ready without having to be needled.

"Okay," I said. "Anything special going on at school today?"

She shook her head. "No. Just…nothing."

I didn't force the issue, and for the rest of breakfast she was quiet.

After she left, I put away the dishes and made a note to pick up some things for dinner. By the time I headed out, it was nearly nine.

I called the front desk of the hotel and asked for Jamie. I was told he wouldn't be in until ten. I asked to be connected to Rulenska's room. The clerk connected me, but there was no answer.

"Okay, Parker," I said, "if at first you don't succeed…"

I had the newspaper with me that I had found in the hotel room and called the number on the ad. When the owner of the car came on the line, I asked about the car.

"Sorry," he said. "But I sold it a few days ago."

I told him that I wasn't really interested in the car as much as I would like to talk with him about the buyer. He agreed, and an hour later, I was standing on his driveway in a neighborhood that was solidly middle-class, with the picture of Rulenska in my hand.

"Sure," he said. "That's him. Only he's a little older now. Hair is graying. He has a goatee and he's…you know, thicker." The man's son was mowing the lawn. We suspended conversation until the boy pushed the mower to the other side of the yard. I wondered why the boy wasn't in school.

"How did he pay you?"

"Cash. Twenty big ones."

In a day when nearly everything, including fast food, is purchased by debit cards, credit cards, and checks, I was amazed when cash was offered for such high-ticket items and no one questioned it.

"Didn't that strike you as a little odd?" I asked.

He was a thin man with thinning hair and an angular face that was highlighted by what I perceived as a perpetual five-o'clock shadow. He was dressed neatly in a polo shirt and Dockers. "Sure. But I thought, hey, the guy's offering cash. It doesn't get any sweeter than that." He paused to take me in for the first time. "You're a private eye?"

I nodded.

He smiled. "Do a lot of divorces and stuff like that?"

"Stuff like that," I said, wanting to get the man back on track. "Did he say anything about where he might be headed?"

The man crossed his arms, taking time to think. Just as he was ready to speak, the lawn mower came back our way again, and again we stopped talking. After the mower moved away he said, "No, I don't think so. At least if he did, I don't remember anything. He just asked to see the car, and I showed it to him. Then he asked if I would take two thousand for it. I said no, and then he said, 'Cash.' I said, 'Show me the money.'"

Rulenska was a professional. If he bought the car to use while in town instead of stealing one, he was going to go to great lengths to avoid detection.

"What about plates?" I asked.

The man said, "Yeah. He seemed like he needed the car real bad. Had some plates with him. Said they came off his other car and he would use them on the Grand Am until he could get home and get proper license plates for it."

"So, he just whipped out some tags and put them on the car?"

"Yeah, that's pretty much what he did."

"How did he get here?" I asked.

The man seemed puzzled. "I don't know, now that you mention it. He knocked on my door. I didn't see him drive up." He frowned. "Yeah. That's right. How did he get here?" he asked himself.

"Did he drive off in the car?"

"Yeah. Put the plates on and drove off."

"Did you happen to see the plates?"

He shook his head. "No, sorry."

"Okay, thanks," I said, handing him my card. "If anything else comes to mind, call me. Okay?"

"Sure thing, buddy. I'll do that."

The carelessness with which he had sold the car to Rulenska, that allowed the killer to drive off with plates he just happened to have available, would cause the man some concern for a while. Or maybe not. In his world, a world centered around lawn maintenance, block parties, and cookouts, the really bad elements were always somewhere else. Somewhere else where men like me were required to confront and deal with them. As soon as it was time to fertilize again, the man would forget about Rulenska and the Grand Am. I wouldn't hear from him again.

I drove to Easy Travel, since I was less than ten minutes anyway, to see if the travel voucher had been redeemed. When I arrived, I found Betty and Sharon sitting at their desks just as they had been when I had last seen them. No one else was in the building. Whatever there was in the way of clientele wasn't exactly cutting in line to buy dreams. Probably explained how they had remembered Claudia so easily.

"Good morning, ladies," I said, strolling into the air-conditioned agency.

Sharon beamed as she had the last time I was in there and was just as pink as ever. Betty came around to Sharon's desk and stood silent guard. I talked to Sharon.

"Has the travel voucher purchased by Frances Seymour been redeemed?" I asked.

"Well, let's see," Sharon said as she began to work the computer's keyboard.

I glanced at Betty, who was staring at me through narrowed eyes.

"Nice day, isn't it?" I said.

Nothing.

"Hear we are," Sharon sang. "It was redeemed yesterday."

"By whom?" I asked.

She traced a finger along the computer screen. "By Vincent Gagliardi."

"How did he do that?" I asked.

"It's easy. He just called and asked that his voucher be applied to the destination of his choice. We do that and send the tickets to his preferred address."

"It's that easy?"

She smiled. "That's our motto here at Easy Travel. We make it easy for you."

Betty kept her narrowed eyes on me.

"Sure," I said. "I'll keep that in mind the next time I want to dream. Can you tell me where you sent the tickets?"

"Why, certainly," Sharon said, as she began to scan the screen again. She gave me the address.

"Are you sure?" I asked.

Betty gave Sharon a look of exasperation and motioned for her to move aside. As Sharon stood, Betty slid into her seat and looked at the monitor.

"The address is correct," she said matter-of-factly.

Sharon looked at the screen again. "It's right here. The computer doesn't lie," she said with a broad smile.

Maybe the computer didn't lie, but it was sure capable of causing confusion. The address was mine.

CHAPTER FORTY-NINE

I raced back to my house. As I sped along the uneven flow of traffic, I dialed the hotel again. This time I got Jamie on the line.

"Do you know who this is?" I asked.

"Yes."

"Has our friend returned?"

"No. But he's not supposed to check out until tomorrow morning."

"Could he have checked out before you came on duty?" "On duty" sounded more cop-like than "came to work."

"No sir. I checked first thing after I got here. I even had the maid go into his room. She said that his stuff was in there and the television was on but that he wasn't there."

That would fit. I had left everything the way I had found it. Unless I missed my guess, Rulenska wasn't going back to the hotel.

"Thank you, Jamie," I said.

"Yes sir."

I hung up, hoping the kid landed a job with the FBI someday.

I took I-65 south off of I-70 and exited onto Raymond. Within a few minutes I was on my street. I skidded to a stop just a few doors down from the house and jogged to the alley that ran along the rear of my street with the .38 in my hand. When I reached my house, I hopped the chain-link fence that separated the alley from my backyard.

I paused at the back door long enough to insert my key and then, as I had done at the hotel, I went in with the gun in hand, sweeping the kitchen.

It was quiet. I paused to listen. Hearing and seeing nothing, I moved from the kitchen into the short hallway that connected the kitchen to the living area. I kept the gun at waist height as I inched through the hallway, pausing to open the closet door. When I did, I was attacked by a mop that I had stashed in the closet a few days before. I caught my breath, put the mop back, and closed the door.

I craned my head around the entrance to the living room with the gun leading the way. The room was silent as I moved cautiously forward, working my way to the hallway that connected Callie's room with mine. By the time I reached that area of the house, I was beginning to perspire.

I crept along the hallway, pausing first to ease into my room. Like the living room, it was empty. I checked the closet and under the bed. Nothing.

I checked Callie's room and again found nothing.

The basement was the last place to check. And the most likely. Basement burglaries are common. Few people lock the windows in a basement, and fewer still alarm them.

It was also the most dangerous.

I opened the door and knelt as I peeked around the corner, gun in hand. Drops of perspiration trickled down my back as my heart felt Krupa start another drum solo.

I had to go downstairs. Like a kid who's afraid of the boogeyman, I wiped my sweaty palms on the legs of my pants, before moving ahead. Each step, like the steps at the cabin in Brown County, creaked. I hadn't noticed the creaks before, and I would never forget them again.

The area was dark. The small amount of light that leaked through the basement windows was just enough to create shadows—the darkened, isolated parts where Rulenksa could be hiding.

I placed my feet onto the last of the steps and then onto the basement floor. From the shadows, I could see the flash of a muzzle blast, knowing it was all in my mind. Dreaded anticipation was tightening its grip and turning the play of the light into something more ominous.

In the corner of the room, the familiar rack of weights were now tall and foreboding like a Russian assassin waiting in gleeful anticipation for his prey.

The house was clean, but by the time I reached the top of the stairs, I wasn't. The perspiration had soaked through, and Mr. Krupa was still pounding his way through his solo in my chest.

I went into the kitchen and opened a bottle of water.

Rulenska was on to me, and he wanted me to know.

I chugged the cold water. My breathing was starting to slow as the rhythm of the drummer of my heart began to adjust.

Rulenska's message had been received. Now, I would send one of my own.

CHAPTER FIFTY

I packed as many of Callie's clothes as I could along with the necessary items that a thirteen-year-old girl would need for the next few days and slipped out of the house.

I threw the things into the trunk of the car and drove to Callie's school. I would need to make another trip to the house before going after Rulenska, but I needed to get Callie to as safe a place as possible, as quickly as possible.

"What is it? What's wrong?" she asked, as she was brought to meet me at the school office.

I could tell from the looks I was getting that the principal and her secretary had concerns as well.

"We have to leave, honey," I said. "We have an emergency." I smiled and thanked the principal for her consideration and ushered Callie through the door and into the hallway as quickly as possible while trying to not arouse further suspicions in the school staff.

"What kind of an emergency?" Callie asked as I helped her climb into the car.

"Just get in, Callie. I'll explain after we get going." I glanced around the parking lot before heading off toward the Shapiros'.

"You know what I do, right?" I asked.

She nodded. "You're a private detective."

"Right. Well, there are some very bad people in the world, Callie, and one of them may be after me." As soon as I said it I realized I had said the wrong thing. A child who has already lost one parent, who had her world inverted, even when she places the blame on the remaining parent, doesn't want to believe it could happen again.

"I'll be alright," I said quickly, "but I just thought it would be best if you stayed with Grandma and Grandpa for a few days. It'll only be a few days," I said.

She sank into the seat. The momentum that I had managed to build during the game was gone.

From her demeanor, I couldn't tell what bothered her the most. Did she not believe what I had told her? Was she angry with me for dumping her off on Anna's parents? Or was she afraid because I was in danger?

She was silent for the remainder of the ride to Carmel, which led me to believe that the silent treatment probably wasn't because someone was gunning for me.

When we arrived, Corrin greeted us at the door with a smile and a look of surprise.

"Colton, Callie! What are you doing here?" Then to Callie, "And how come you're not in school?" She stepped aside to allow us in. When she saw the suitcases, her expression changed from surprise to concern.

"Sorry to drop in on you and Frank like this, Corrin," I said, setting the suitcases down.

"What is it, Colton? What's wrong?" she asked.

I sidestepped the question. "Is Frank home?"

"No, he went to the store to pick up a few things for me. What is it? What's going on?"

I closed the door behind me as Callie went to her old room in silence.

"What is it?" she asked again, more insistently this time.

"Corrin, I've stumbled into something on the case that I'm working. I think that I may be under a threat, and I would feel better if Callie could stay with you and Frank for a while."

"Oh my," she said. "What kind of threat?"

I didn't want to tell her the details. I had already said too much to Callie. "I don't think there's too much to it, but—"

"If you thought there wasn't too much to it, you wouldn't be here with Callie."

I sighed. "Okay. I'm trying to find a hit man out of Florida who is going to kill someone in Indianapolis sometime in the next forty-eight hours or so. I need to find him and stop the hit. The problem is that he now knows I'm on to him, and he knows where I live. I can't let Callie stay in the house if there's any chance she could get hurt. This whole thing has to come to a head in the next couple of days. After that, it'll all be over."

She stood for a minute in stunned silence.

"Don't worry," I said. "I kept an eye out for a tail, and I took the long way around. In fact, I've been driving around Carmel for the past forty minutes. He didn't follow me."

The stunned look was replaced by one of indignation. "I'm not worried about us. Frank has a shotgun, and we both know how to use it."

"Sure," I said. "If I thought either of you was in danger, I wouldn't have come here. But I need to know Callie's safe."

"She's safe here. Frank and I will see to that."

"I know you will," I said, leaning to kiss her on the cheek.

"But what are you going to do?"

"I'm going to stop him," I said.

CHAPTER FIFTY-ONE

I drove back to the house and grabbed two boxes of shotgun shells, each containing twenty-five rounds, and two boxes of .38 shells, each containing fifty cartridges. I put the ammo in a gym bag, locked the house, and left. On the way out, I checked the mailbox. There was a one-way ticket on AmeriCon Air to Destin.

I tucked the ticket in my hip pocket and tossed the gym bag of ammo into the trunk. I slid the shotgun behind my seat, the same place that I had kept it the night I tossed Vinny's place.

I pulled away from the curb as inconspicuously as possible and drove to the office. I arrived five minutes later and called Mary.

"I have a bit of a situation," I said.

"What kind of a situation?" she asked.

"It seems that the hunter has become the hunted," I said, "if I could borrow a cliché." I told her about my near miss with Rulenska and how he had signaled me that he was aware I was working him.

"You're right. You have a bit of trouble. Don't you think it's time you told me what this is all about?"

"No."

"No?"

"I don't want to compromise you."

213

"I don't think at this point that's a big concern. If you're in trouble—"

"No, Mary."

She sighed. "Then why did you call?"

"I have Callie with the Shapiros. I need for you to look in on them."

"Do they know what's going on?"

"Corrin does. Frank was out, but I'm sure he'll know soon."

"Are you staying at the house?"

"No. That's what he wants me to do."

"I agree," she said. "He wants you to hide so he can do his business. Whether he kills you or keeps you running, he wins."

"Right. Which is why—"

"Who's he going to hit, Colton?" Her tone had changed from friend to federal agent.

"Sorry. I can't tell you that."

"You're putting yourself in legal jeopardy."

"I was born in legal jeopardy," I said. "I wouldn't know how to live any other way."

There was a long moment of silence. "Okay. But if you get in too deep, we will have to take you down along with everyone else."

"I know," I said.

"Colton?"

"Yes?"

"Be careful." Her tone changed again. She was my friend this time.

I assured her that I would.

After hanging up with Mary, I pulled the phone book from my desk drawer and began calling the cab companies that serviced the airport. With each one, I told them that I had lost my watch in the cab and that I had been picked up at the airport and taken to the hotel where Rulenska had been staying. I knew the date he checked in from Jamie, so I had some added plausibility. After four phone calls, I found the right one.

"Yeah," the whiskey voice on the other end of the line said. "We picked you up at around nine."

"That's right," I lied. "Who was driving that night?"

"That would have been Corn."

"Will Mr. Corn be driving tonight? I'd like to ask him—"

"It's Miss Corn," he said. "Louise Corn. If she had found a watch she would've turned it in. My drivers don't steal, pal."

"No, of course not," I said. "But she may not have found it. If it's there, I would like to give her a reward. The watch means a lot to me."

He never questioned why I would give her a reward for something she didn't do, but it seemed to work. It was the best I could come up with on short notice.

He put me on hold. No music, just hold.

"She's driving now," he said after coming back on the line. "Airport. Cab thirty-two."

I thanked him and headed out for the airport.

CHAPTER FIFTY-TWO

I found myself in short-term parking at the airport again, but this time I was heading for the arrival deck outside the terminal. I had flown out of Indianapolis International often but had never really grasped just how big the airport had become until I began walking around the arrival deck, looking for cab thirty-two. The size of the arrival deck alone showed that the city had indeed become a place of international exchange. A far cry from the "Indiana no place" of my childhood.

I made several trips back and forth along the arrival deck but didn't see cab thirty-two. So I went to the departure terminal on the next level and walked the deck there, looking for the cab. No luck. I did this a couple of times and then went inside to cool off. I found the food court and grabbed an iced tea.

As I sat in the cafe, drinking the tea and trying to reestablish normal body temperature, I watched the people as they milled about. Some were dressed to be seen, wearing expensive suits with all the appropriate paraphernalia: expensive gold jewelry, briefcases with just the right monogram, and invariably, a recent incarnation of the cell phone attached to one ear. Others, though, were less well dressed and were clearly struggling just to make ends meet. And still others probably shouldn't have been seen at all. Pants were at half-mast, mid-drifts that should have been covered were exposed, and an array of various other body parts were bared to some degree or other.

Some of the people who I saw were obviously excited to be traveling; some were not. Some were alone; some were not. Some were dragging small children who were tired and didn't want to go any farther; some were pushing elderly parents around in wheelchairs. But of all the people I saw, none of them looked like a Russian assassin living in Florida.

I finished the tea and went back into the heat to begin my trek again. After I rounded both decks, I was beginning again when I saw a female cabbie pull into a slot a dozen cabs ahead of where I was standing. A bold 32 was on the trunk.

I began running toward the cab, darting around clusters of travelers as I tried to reach her before she picked up another fare. I got lucky. She was far enough down the line that she had time to get out of the car. By the time I reached her, she was leaning on the hood with her arms folded.

"Where you headed?" she asked.

"Are you Louise Corn?" I asked.

"Maybe." She backed up a bit.

"It's okay," I said, displaying my ID. "I'm a private investigator. I just need to ask you some questions."

She was short, round, and had an edge to her that spoke of too many nights driving the city's streets. And yet there was a sense of vulnerability about her too. One that would cause her to back away from me when I approached her. She eyed me cautiously as she glanced at my ID. "Oh yeah," she said, "the dispatcher radioed me. Said you might be looking for me. But I didn't find a watch, you know? If I had I would—"

I held up a hand. "I'm more interested in a fare you had a couple of nights ago. About nine PM you took a man to a hotel. He —"

"I do that every night, mister. You're going to have to be a lot more specific."

"Here," I said, showing her the photo of Rulenska. "This is the man."

She took the picture from me and moved to a position under the light to study it. "Yeah, maybe. It could've been him." She handed the picture back to me.

"Tall, strong accent," I said, trying to jog her memory.

"I remember a tall man with a Russian accent. It's just that I'm not sure if your picture there is the same guy."

"Do you remember where you dropped him off?"

"I think so," she said. "If it's the same guy, he seemed to have a lot of questions about strip joints and such. The fleabag he stayed in seemed just about right for a guy like that."

"Where did you take him?" I asked.

"Some dive off of the interstate." She turned to motion to an area east of the airport. "The Rest and Eat."

Jamie's hotel. "Do you remember anything else?"

"Why?"

"I need to find him," I said. "It's important."

She crossed her arms and leaned on her cab to think. "This isn't about your watch, is it?"

"No."

"I knew it wasn't." She continued to lean against the cab, looking me over. Then she sighed and said, "I remember he asked if I knew of any good seafood places."

"Seafood?"

"Yeah. I told him about Jake's. And he wanted to know if I knew of any clubs around. Strip clubs. I thought he was trying to hit on me."

"Did you give him the names of any places?"

"Sure. I wanted him out of my cab. I would have sent him to a grocery store if it would have gotten him out. There was something about him that just gave me the creeps. I couldn't put my finger on it. I just didn't like him. Why? He a friend of yours?"

"No, I've never met him. Where did you send him?"

"That place next to Jake's. It's called Grin and Bare It."

"Thanks," I said. I handed her a twenty. "You've been a big help."

"You won't say that when you meet him," she said, folding the twenty as she slid it into the pocket of her jeans.

"Why's that?"

"Because I've been in this business a long time, you know? I know people. It's how I knew this wasn't about a watch."

"And?"

"And that guy is dangerous."

I smiled. "Maybe I am too."

She shook her head. "No, not like him. If you're not a cop now, you used to be. I can tell. You play by the rules. But he don't play like that. You take people to jail. He probably sends them to the grave."

CHAPTER FIFTY-THREE

The information Louise had given me was helpful. The restaurant and the club shared a common parking lot. If Rulenska had dinner at one and then went to the other, his chances of being seen or getting involved in a conversation or leaving some other piece of himself behind were pretty good.

I drove east on US 40 to the east side of Indianapolis. Jake's was a well-known establishment that had made a name for itself as the place to go for seafood long before the big-name national chains came to town. Over the years, the place had not moved on when the city had begun to decay around it, and it now found itself surrounded by places that drove away its previous clientele. Most of the people who ate at Jake's now ended up in the nearby clubs or bars. Jake's had become just another statistic of urban decay.

The restaurant was dark, even on a bright August day, with a decor that was very retro. Dark paneling lined the dining area as a few diners ate at tables adorned in stained tablecloths. The rest of them were sitting at the bar, and some I recognized from my days with the bureau as the city's less desirables. All in all, a rosy picture.

"You the manager?" I asked a stone-faced man with a cauliflower ear. He was leaning on a display case full of gum, candy, and mints.

"Uh-huh," he said, barely looking in my direction as he punched a calculator with one hand and counted receipts with another.

I held out Rulenska's picture. "Has this guy been in here recently?"

He punched the keys a few more times, cursed, and penciled something onto one of the receipts before sliding the pencil back behind one ear and taking a look at the photo.

"Yeah." He went back to his receipts.

"Yeah? Just like that?"

"That's what you wanted, isn't it?"

"I want the truth. Did you see this man in here?"

He counted out a few receipts, licked his thumb, and counted out a few more. He put those into a small cash box and reached under the counter to pull out a new stack of receipts that were held together by a rubber band. "If I say yeah, it's yeah." He punched the total of the first receipt from the new stack into the calculator.

"How can you say yeah? How can you remember seeing this—"

He stood up straight. "Look, if I say I saw him, I saw him."

"When?"

"A couple of nights ago."

"This picture is ten, maybe fifteen years old. How can you know for sure it's him?"

"Look at me," he said. "See this ear? You think I was born like this? I'm a fighter. I know it's him because I know a fighter when I see one."

I put the picture away. "Has he been in here since the other night?"

He leaned on the counter again and began adding up the receipts. "No."

"How long was he here?"

"Long enough to eat."

"Did he have anything to say?"

"Not to me."

Man of few words.

"Talk to the server? Another customer?" I asked.

He straightened up again, clearly annoyed. "Look, I don't know who he talked to except for the guy he was with."

"He was with someone?"

"Wow," he said, "you ain't so dumb after all." He leaned on the counter again and began adding receipts.

"A guy that looked like Clint Eastwood? Maybe John Carradine?" I asked.

He shook his head. "Nope. A little guy. Looked like Raoul Dominguez."

"Who's Raoul Dominguez?" I asked.

"My wife's ex. A little Hispanic dude."

The Hispanic man who had met with Rulenska may have looked a lot like Raoul Dominguez to the manager, but I was willing to bet that he would look a lot more like Cortez the dry cleaner to me.

CHAPTER FIFTY-FOUR

Time was running out, and my options were dwindling. If Cortez had met with Rulenska, there was a chance that he knew where to find him. That meant I was going to have to talk to Cortez again, which meant going into the dry cleaners again. But this time, they wouldn't be caught off guard so easily. I was going to need help.

I climbed the steps again to Sean's second-story apartment. He answered with a Guinness in hand.

"Got a minute?" I asked.

He stepped aside to let me in, this time not bothering to take a look at the street below.

"This is getting to be a regular thing, friend," he said. "Let me know a little earlier next time and I'll set a place for you."

"I may know how to find Rulenska," I said.

He arched an eyebrow as he hoisted the bottle of brew.

"But I'm going to need help."

"What kind?"

"Your kind," I said.

He slowly shook his head. "Sorry," he said, "but I'm out of the game."

I looked around the kitchen and at the beer in his hand. "You're out of life," I said.

He nodded. "Maybe, but at least I'm alive." He took another long pull from the bottle.

"No you're not, Sean" I said. "No offense."

"None taken."

We were standing in the barren kitchen. The light overhead was dim, and a stack of empty McDonald's cartons were overflowing the trash can.

"You haven't been alive for years," I said. "You can't run from what happened in Hastings." I nodded toward the bottle. "You won't find what you're looking for there either."

"And how would you know what I'm looking for, my friend?"

"Because I've been there."

He arched the eyebrows again. "Have you now? You've killed dozens of people?" He drank from the bottle as he kept his eyes focused on me, waiting for an answer.

"No, but I—"

"You've murdered children?"

"No, Sean. I haven't done that. But I have been in the hole. I'm in it now. And I know that life goes on. If you don't help me with this situation, someone else is going to get killed. And you will have to live with the fact that you could have helped me stop it."

He polished off what was left of the beer and tossed the empty into the trash. "Aye. But, am I supposed to stop everything that's happening? Do you think I sleep well now? Let me tell you, Mr. Policeman," he said, "I don't. I've killed men before." He began to pace the kitchen. "And they deserved it. But I didn't sign on to kill children." He turned and opened the door, pointing to the street below, as he raised his voice. "Look outside, Mr. Parker. People die everyday. They die everyday, and they aren't my fault."

"I need to find Rulenska," I repeated. "I need to find him and stop the hit before it goes down. You can help me."

He shook his head as he closed the door. "I don't know where to find him. I haven't seen him in years."

"I met with Cortez," I said. "Cortez has met with him since he came to town."

He shook his head again. "Sorry, I'm just not your man."

The room was quiet except for the buzz of the traffic downstairs. His last words hung in the air like the words in a comic strip balloon. But there was no comedy in what we were discussing.

He stopped pacing and stood with his back to the kitchen counter, leaning on the heels of his hands with his head down.

"Okay, Sean," I said, breaking the silence. "I'm sorry to have troubled you." I went to the refrigerator, got a bottle of beer, and handed it to Sean. "Here," I said. "You're going to need this. It's probably the only friend you have left who doesn't expect anything from you in return."

Chapter FIFTY-FIVE

I called Beverly. She was staying put, but the tension in her voice told me she was growing increasingly uptight with each passing hour.

After hanging up, I called the Shapiros and found that Callie was as sullen as ever. They told me that Mary had already been by once to check on them. Otherwise the home front was quiet, even if unchanged. Neither of the Shapiros expressed any concern for their own safety, but I detected a hint of resentment toward me for endangering their granddaughter.

Without Sean's backup, I was going to have to approach Cortez alone. That meant that if I were going to even the odds in my favor, I would need to use the element of surprise. I would need to catch him without his entourage of guards. I would have to do it the FBI way.

During my tenure with the bureau, we recognized that our best approach in apprehending a suspect, particularly a dangerous suspect, was to approach him while he was sleeping and overwhelm him with firepower. That way, he was less likely to resist, which left everyone a lot safer. Unlike the local police, the FBI wasn't geared for confrontations that arise suddenly and without warning and that often end just as abruptly, usually with someone dead. A group of FBI agents in Miami had tried a felony car stop leaving two agents dead and several others wounded. That disaster led to a change in training at the FBI academy in Quantico, Virginia.

But I was still old school. I didn't have overwhelming firepower, but I could have the element of surprise.

I drove to the shopping area where the Cortez operations were located and parked across the street in the parking lot of a smaller strip mall that housed a barber shop and a storefront church.

The day was still going strong but would be spent in a few hours. I sat, watching the front of the dry cleaners, hoping Cortez would be leaving soon. And if I was lucky, he would be leaving alone.

If I could tail him and approach him when he wasn't looking, I might be able to find a location for Rulenska with a minimal amount of fuss. Of course, if Cortez wasn't alone, I could do it *with* a great deal of fuss. All in all, I preferred the former.

I pulled the shotgun from behind the seat and checked to be sure I had enough rounds in the chamber. Having become the hunted myself, I didn't want to be caught off guard.

The movies often show the staid PI drinking coffee as he patiently waits for his suspect to come into view. Sometimes our hero will even fall asleep but always seems to wake just as his suspect is making a move. Then our hero, with unshaven face and bloodshot eyes, tails the suspect, staying just a car or two behind, until the bad guy makes the move that will eventually lead to his downfall. Our PI swoops down and cleans up the mess in time to recap the whole story for his adoring and hard-working secretary. The story line may produce an Emmy, but it has little to do with reality.

Biologically speaking, anything that goes in must come out. Drinking coffee on a long stakeout is going to require a nearby restroom. Since Murphy's Law does seem to prevail during moments like these, one can reasonably expect the suspect to make a move while the hero is doing his business in the Port-a-Potty or other nearby facility.

Sleeping is out too for the same reason. So our hero—in this case, me—sits and waits and tries not to arouse the suspicion of the store owners, who wonder why a strange man has been sitting in their lot for so long. I had waited six hours when Cortez finally came out of the cleaners.

He was dressed in the same type of buttoned short-sleeved shirt as before with the tail hanging out. One hand held a cigarette, and the other hand was buried in the pocket of his jeans. Two men accompanied him, both considerably taller than Cortez. I recognized one of them as the armed man in the drug cutting room.

The group approached the right rear of a Lexus RX, where Pancho opened the door for his employer. After Cortez climbed in, the other guard got into the left side of the rear seat, sitting next to Cortez as Pancho moved back around to the driver's door. As the Lexus pulled away, I started the Escort and moved into traffic behind them, staying back several blocks.

We worked our way onto Thirty-eighth Street and moved west. Traffic was becoming heavy, so our progress was slow. Staying close enough to follow but far enough behind to avoid being spotted was becoming increasingly difficult. I tried using larger vehicles for cover, but that too was nearly impossible as they jockeyed for a better position in traffic. Concerns for my own safety were coming into play as I thought I recognized a tail behind me. Each time I maneuvered into position to see Cortez, a dark sedan did the same. Eventually it dropped off, and I was glad to know I was just paranoid and not yet in any real danger.

We crossed over I-465 and continued west to the Eagle Creek area. Eagle Creek was made up of land that had originally been owned by Josiah Lilly, of the pharmaceutical Lillys, and was sold to the city of Indianapolis for one dollar because of extensive flooding. The city built a reservoir to control the problem. The area was now a park and served as a recreational facility with camping, fishing, and boating activities. The area even boasted a small airport now, and several upscale neighborhoods had sprung up along the park. From what I could tell, the RX was heading for one of those areas.

We turned right and drove north between the reservoir, with its late evening boaters, and the airport, which was beginning to glow with the blue landing lights that had made it famous as a lovers' lane. Traffic along the roadway was thinning out, forcing me to keep an even greater distance than before. In two instances, I was forced to pull over in rest stops to avoid being noticed.

We crossed the reservoir on Fifty-sixth Street and eventually came to a row of houses that sat on a bluff, facing the water. The RX turned onto one of the side streets and pulled into a three-car garage. I drove past, turned around in a cul-de-sac, and came back to the street where I had seen the RX enter the garage. The sun would be down in a few minutes, so I parked the Escort alongside the curb, near the intersection, and waited. I was in the lion's den now, and I was glad to have the shotgun with me.

About an hour after sunset, the garage door opened and the Lexus backed out. It drove to the intersection and turned, shining its head-lights across my windshield and forcing me to slink in my seat. When the danger passed, I sat up and tried to see how many people were in the Lexus, but it was too dark to tell.

I glanced toward the house. The lights were on, which could mean that Cortez was still in the house. If he was, whether alone or not, I was going to have to go in and talk to him. I needed to find Rulenska, and Cortez was now my only hope. Unless I misinterpreted the letter, the hit was going down in less than twenty-four hours.

Time had run out.

CHAPTER FIFTY-SIX

It was too dark to see my watch, and I didn't want to run the risk of turning on the car's dome light, but I guessed that I had been sitting for almost four hours since the RX left the house. That would make the time to be around midnight.

I looked at the house again. The lights were still on, which meant Cortez was still up or he had left in the Lexus. At any rate, I needed to find Rulenska. If Cortez was home but didn't know where Rulenska was, then I was out of leads, and my chances of avoiding trouble were gone. It was time to move.

I got out of the car with the shotgun and eased the door closed. The evening air was as humid as it had been all day, and the neighborhood was alive with the drone of air-conditioning units.

I jogged across a lawn and then the street to the house where Cortez was located. The backyard was surround by a nine-foot tall privacy fence, and the gate was locked.

I looked for something to help me climb the fence and found a couple of flowerpots. I overturned them, spilling the flowers onto the ground, and stacked one pot on top of the other. Holding the shotgun in one hand, I placed the other hand on top of the fence, planted one foot on the pots, and put the other foot on the lock and latch mechanism. When I hoisted myself up and over the gate, motion-detector lights kicked on, illuminating the backyard and revealing an in-ground pool, a hot tub, and enough landscaping to make the Indianapolis Parks Superintendent salivate.

Hearing stirrings from the patio door at the rear of the house, I tossed the shotgun behind some forsythia bushes as I ran for the pool and eased myself into the water as quietly as possible.

I kept my head above water and listened as the patio door slid open. "Hurry up, you dumb dog." It was Cortez.

I could hear the dog's tags jingling as it moved about the yard, finding the perfect spot to do its business. I kept my feet on the pool's ladder and one hand on a rung. I didn't want to start drifting, and I was trying to keep quiet. If the dog was aware of me, it didn't give any indication.

"Get in here, you dumb mutt," Cortez said. I could hear the jingling tags move toward the house, followed by the sound of the patio door closing.

I eased my head out of the pool and could see that the drapes over the patio door had been drawn closed. Climbing out of the pool, I went back to the forsythia bushes and retrieved the shotgun. It was late, but if I could wait just a little longer, Cortez would soon be in bed, which would make my job of talking with him less dangerous for both of us.

I didn't have to wait long. The lights of the house soon went out, and twenty minutes later I moved along the back of the house, where I found the telephone wires. Most home alarm systems are wired through the home's phone wires, so cutting them will usually disable the alarm system. It was the best I could do on short notice, so I cut the wires and hoped Cortez had been shortsighted on his home security.

I crept along the back of the house and found the bathroom window. I didn't want to enter through the bedroom and have Cortez catch me half in and half out. Other than the bedroom, the bathroom seemed to be the best point of entry.

The window was about chest height. I looked around the yard and saw two flowerpots, similar to the ones I had used to climb over the fence, sitting on the patio. I grabbed them, dumped out the plants and potting soil, and stacked one on top of the other. The pots allowed me to reach the upper half of the pane.

The lock was a simple latch, and when I tried to open the window, it was locked. I cursed and decided that in the interest of time, I was going to have to take a chance on making a little noise.

I tapped the glass in an area just over the latch with the butt of the shotgun. The glass cracked. I wrapped my hand in my shirt and pushed the broken glass on through and turned the latch. Within a minute, I was standing in the bathroom, soaking with chlorinated water and sweat.

I paused to listen. I was concerned that I may have alerted Cortez, but the house was quiet. And not as dark as I had anticipated. The security light from outside was illuminating most of the bathroom. From what I could see, it was nice, with plush carpeting and a large Jacuzzi sitting in the middle of a marble platform and surrounded by steps. The towel racks were adorned with the type of towels that most people use for show, and the fixtures were gold-plated. Nice, if you like luxury, comfort, and that sort of thing.

I moved into the hallway and saw that Cortez had plugged night-lights into the outlets, further illuminating the way.

The hallway was exceptionally wide and carpeted with thick-piled, well-padded carpeting. As I moved along the pathway, I kept my eye on the room just ahead, at the end of the hall. I could hear snoring, and unless I was missing my guess, it belonged to Cortez. As I moved forward, the plush carpeting made each step virtually silent.

I paused at the first room to my right and peered in to see a bed, made and empty. I moved down the hall and looked into the room on my left. Another made and empty bed. That left the last room on the right—the one I had heard the snoring coming from and the one I had been watching.

The house was two-story, but there were at least three bedrooms on the first floor. The snoring I heard coming from one of them wasn't guaranteed to be Cortez, but I couldn't afford to overlook it either.

When I moved around the corner, I saw two lumps under the covers of the bed. Both were motionless, and at least one of them was snoring loudly.

I moved into the room, switched the shotgun to my left hand and reached for the light switch with my right. When I did, a searing pain shot through my arm, and I went down.

Chapter FIFTY-SEVEN

The dog, a very large and very motivated German shepherd, had lunged for my arm. When it did, I instinctively struck at it with the shotgun in my left hand, which had deflected its full-on bite. Still, it had managed to tear the flesh of my arm, and blood was pouring from the open wounds. The impact of the shepherd's attack drove me to the floor, where I landed on my left side. I dropped the shotgun.

I kicked at the dog with my right foot and managed to shove it aside as I reached for the shotgun. Cortez and his companion were coming awake and moving from under the covers.

"Sic him, Buck," he said. "Tear him apart."

I kicked at the dog again and extended my reach for the shotgun. Cortez saw what I was trying to do and reached for the nearby nightstand. A young woman who had been lying next to Cortez turned and saw me wrestling with the dog. She screamed.

The dog lunged for me again, grabbing one pant leg. It began to pull, dragging me across the floor, as I kicked at it in an attempt to free myself. I reached for the shotgun again. My fingers slipped past the stock but managed to spin the gun around on the padded carpeting. I grabbed it with a firm grip around the barrel and swung it, bringing the shoulder stock down on the dog's head. It yelped just as Cortez was pulling a stainless steel nine-millimeter from the nightstand drawer.

I brought the stock around to my right hand, while still kicking at the dog with my right foot, and jacked a shell into the chamber of the shotgun.

"Raise that gun at me and I'll cut you in half," I said over the growling of the dog and the screams of Cortez's bed partner.

He froze with the nine-millimeter in his right hand.

"Call the dog off of me," I said, still pushing it away with my foot. "Call him off of me or I'll shoot him."

Cortez hesitated, so I swung the barrel toward the dog.

"Buck! Over here, Buck." Cortez motioned with his free hand for the dog to come to him. "Come here, boy."

The dog was still snarling but began to back up, keeping its eyes focused on me. I redirected the shotgun toward Cortez, who still had the semiautomatic pistol in his hand.

The young woman had stopped screaming but was sitting up against the headboard with her knees drawn up and the blankets pulled tightly around her. Only her eyes could be seen.

"Put it back in the drawer," I said. "Grab the barrel with your left hand and put the pistol in the drawer. Slowly."

The dog had moved to the other side of the bed, near Cortez, and was out of my line of sight. But I could still hear it's guttural sounds.

"Do it now," I said.

The dry-cleaning drug lord reached with his left hand and took the pistol, by the barrel, from his right. He put it back into the drawer and closed it. He did not take his eyes off of me.

"How did you get in here?"

I climbed to my feet. My right arm was bloody. "A man like you, with your stature, ought to spend more on his security." My arm was burning, and I winced from the pain.

His expression, a mix of anger and mirth, had an overlying look of pleasured animosity. "My alarm system may need to be updated. I will have my men look into that." He rose from the bed, standing in a partially stooped position as he rubbed the dog's head.

"Might be a good idea," I said. "A lot of guys like me are running the streets at night. Getting to be so that a decent, hard-working man like yourself isn't safe in his own home."

"It might be easier to deal with the men like you," he said. "It costs less and is a lot more enjoyable."

I directed my attention to the woman. "Who are you?"

"She's no concern of yours," Cortez said. "Your business is with me."

I switched the shotgun to my left hand again and rested the butt of the stock against my left hip with the barrel pointed toward the ceiling. My right arm was very painful, and I could feel the tips of my fingers getting sticky from the flowing blood.

Cortez nodded toward my arm. "It seems that Buck was effective."

I nodded. "Yes. Almost got him killed though."

Cortez' expression changed. Instead of a sneer and a smile, I was getting just the sneer. "That would have been another grave mistake, my friend."

"Sure," I said. "And that scares me, seeing as how I haven't made any of them so far."

He ceased petting the dog and straightened to his full height. "What do you want?" he asked. "What is worth losing your life for?"

"I found Gagliardi," I said.

"And?"

"And he's dead."

"Death is a part of life," he said.

"Maybe," I said. "But the man I'm looking for has made a nice living from it."

Cortez sighed. "It is late and we are tired. Why don't you tell me what you want and I will let you know if I am willing to let you have it."

"You had a meeting with Rulenska. I want to know where I can find him."

Despite what most people may think about themselves, very few have a poker face. Even those whose business interests require it. I saw an almost imperceptible flicker in Cortez's eyes. It gave him away and made it impossible for him to recover.

"I know of this man," he said, "but you are mistaken if you think that I have—"

"Stow it," I said. "You met with Rulenska at Jake's. I want to know where I can find him."

His eyes betrayed him again as they bobbled toward the shotgun and back again.

"I don't want to kill him," I said. "I don't want to kill anyone. In fact, I'm trying to stop a killing. He can even keep the fee. I just want him to walk away."

Cortez smiled. "You do not know him, do you?"

It was getting late. My arm was hurting, I was hungry, and I was growing increasingly agitated by the minute. "No," I said, shaking my head. "I only know of him."

"Then you should know that what you ask is an impossibility."

"So was breaking into your house an hour ago. Yet here I stand. Impossible or not, I'm going to stop him."

"Then," Cortez said, nodding toward the shotgun, "you will have to kill him."

"Like you said, death is a part of life."

He watched my face. He wanted to see if I was bluffing. He wanted to see how good of a poker player I was. After a few moments, he knew I wasn't bluffing.

"He is on the move. He never stays in one place two nights in a row."

"Where was he last?"

Cortez shrugged. "I only know that he was staying at the airport. A place called the Rest and Eat."

"How did you contact him?" I asked.

"He contacted me," Cortez said.

"What did he want?"

He shook his head. "For that," he said, nodding again toward the shotgun, "you will have to use it."

I lowered the barrel and pointed it at Cortez' abdomen. His non-poker face gave him away. He was scared, but he did not back down. Whoever Rulenska was, whatever he had, it was enough to scare one of the city's most notorious and most ruthless cocaine dealers.

I watched as Cortez held his breath but did not take his eyes off the gun. He was steeling himself in preparation for the blast.

I raised the barrel to its previous position. Cortez let out his breath.

"You're in the wrong business," I said. "You fear death. And for you, for a man who does what you do, that's a defect."

He nodded his head. "Yes. I do fear death. I know where I am heading and I am in no hurry to arrive."

"And yet you were willing to let me shoot you? To protect a murderer?"

He nodded. "I know that you are capable. You see, a blast from your gun is quick. But with the man you seek, death comes much slower. And much more painfully." He stooped to pet the dog again. "I fear death and I fear hell. But I fear the way that they come much, much more."

CHAPTER FIFTY-EIGHT

I left Cortez' place and walked back to my car. I was wet, tired, hungry, and bloody. But also wiser.

Rulenska wasn't going to be easy. Cortez had not only ruined many lives but was probably responsible for ending a few of them as well. Undoubtedly, some of them were by his own hand. He lived and worked in an area of life where death comes quickly and violently. He had lived with it all his adult life. And yet the fear in his eyes was real. His fear of death and the hell that awaited him was genuine. But the fear of them was not so great that he wanted to live with the risk of dealing with Rulenska. And for a man like Cortez, that said something.

I started the car and began to work my way back to Fifty-sixth Street. It was almost one o'clock in the morning, which meant Chatham's last day on earth would be dawning soon. My best chance of finding the Russian before he carried out his task had evaporated in Cortez' bedroom. Now, if I was going to stop the hit, I was going to have to get Chatham out of the way. And unless I could come up with a plan, that would mean letting Chatham in on the deal. My effort to keep everyone involved in the dark as much as possible wasn't working out as I had hoped.

As I drove toward the south side of Indianapolis, I began thinking of a plan to get Chatham out of the way. By the time I reached home, I had one. It wasn't a great one, but given the circumstances, I didn't have time for anything else. It would be a gamble and involve some element of risk. The big unknown was whether Rulenska would take the bait and try to hit Chatham at home. I was hoping he would, and I was betting my life, Chatham's life, and Lester's marriage on being right.

I fixed a sandwich and ate standing over the sink. I hadn't eaten for a while and would most likely not eat again for a long time.

After I finished my sandwich and downed a Coke, I cleaned up, bandaged the dog bite as best I could, and slipped into my shoulder holster, carrying my Ruger nine-millimeter and two fifteen-round magazines. I decided to leave the .38 behind in favor of the higher capacity of the Ruger. Fifteen cartridges in a magazine was better than five in a cylinder. If all went well, I wouldn't need any of the firepower. Rulenska would take the money and walk away. But things seldom go as planned. Sean and Cortez both knew the hitter better than I did, and what they knew didn't give me a lot of hope for a peaceful resolution.

Before leaving the house I called Beverly. She answered on the third ring.

"Yeah?" She was groggy. I looked at the clock over my stove. It was two thirty AM.

"It's Colton. I'm going to be coming over in a little bit. Make some coffee." I hung up. It might have been stark, even rude for me to talk to her as I did. But I had little feeling for her, and I didn't see that changing any time soon.

"I have a plan," I said, "but you're going to have to help." I was standing in the kitchen, leaning against the counter. I had just poured a cup of black coffee and was holding a blue plastic mug of it in my hand.

Beverly was dressed in a blue bathrobe. Her face was still swollen from sleep, and her hand shook as she stirred the cream into her cup.

"It won't be easy," I said, trying to get a response.

"Nothing's easy."

"You made this mess," I said. "You should help clean it up."

She dropped two sugars into the cup. "What do you need from me?"

"I want you to call Chatham. Tell him you've reconsidered. Tell him you will give him what he wants, but you need a place to stay." I gestured around the kitchen. "If he pays your rent here, you'll provide the services he wants for as long as he is willing to pay."

She shook her head. "No. I can't stand that man. He's cost me everything I have."

"If you don't do this, Beverly, I have no way of getting him out of his house without him finding out about the contract you have on his head. That means you don't have a chance of ever getting your life with Lester back on track. You go to jail, he gets a divorce, and Chatham walks away."

"No," she said. "He won't walk away. He'll be dead." She blew on the coffee before drinking.

"No," I said, pouring more coffee. "Chatham won't die."

"But—"

"He won't die because I have a duty to prevent a murder. I'll have to tell him about your hitter, and he'll go into protective custody until the man you hired for the job can be stopped."

"You would do that? You would tell him? Let him live?"

"I don't have a choice."

She glared at me as she poured what was left of her coffee down the drain. "When do I do this?"

"Daylight. I need him out as soon as possible. Tell him to meet you for breakfast. Tell him you need to talk about the offer. Let him know you can get the information he wants from Lester's office but that you want to be compensated for it. Tell him you will need him to finance you so you can get away from Lester." I locked eyes with her to underscore the seriousness of the situation. "You've got to make it seem real. Play it up. Do whatever you have to do to get him out of the house and keep him out all day."

She was shaking her head in disgust.

"And I mean *all* day. Do whatever you have to do."

"And where will you be when all of this is happening?"

"Don't worry about me. You just take care of your end."

She took the still full cup of coffee from my hand. "It isn't you I'll be worrying about."

Somehow, I believed her.

CHAPTER FIFTY-NINE

I left Beverly's apartment and was in front of Chatham's house within the hour.

The attorney lived the life of a country squire. A two-story English Tudor stood amid a grove of pin oak and maple trees with a winding driveway that led from the narrow road in front of the house to the three-car detached garage that was located at the rear. The house was large—I guessed about seven thousand square feet—and was surrounded by acres of gently rolling ground. All in all, the picturesque home of a gentleman. But any suggestion that Chatham was a gentleman was false.

It was just past three-thirty in the morning. If Rulenska were going to hit, this would be a good time. If he had already done so, then I was too late. If not, I had time to save a man I had met only once and who had not proven to be very endearing.

I left the car with the shotgun in hand and jogged down the driveway to the front of the house. I made a quick survey and saw no open windows. The door was still locked and hadn't been tampered with. I ran alongside both ends of the house and eventually the back, making similar checks. From all appearances, I wasn't too late.

The garage wasn't attached to the house, and it did not appear to have been penetrated. From the side of the garage farthest from the house, I had a good view of the front, back, and one side of Chatham's home. I could also see the street. If Rulenska decided to make his move before dawn, I was in a good position to stop him.

I had settled myself in a flower bed beside the garage with the shotgun in my lap. For the next three hours, I kept a steady watch on the house and the street. And for three hours I saw nothing but a newspaper delivery.

Then, around six AM, the lights in the house went on, and a copy of the newspaper was tossed onto the front lawn. I saw Chatham, in his bathrobe, come out of the house shortly afterward and pick up the paper. He had a cup of coffee in one hand and casually flipped open the paper with the other as he sauntered back toward the house, where he would be dry and cozy while I sat in a dew-soaked flower bed, trying to save his life.

The working assumption was that Rulenska had already planned the hit on Chatham. According to Sean, the Russian liked to do the deed up close. A knife or garrote. If Beverly executed things properly, Chatham would call in sick. When Rulenska didn't find his mark, he would call the office too and would be told that Chatham wasn't in, or better yet, that he was ill and at home. Having your mark at home, sick, and alone would be any hitter's dream. I was hoping it would be Rulenska's.

At seven, Chatham came out to the garage in a light brown pin-striped suit, white shirt, and dark brown silk tie. He had a leather brief-case in one hand and a travel mug of coffee in the other. By all appearances, he was dressed to sue.

Within a minute, he was backing his Mercedes out of the garage. I kept out of sight until he was gone and then jogged across the yard to the house. I let myself in, disarming the alarm as I had done at Cortez' place by snipping the phone wires at an area that was close to the ground. The ease of disarming these things was beginning to make me wonder why anyone bothered.

The interior of the house was as ornate as I had imagined it would be while I was sitting in the dew-soaked shrubbery. The kitchen, through which I had entered, was as large as my half of the rented duplex I lived in, and very well equipped. A large semicircle of oak cabinetry surrounded a center island. At one end of the kitchen was a brick encased oven, and at the opposite end, a dining table positioned in front of a fireplace. The table looked hand carved. I guessed that it had probably been imported at a cost that exceeded my fee for this job.

I opened the refrigerator and found it fully stocked. I fished around and extracted a package of thinly sliced ham. I was still hungry, so I found a loaf of bread in a bread box on the counter, a tomato that had already been sliced, and some green peppers. When I was done, I took the sandwich into the living room.

Like the kitchen, the living room was large—maybe forty feet by fifty—and nicely furnished. The fireplace that was in the kitchen doubled as the fireplace in the living room. Leather sofas and reclining chairs were grouped around a mahogany coffee table with a chess set on it. The game pieces appeared to have been made from hand-carved ivory.

I ate the sandwich as I moved around the house. To one side of the grouping, I noticed a plasma television suspended on the wall and book-shelves, also of mahogany, filled with DVDs of Hollywood's latest hits. I perused some of the titles on his shelves. I was glad to see that Chatham had some Bogie classics along with Errol Flynn and John Wayne. If events did not go as planned or I was wrong about Rulenska and Chatham, at least I would eat well and be entertained properly while committing the felony that would land me in jail.

Not to be outdone, the entryway of the house was as ornate as the living room, with a mahogany staircase that descended in dramatic fashion from the second floor. A large, solid mahogany door with a small crystal window sat at the bottom of the stairs and opened to the outside.

Two ornate iron soldiers, resembling the kind often seen in the *Nutcracker Suite,* stood guard on each side of the door. They were nearly three feet tall and probably weighed more than fifty pounds each. Overall, gaudy and out of place items in a house that was otherwise tastefully decorated.

I continued eating the sandwich as I moved upstairs. The staircase was decorated with several brass planters that each contained a different type of plant. They were spaced approximately every third step. A little heavy on the foliage for my taste, but nice nonetheless.

The master bedroom was furnished with a four-poster bed, mahogany like everything else, and equipped with a small study off to one side. It was somehow still within the bedroom, yet somehow separate. I moved to the study and examined the bookshelves. On them were books that no one ever read but that looked really nice when company came to visit. I didn't think, though, that Chatham had me in mind when he decorated.

I went along the upper-floor hallway, checking out the other rooms. All of them had a significant amount of mahogany, and all of them were significantly impressive.

I went through the closets and drawers, looking for anything that might help me get a better handle on Chatham. Not that he was the focal point of why I was there. Lester was. But if I could find anything that might help me persuade him to go on about his life and stay out of the Cheeks', I wanted to have it. The more persuasion I had, the better and smoother I could expect things to flow. But after nearly an hour of searching, I didn't find anything in the house to suggest that Chatham was anything other than a successful businessman. Still, he had managed to irritate someone enough to have him killed. And here I was, committing an offense that would probably get me jailed, just to save him. Lucky me.

Chapter Sixty

I watched one of the morning shows on Chatham's big-screen television as I had a cup of coffee. Chatham apparently preferred the grind-it-yourself kind and had all the equipment available to do it. I sat on one of the leather sofas and watched as an anchorman with nicely coiffed hair sat next to an academy-award-winning actress. They were talking about her latest role and her hopes for mankind. As they began to drift into her political views, which he pursued with the same intenseness as if he were talking to the president of the United States, I changed the channel.

On the next one, I saw another anchor talking to a video screen behind him. The topic of acupuncture versus skin cream for the treatment of psoriasis wasn't something that interested me, so I changed the channel again. Much more of this, I thought, and I'm going to need a lobotomy.

I turned off the TV. The house was quiet. That wasn't what I wanted to hear. I didn't know how long Beverly was going to be able to keep Chatham at bay or how much longer she would even be willing to try. If the Russian was going to hit Chatham at the house as I had assumed, now would be a good time to do it before Chatham was in busy downtown Indianapolis all day.

I stood to stretch and move around the house. I kept the shotgun in my hand and kept the shoulder holster on as well. I also kept the doors locked. If I made it too easy for Rulenska, he would sense the trap and leave.

As I rechecked the doors, I glanced out the window through a gap in the nearly closed drapes. I saw a dark sedan pull into the driveway. It was a late-model BMW. I watched as it sat for a minute or two with the engine idling and then backed out, turning and moving on down the street.

The car was familiar. It looked a lot like the one I had seen tailing me the night I was tailing Cortez, the one that I had dismissed as nothing.

I closed the drapes, assuming the car was Rulenska's. He had made me at the hotel and had probably been tailing me when I was tailing Cortez. Which meant he would know my car, which I had left parked along the street just a few doors down from Chatham's house.

I had wanted to make it easy for Rulenska without making it look like a trap. If I didn't move my car, he would notice and flee, leaving the contract on Chatham open-ended. The chances of finding him then wouldn't be good, and everything that had been done to this point would have been for naught.

I slipped out of the house and jogged to where I had left my car. I drove a bit farther down the road and around a curve, where I parked the car just off the shoulder. Although it wasn't completely out of view, it was partially obscured by a veil of dense roadside foliage. Not the best camouflage, but it would have to do.

After parking, I ran back to the house and noticed the phone lines I had cut earlier and forgotten to repair. I went into the house, rummaged for supplies, and came back outside with black electrician's tape. I re-taped them as inconspicuously as possible. I suspected that Rulenska would enter the house pretty much the way that I had and would cut the line, most likely at mid-wall level. He wouldn't notice where I had cut the line and would think he was disabling the alarm system.

I stood back to admire my taping job. The phone and the alarm wouldn't work because my repair was solely cosmetic. But the phone lines didn't look like they had been tampered with, and that was all I cared about. I didn't want to tip him off. I wanted everything to look as normal as possible.

Once I was back in the house, I began setting the bait. I relocked the doors and positioned the drapes as Chatham might have done for early evening. I put away the dishes I had used and cleaned up the kitchen. Afterward, I checked and rechecked the house, upstairs and down. The trap had been set. There was nothing left to do now but wait.

I poured myself a glass of orange juice, compliments of Chatham, and watched baseball on his plasma TV with my feet up on his mahogany table. I had all the comforts of home. A remote in my left hand, a drink in my right, and a twelve-gauge Winchester pump shotgun on my lap.

A baseball game and a Bogart movie later, Rulenska had still not shown. It was nearing three in the afternoon, and I was getting concerned.

I didn't know for sure how Beverly was managing to keep Chatham at bay for so long, but I could guess. At any rate, I didn't care. In fact, I was grateful.

I stood to peer out the window. The area remained quiet.

Restless, I used my cell phone to call Mary and check on Callie. All was well, and Callie and Mary were making dinner plans. The Shapiros, who saw Mary as an interloper on their deceased daughter's family, would not join them.

By the time the sun had gone down, I was getting concerned that I had misinterpreted my leads. What if Rulenska wasn't going to hit Chatham tonight?

I pushed the thoughts from my mind and, for the fifth time, ejected the magazine from my Ruger and checked the ammo before sliding it back into the butt of the pistol. If I read Rulenska wrong, if he didn't show, I was going to be neck deep in trouble.

I made one last check of the house. It was pretty much the same as I had found it when I first arrived earlier that morning and a lot like it was when I had checked an hour ago.

I made my way upstairs. The upper level would give me a bird's-eye view, which would help me spot the dark sedan again if it was still in the area. When I reached the top of the stairs, I turned left and went into the master bedroom and flicked on the light. When I did, I found Rulenska.

CHAPTER
SIXTY-ONE

The garrote was around my neck, causing me to drop the shotgun as I instinctively grabbed at the wire.

"You looking for me, my friend?" Rulenska said in a thick Russian accent. He had grabbed me from behind. I could feel his breath on the back of my neck.

I drove my left elbow deep into his ribs. I could feel the air rushing out of him as he exhaled. His hot breath was stale, and I could smell the afterburn of several cigarettes. Still, he hung on, heaving me backward, nearly lifting me off of the floor. He had a powerful grip on the garrote. And me.

It's instinct, when being strangled, to grab the instrument that is being used with both hands. I had attacked him with my left elbow because I didn't want to let go of the garrote with my right hand. But Rulenska was big and very strong. I could feel my feet leave the floor as he tried to strangle me or break my neck.

I let go of the garrote and began driving both elbows into his ribs with as much force as I could muster. I wanted to break his ribs and drive them into his lungs.

But he was prepared this time and chuckled with each attempt.

I drove my head backward, trying to break his nose. He grunted in pain.

"You are feeble," he said as he tightened the garrote and swung me around the room. "Feeble like a woman."

The suddenness of the attack had caused me to forget that I was armed with more than the shotgun. I pulled the Ruger from my holster. Rulenska took note and spun around, driving me into the wall face-first again and again. Each time he pulled back on the garrote, he slammed into the wall with more force as he attempted to drive the gun from my hand.

"I am going to kill you, my friend. I am going to kill you and send you to hell."

As he began to shove me forward again, I placed both feet on the wall and pushed, using it as leverage. Rulenska and I fell backward onto the floor, but he maintained his grip on the garrote. I kept mine on the Ruger.

I maneuvered the pistol to a position where I could shoot him, but he adeptly rolled over, placing me face down in the carpet with the gun lying underneath me. Rulenska was sitting on top of me now and began to pull on the garrote like he was pulling on the reins of a horse. It was becoming increasingly difficult to breathe, and my vision was beginning to dim.

As his weight bore down on me, I could hardly move. I began to shift to my right, trying to find some space under his right knee. The limited space gave me some maneuverability. As I shifted, I was able to free the barrel of the Ruger from its constrained position between my chest and the carpet. I pointed it at his left knee and fired.

Rulenska cried out in pain and immediately loosened his grip on the garrote. When he did, I rolled farther to the right. As I cleared myself from under his crushing weight, I pointed the Ruger at his chest. He swatted at the gun, knocking it from my hand.

I shifted again, rolled to his left, and climbed to my feet. Despite his wound, Rulenska was staggering to his feet. I lunged at him, driving my head into his abdomen. He collapsed on the carpet. I stood and moved toward the hallway. I needed to get away and regroup. Rulenska was a trained killer and too powerful for me to handle one-on-one. As I moved into the hallway outside the bedroom, I pulled the door shut. Rulenska had not yet gotten to his feet, but he would soon. And this time, he would have the Ruger and my shotgun.

I half ran, half fell down the winding staircase. My head was throbbing and my throat was on fire. Each breath I took felt as if it had been heated with a torch. I had come here to reason with Rulenska. To offer him a chance to keep the money and leave Chatham alone. But I had underestimated him. Cortez had been right. I didn't know Rulenska. He didn't kill for money. He killed for fun—and he was right behind me.

I ran to the kitchen, hoping to find a weapon.

"You will not run, my friend. You are no coward. You will stay and fight. And you will die." Rulenska's voice was much closer now.

I didn't see a knife block on the counters or any hanging pots and pans, and I didn't have time to search the drawers. I would have a better chance if I ambushed him from one of the rooms down the hall. I moved into the living room as I kept an eye on the staircase. I could not yet see Rulenska.

I began to move along the wall, away from the kitchen and toward the first-floor guest rooms. As I did, I pulled the plug on any lamp in my path. I wanted the house dark. I wanted Rulenska to have to work to find me. The breaker panel would have been better, but I didn't know where it was located. I had been in the house several hours, and I hadn't bothered to look for the breaker panel. It was an oversight, and I wasn't pleased with myself. Pulling lamp plugs was as good as it was going to get.

"Where are you, my friend?" Rulenska said. I could hear him jack a shell into the chamber of the shotgun.

I moved along the hallway and found a bathroom. I rolled into the room, trying to listen for Rulenska. I opened the medicine cabinet and found nothing but toiletries. I opened the cabinet under the sink and found towels, a mirror, and a can of hair spray. If I had matches, the hair spray could be useful. As it was, I could probably throw it at him, but it wouldn't go far against the buckshot he could throw back at me.

He fired a blast from the shotgun and immediately jacked another shell into the chamber.

I turned the light on in the bathroom, closed the door of the bedroom across the hall, and climbed into the shower stall just as Rulenska rounded the hallway from the living room.

"I know you're back here," he sang, followed by another shotgun blast.

It was getting hard to hear, which was probably part of his plan. He didn't need to fire the shotgun because he had the Ruger. But the blast drowned out any chance of me hearing him approach. It also had tremendous psychological affect.

He fired again, closer this time, and the blast of the gun was deafening. I couldn't hear, but as he moved down the hallway, I could see his reflection in the bathroom's mirror. He paused at the door. I positioned myself flat against the shower stall.

I watched his reflection as he peered around the corner of the bathroom door. His face was less than a foot away. He turned as he saw the closed bedroom door across the hall.

"You think you are smart enough to detour me?" He turned to face the bedroom door, which placed him out of my sight. He fired the shotgun. As he did, I jumped out of the shower stall and into the hallway.

The bedroom door was in splinters and Rulenska's back was facing me. I tackled him, driving him face forward through the remnants of the bedroom door and into the bedroom. As we fell into the room, the shotgun lurched from his hands and fell to the plush carpeting, where it spun away from us, bouncing under the bed.

Despite his size and the gunshot wound to his knee, Rulenska moved with the agility of a cat. He kicked at me with the uninjured leg, sending me sprawling into the doorway. As he rose to his feet, I struggled to mine.

"I just want to talk," I said. "I'm trying to—"

He swung at me with a right hook. I ducked and swung at him, connecting under his jaw. It had no effect.

"That is it, my friend? That is the best you have got?"

"I just want to talk," I repeated. "I want to call off the—"

He swung at me again. I was able to partially deflect the punch, but what was left of its trajectory knocked me off of my feet and deeper into the hallway. Rulenska stepped over the shattered door and came after me.

I climbed to my feet and ran down the hallway and into the kitchen. Rulenska hobbled after me.

When I got into the kitchen, I stood flat against the wall on one side of the entryway. I saw a fire extinguisher that I hadn't noticed earlier next to the kitchen counter. I grabbed the extinguisher just as Rulenska came around the corner and I hosed him with the carbon dioxide. The sound was loud and threatening, but the CO_2 did little to slow him down.

I swung the fire extinguisher at him, hitting him square in the face. He went down with a groan. His nose was bloody, and from its new shape, I could tell that it was broken.

The hitter was a big man, taller than me by better than six inches and outweighing me by fifty pounds. Fifty *muscular* pounds. My only chance at subduing him would be at the end of a gun barrel.

I leapt over the stunned hit man and ran down the hall to the bedroom. I reached under the bed and felt for the shotgun. As soon as my fingers clamped around the stock, I ran back to the kitchen.

Rulenska was gone

The blood from his broken nose left a trail that extended from the kitchen into the living room. I followed the dime-sized spots of blood that stained the plush carpeting through the living room and up the staircase. He had gone upstairs, where I had left the Ruger during our struggle. He would be waiting for me with the gun in hand. And, unless I missed my guess, he would be hiding in one of the other bedrooms.

I jacked the pump on the shotgun and began my trek upstairs. As I moved up the winding staircase one cautious step at a time, I kept the barrel of the gun extended forward. With each step, I paused to listen, keeping my neck craned around the next twist of the staircase. As I moved along, I glanced down at the step that was just ahead of me. In my haste to assume Rulenska was upstairs, I hadn't noticed the trail of blood on the carpeting had ended. By the time I did, it was too late.

CHAPTER SIXTY-TWO

I felt the penetration of the bullet, before I heard the sound of the shot. The impact spun me around, knocking my feet out from under me. I landed on my back and dropped the shotgun. It was lying on the step next to me.

Rulenska was standing behind one of the two sofas in the living room. He had used his blood to lure me up the stairs and had then gone into hiding. It was a very effective trap, and I had fallen into it.

A large dark stain on the front of my left leg was growing by the second. I could see a hole, which meant the bullet had passed clean through. During my years in law enforcement, I had always lived with the possibility of getting shot and had always assumed it would generate incredible pain. Oddly enough, this did not seem to hurt that much. I had only a mild burning sensation.

I saw Rulenska limp from behind the sofa. He kept the barrel of a Glock nine-millimeter semiautomatic trained on me, and he grinned as he wiped the blood from his nose with his sleeve. He must have had the gun with him all along. If he had wanted to kill for the contract, he would have used it earlier. The fact that he preferred the garrote told me he relished his job. He began to move toward the staircase.

The fingers of my right hand were within an inch of the stock of the shotgun. I began to slowly work the gun toward me as I lay on the staircase. The hitter had the drop on me, and any sudden movement from me now would bring more shots my way. But I had no real options left, except for the shotgun that was within an inch of my hand.

As Rulenska moved to place his foot on the bottom step, he had put himself in a position that forced him to come around the newel post. The large ornate post, along with the innate spiral of the staircase, would temporarily block me from his view and give me the time and the cover I needed to grab the shotgun. As he came around the post, I pulled the gun toward me, leveled it at the still grinning killer, and pulled the trigger.

Click.

I jacked the pump and pulled the trigger again. *Click.*

"You are too emotional," he said as he stood on the bottom step just fifteen feet away. "You must learn to use your head in confrontations. You only had four shells in the chamber. Didn't you hear me fire them?"

"I just wanted to talk," I said, preparing for the final onslaught. "You're contract on Chatham has been voided."

He slowly shook his head. The grin never left his face. "I decide when a contract is voided. After all," he said, leveling the barrel at me, "I have a reputation to uphold."

"Is that why you killed Vinny? Because he knew too much?"

He shrugged. "He was a stupid man. He held out on me."

I recalled my own suspicions that Vinny had withheld part of the money due to Rulenska.

"But he also knew you," I said. "Knew your reputation. He didn't just withhold, he also took out insurance. He took care of business." I didn't know what "business" that would be, but I was hoping to buy time to make another run at Rulenska.

"What business?" the Russian asked.

"Yours. How else did I know you'd be here?"

His face contorted as he thought over the possibilities.

I wanted to press him, rattle him. "I was an FBI agent. Do you think I would come here without setting a trap first? Think about it. Didn't you come here looking for Chatham and find me instead?"

His smiled evaporated as he lowered the gun. His face told me he was continuing to think. Men like Rulenska can survive only if they clean up after themselves. They can't afford to leave loose ends, and I was playing on that fear.

"I can kill you," he said. "I can—"

"Sure. But you won't get away. The bureau will hunt you down. Interpol will leave you with no place to go."

He smiled again, but this time it was forced. "I am well-known to Interpol. That is nothing new, my friend."

"It'll be new this time," I said. "You'll have killed one of the bureau's own." I slid upward to a sitting position, using the staircase for leverage.

"Enough talk," he said. "I've got a job to complete."

As he began to raise the barrel again, I kicked one of the potted plants that I had seen earlier, sending it hurtling toward him. His momentary deflection gave me enough time to push off the staircase and dive head-first into him.

We tumbled down the stairs as I fought for control of the Glock. But Rulenska's strength and my wound were working against me.

We landed at the bottom of the staircase. Rulenska was on his back, and I was on top of him, straddling him with my feet spread broadly apart to maintain leverage. I had both hands on the weapon, as did Rulenska. We each fought to wrestle the pistol away from the other.

But the Russian was incredibly strong. And savvy. It didn't take him long to exploit my weakness.

He let go of the weapon with one hand and punched me hard in my wounded leg. The pain seared through my wound and into my back, causing a transient numbness as I lost my two-handed grip on the nine-millimeter. Sensing final victory, the smile flashed across Rulenska's face again as he grabbed the pistol with both hands and wrenched it free from my grip.

I struggled to reach for the weapon, but the Russian brought it down on the side of my head with devastating force. The Glock didn't have the traditional weight of most nine-millimeters, but the force of the Russian's blow had its intended effect. I rolled off of Rulenska and to his left side as my head rang like bells of a Las Vegas wedding chapel.

I was lying side by side with the Russian as we both were on our backs at the base of the staircase. I looked at Rulenska in time to see the assassin begin to move to his feet. The Glock was still in his right hand. Although my leg was searing and my head was banging, I knew I had to react and move quickly to try and get the gun from him.

As he began to push himself to his feet with his left hand, I spun on the tile of the foyer and kicked him hard. I landed the blow to his left arm, knocking the support from under him as he fell to the floor again.

I pushed myself off of the floor and kicked him again as the gun spun from his hand. Taking advantage of the moment, I dove over Rulenska to where the gun lay, three feet off to his right side. He let out a short gasp of air as I landed on top of him in my struggle to reach the gun.

"Enough," he said. He worked both hands under my torso and began to lift me off of him. I was less than two feet from where the gun was, so I drove my right elbow into Rulenska's rib cage just as he began to push me off. The blow collapsed his right arm, leaving the full force of his thrust to his left. That sent me sprawling onto the foyer's tile to his right. The pistol was less than a foot away.

I scooted across the tile and reached for the gun. As my fingers hit the pistol's butt, it spun away. Behind me, I could hear Rulenska scurrying to his feet. I made one final thrust and gripped the Glock with my right hand. As soon as my fingers closed around the gun, I rolled over onto my back and pointed it at the Russian.

He was standing over me, holding high over his head one of the iron soldiers that Chatham kept standing to each side of his door. He was about to bring it down on me when I fired.

Chapter Sixty-Three

The shot propelled Rulenska backward, where he landed on his back, motionless. The heavy statue had landed on the foyer floor, less than a foot from me, crushing large sections of the inlaid tile.

I eased myself to my feet, wincing in pain from the gunshot wound, which was now beginning to throb, and from the blow to my head. I kept the gun trained on Rulenska as I moved forward.

He didn't move. No breathing. No sounds. I placed a finger on his neck. There wasn't a pulse.

"Dead?"

I spun around and brought the gun to bear on the voice. It was Sean.

"Easy there, mate," he said, coming from the kitchen. "Let's not get trigger happy, shall we?"

"How'd you get—"

"Same way you did. I came through the door." He looked at Rulenska and then knelt to feel for a pulse.

"He's dead, Sean," I said.

"Aye. He's as dead as Lenin." He looked at my leg. "You okay?"

"I think so. He shot me from behind and I can see the exit wound on the front of my leg." I showed him the bloody hole in my jeans. "I think it passed through. The bleeding seems to have stopped too."

He nodded and then stood. "Get in the car," he said. "I'll take care of him."

I stood. "I've got to get my gun first."

"Where is it?"

"Upstairs," I said. "I've got to—"

"Go. Now. The police may be here soon." He put a hand on me and steered me toward the kitchen. "I'll clean up."

I hesitated for a moment but began moving toward the kitchen.

"Hey," Sean said.

I turned to face him.

"Take these." He tossed me the keys to his car. "I'll be out in a minute or two."

I went outside and saw a dark BMW sedan. It was the same car I had seen in the driveway earlier in the day. Probably the one I had seen following me the night I was tailing Cortez.

I got in the car and sat in the right front seat. Within a couple of minutes, I saw Sean pushing a wheelbarrow containing my shotgun and an ornamental rug rolled up like a cigar. He had my Ruger tucked in his belt and was whistling like any other handyman who was just doing his job.

"Excuse me," he said, pausing at the window. "But could you be so kind as to open the trunk?"

I pushed the trunk-release button under the dash and waited while Sean deposited the rug into the trunk. After closing the lid, he pushed the wheelbarrow back toward the garage and, within in a minute, was in the front seat of the BMW.

"Nice car," I said.

"I thought so too," he said with a grin. "I wonder what it cost?"

He started the car and began backing out of the driveway.

"It was you I saw tailing me, wasn't it?" I asked.

"Aye."

"Don't think I'm not grateful," I said, "but you let it get a little close back there, didn't you?"

He smiled as he shifted the car into drive. "I came by once, pulled in the driveway, and watched the house. I didn't see anything, so I drove around the area for a while. When I came back, I saw your car was gone." He punched the accelerator and the car lurched forward.

I shook my head. "That must have been when I moved it. I figured Rulenska knew the car too, and I didn't want him seeing it."

Sean nodded. "I was thinking maybe you left. But I sat around for a while anyway and then took another drive around. I came back for one last check and heard the gunshot."

"How many shotgun blasts did you hear?"

He looked at me with a quizzical expression. "I didn't hear a shotgun. What I heard was a pistol."

"You didn't hear the shotgun?"

He shook his head. "No. I had pulled back into the driveway and decided to wait there for a bit, when I heard a handgun. That's when I came in the house."

"That must have been when Rulenska shot me," I said.

Sean shrugged.

"I'm sorry I got you involved," I said.

He smiled. "It isn't the first time that Sean O'Connor was involved."

"Is that it? O'Connor? I've always wondered what your real name was."

He smiled. "The O'Connors of Belfast," he said. Then, as the grin faded, "I come from a good family. A mother and a father who loved their children." An expression of sadness creased his face. "Somewhere, I went off track."

"We've all gone off track," I said. "In my case, I was born there."

Sean nodded. "Well," he said, "I wasn't. I've let my family down." He didn't say anything for a moment as the sadness seemed to linger. Then, as if he had washed it all behind him he asked, "Where's your car?"

"Around the corner," I said.

He pulled alongside the curb where I had left the Escort. I paused as I got out of the car. "What will you do with Rulenska?"

He smiled, but there was no mirth in his expression. "Leave that to me."

"Why are you doing this, Sean?"

Sadness filled his face again. "I thought about what you said. About how I didn't have a life."

"Sean, I—"

He shook his head. "No. You were right. I've been running from my past. This was a chance to redeem myself. Or something like that, I guess."

Our eyes locked briefly. Again I started to say something, but he stopped me.

"It's all right," he said, and then he pulled away. I watched him till he rounded the corner out of my sight, and then I eased my way into the Escort, my leg still throbbing.

I headed back to my house. I needed to attend to my wounds, change my bloody clothes, and get back to Beverly's as quickly as possible. I wasn't sure how she had detained Chatham, but I knew if I didn't show soon, there would be problems that even Sean couldn't help solve.

Things had gotten out of hand. I had wanted to convince Rulenska to go home. I had wanted Lester to get his life back, and I wanted to keep mine as it was. The confrontation with Rulenska was violent and had ended badly. If Sean hadn't gotten involved, I would have had to call the police, and the whole thing would have tumbled down. But he *had* gotten involved, and his help would give me a chance to put everything right.

I headed south and called Beverly. When she answered, she was clearly annoyed.

"It's me," I said.

"Yeah."

"Chatham never showed. How did you keep him this long?" I asked.

"Why don't you come and see for yourself?"

I didn't like the tone in her voice.

"What have you done?" I asked.

"Why don't you come and see for yourself?" she repeated before hanging up.

CHAPTER SIXTY-FOUR

The drive home was grueling. The dense rush-hour traffic, the lack of sleep, the fight with Rulenska, and the wounds to my leg and head were making my life miserable. By the time I finally parked in front of my house, I was exhausted.

The walk from Chatham's house to Sean's car and from my car into my house had made the pain in my leg much worse, and my head still hurt from Rulenska's blow with the Glock. I opened the medicine cabinet and took two Tylenol. I knew I needed something stronger, but it was all I had. I probably needed an antibiotic too. But given the circumstances, I didn't have the luxury of walking into the nearest hospital.

I changed clothes and took the time to examine my leg. The wound was painful but there wasn't any drainage or odor, and it was only slightly red. I took all of these as good signs and cleaned away the blood, applied some antiseptic, and wrapped it with gauze.

I checked the Ruger to make sure it was still loaded and slid it back into my shoulder holster in preparation for whatever might await me at Beverly's. All I had been able to do so far had been done at considerable risk. Now, in one fell swoop, she could jeopardize all that I had accomplished.

I drove to Beverly's apartment as quickly as traffic would allow. When I arrived, she buzzed me through the security door and was waiting for me in the doorway of her apartment as I limped up the stairs. She was dressed in a bathrobe over a negligee and smoking a cigarette.

When I reached her apartment, she didn't acknowledge my presence. She merely stepped back into the room and allowed me to follow her.

When we crossed the foyer, she stood in the middle of her living room with one hand on her hip as the other fed her the cigarette. She exhaled, blowing the smoke out of the corner of her mouth, and nodded toward the sofa.

Chatham sat on it with his hands in front of him, duct taped at the wrists. A second piece of duct tape was over his mouth.

I turned to Beverly. "What do you think you're doing?"

"I'm going to kill him myself," she said. She had her arms crossed, resting one elbow on the other as she held the cigarette to her mouth.

"Not while I'm around. He's my concern now," I said.

Her face was flushed. Her eyes were wide and bloodshot. "He belongs to me."

"Wrong, Mommy dearest," I said. "He's now mine. I put a lot at risk for Lester, and others have risked a lot more."

"I don't care," she said. "He's mine."

I sighed as I ran my fingers through my hair. I walked over to the sofa and ripped the tape off of Chatham's mouth. He yelped as the tape came loose and then immediately began making lawyerly threats.

"I'm going to sue you for everything you own," he said. "And then I'm going to file—"

I put the tape back over his mouth and turned to Beverly. She had the gun from her end-table drawer in her hand.

"Put that away," I said.

She shook her head. "He robbed me of everything."

"He's paid. And he'll continue paying. But there's no reason for Lester to keep paying." I reached out to her. "Give me the gun."

She shook her head again. Her eyes were focused on Chatham. "No. I'm going to kill him, and I want you to see this. I want someone to tell the world that there are people who will fight back." She turned her face to look at me for the first time since I came into the apartment. "I want you to tell people that I'm not a piece of meat. I have feelings. I want everyone to know how much this man took from me. And how much he had to give up for the privilege."

She raised the gun and pointed the barrel at Chatham. It was no longer a threat. Her finger tightened on the trigger, and she began to close her eyes in anticipation of the gun's report. The time for talking was over. She was going to kill the attorney.

I acted in the only way I could, grabbing the gun just as the hammer began to pull back. I wrestled the pistol away from her and shoved her onto the sofa.

I opened the cylinder. The gun was loaded. She had meant business.

"Stay there," I said, ejecting the cartridges and pocketing them.

I moved toward Chatham as I slid the pistol into my hip pocket. "I'm going to remove this tape again. I have something to say to you and I want you to listen. If you begin making threats, I'm going to give her this gun and walk away. Do you understand?"

He nodded, his eyes wide.

I tore off the tape. "You have been making threats against this woman." I pulled the cassette tape that I had taken from Beverly's machine from my pocket and showed it to him. "And your attempts to destroy Lester, his business, and the Cheek marriage are now documented."

He looked at the tape in my hand. "If that's all you've got, you—"

"It's not," I said. "There are some volunteers at Mother's Advocating for Children, who, I am sure, will recognize this voice as the one who has been calling her." I gestured toward Beverly. "We have enough, counselor. Enough for her to go after you in court."

"Let her. Let's see how far a—"

"Or we can let her do this the way she prefers."

His eyes were full of indignation. "You're in this too, aren't you?" he said. "That's why you came to my—"

"Shut up, you pompous jerk," I said, feeling the anger beginning to rise. "I just killed a man in your house. A man who was hired to kill you.

I've spent the past several days trying to save your life. If I wanted you dead, all I had to do was to walk away."

"Someone was hired to kill me?" he asked. Some of his legal bullying had begun to wither.

"Haven't you been paying attention?" I asked.

"Who?"

"Me," Beverly said. "I did it."

He looked at her and then back at me.

"Lester may or may not have wronged you. But that doesn't give you the right to use the law as your personal tool to destroy his business or his marriage."

"Or my life," Beverly said.

"You see," I continued, "some people don't address their grievances through attorneys. Some people," I motioned to Beverly, "would rather just kill you and be done with it."

He glanced at her again and then back to me.

"I stopped this one. And I'll make sure she never does this again if you walk away and drop the whole thing. But I can't be responsible for what she might do if you attempt to blackmail her again."

He sighed and lowered his head. "How do I know I can trust you?"

"You don't," I said. "And I know I can't trust you. That's why I will keep this little piece of incriminating evidence, just in case." I tossed the tape into the air and caught it in my hand. "If you attempt to make any contact of any kind with her," I said nodding toward Beverly, "or Lester, or pass on any information that could be harmful to them, I'll see to it that you never practice law again. And I think we both know that she will probably arrange another surprise for you as well."

He nodded. "Okay," he said. "Okay. You win. But if that tape is leaked—"

I sighed and put the duct tape back over his mouth.

CHAPTER SIXTY-FIVE

We drove Chatham back to his house. I walked him through it, so I could gauge his reaction to the events that had occurred. If he reacted negatively and began making threats, I was going to have to find another way to deal with him. But as he walked through his home and saw the blood on the carpet, the blood on the staircase, the broken floor tiles, the buckshot in the walls, and the bedroom door that had been blown to splinters, his face began to drain of its color. When he finished his tour, he sank into one of the living room sofas. He had gotten the message. We wouldn't be hearing from Chatham again. Neither would Lester. Whatever feelings that existed between the two men had been enough to drive Chatham to blackmail Lester's wife into handing over sensitive information about her husband's business. Those feelings were now dead in the stark reality of the revenge they had engendered.

I drove Beverly back to her apartment and gave her time to prepare to meet with Lester. As she readied herself, I called my client and told him I had found his wife and would be bringing her home soon. I depressed the call button and then called the Shapiros. Frank answered, and from the sound of his voice, he was clearly agitated.

"Where have you been?"

"Working, Frank," I said. "I'm almost through. How is Callie?"

"Worried. None of us has heard from you."

"I know," I said. "I've been busy."

"And what about the danger to your daughter, Colton? Is that almost over too?"

I didn't want to tell him about Rulenska. He knew too much already. Yet he needed to know that Callie was safe.

"She's okay, now, Frank," I said. "I just have a couple of loose ends to tie up, and then I'll be there to get her."

"So the killer has been taken care of?" Frank asked.

"Yes," I said. "He won't be a problem for us again."

There was a pause. "Right," he said. "She'll be ready."

I was putting down the phone when Beverly came into the room. She looked more like a high-society hostess than an ex-hooker. The transformation was indeed remarkable. I stood.

"Before we leave," I said, "we need to get something straight. You're going to tell Lester everything."

She lowered her eyes as she nodded in agreement.

"Unless he knows all about you, the possibility of future blackmail will exist. Eventually, someone else will figure out who you are and will use it as leverage against your husband."

"I know," she said softly.

"Then you know that he has to know everything."

"Yes."

"But not about me."

She looked at me.

"There's no need to tell him. I can't be a source of blackmail since no one knows I'm your son. And, I'd like to keep it that way. Understand?"

She nodded again.

We turned to leave. As we reached the door, she put a hand on my arm. "Tell me," she said. "Am I a grandmother?"

I hadn't been prepared for that question. I had assumed that a mother who would be willing to deny the most basic relationship would never need to know how much further it had gone.

"Yes."

She smiled. "A boy? Girl?"

"Girl," I said.

"Can I ask…what's her name?"

I hesitated for minute. I didn't want this woman in my life—not now. I sure didn't want her in Callie's. But I answered.

"Her name is Callie," I said.

"That's a pretty name, Colton. Can I ask…how old is she?"

"She's thirteen."

"Her mother must be very proud of her."

I nodded. "She was. Anna passed away last year."

"Colton, I'm so sorry."

I shrugged. "It's been tough, but we'll manage."

"Is Callie okay? Is she able to deal with it?"

It seemed like an odd question coming from her. She hadn't asked how I had dealt with the loss of my mother.

"She's had her ups and downs," I said.

"I hope she doesn't have any of me in her, Colton."

Me too, I thought. I remembered my first visit to Lester's. About the art I had appreciated and that he had told me Claudia had picked it out. Whatever part of Beverly was in me, good or bad, I didn't want it going to Callie. I wanted her to be her own. And maybe a little of Anna too.

"I hope she does better than both of us," I said. "A lot better."

I opened the door of the apartment and motioned for her to pass. As she did, I followed and closed the door behind me.

Chapter Sixty-Six

When we arrived at Lester's, I drove up the semicircular driveway and found him standing on the front stoop.

We parked, and as Claudia got out of the car, neither of us was sure just how he would react. I had done all that I could for Lester. Whatever happened now was up to him.

The two of them stood facing each other, seemingly oblivious to me. After a while, Claudia lowered her head. Lester stood with his hands to his side, studying her. Then, like a dam that had burst, he moved off of the stoop and hugged her with tears in his eyes. Neither of them said a word.

"Lester," I said, "let's go into the living room. Claudia has something to tell you."

We moved into the living room and sat in the same grouping of chairs Lester and I had sat in two weeks earlier. I knew Beverly didn't want to tell him about the events in her life. But I also knew that if she had any chance with Lester, he was going to have to know the truth.

"What is it?" Lester asked. From his demeanor, he clearly anticipated bad news.

"Lester, I need to tell you something." She took one of his hands in both of hers.

He stiffened, preparing himself for what she was about to say. The tension was palpable as he looked to me.

"You need to hear this," I said. "If there is going to be any healing, you need to know."

He looked at Claudia. "What? What is it?"

She told him the whole story. Her past, the many men in her life, and Chatham. She told him she had hired Rulenska, through Vinny, and that Rulenska had killed Vinny. She told him about her attempts to kill Chatham and the tenuous standoff we had had with the attorney. She did not tell him about me.

After she finished, Lester hung his head and let go. He began to sob.

"I'm so sorry," she said as she took one of his hands in hers, her own tears flowing as freely as his. "I never meant to hurt you. I left because I didn't want to see the look on your face when you found out that…I didn't want to hurt you." She brushed a lock of hair from his forehead with one hand. "I'm sorry. I'm really sorry."

He shook his head. "I don't care what happened before you met me, Claudia." He raised his head to look at her. "When I told you I loved you, I meant just what I said. Whatever has happened in the past is in the past."

A look of confusion crossed Claudia's face. "You mean…this doesn't matter?"

He shook his head. "It matters, but not enough. Whatever has happened is forgiven. I just want to move ahead. I want us to be happy."

I eased out of the room and out of the house. The two of them had things to talk about, and they didn't need to have me around when they did.

As I walked into the brilliant sunlight, I remembered the story of the prodigal son and what Millikin had said about love covering a multitude of sins. Lester's love for Claudia covered her failures and allowed him to forgive her. God's love covered our failures and sent Christ to the cross so God could forgive us. And love would someday allow Callie to forgive me. But I realized I had to ask for that forgiveness. Anything less was to not acknowledge a wrong that had been done. And Callie needed to have the opportunity to forgive. Taking that away from her would only prolong her pain and forestall our reconciliation.

I paused and looked back at the Cheeks' house. I wanted Callie to forgive me just as Beverly wanted me to forgive her. Seventy times seven seemed like a lot to ask. But as I thought about it, I realized I couldn't expect Callie to do something I wasn't willing to do myself. I realized that forgiveness had to start somewhere. I took a deep breath and walked back to the house.

THE END

© Susan Gerth 2005

About BRANDT DODSON

Brandt Dodson was born and raised in Indianapolis, where he graduated from Ben Davis High School and Indiana Central University (now known as the University of Indianapolis). A creative writing professor told him, "You're a good writer. With a little effort and work, you could be a very good writer." That comment, and the support offered by a good teacher, set Brandt on a course that would eventually lead to the Colton Parker Mystery series.

"I tried to write for the secular world, but it left me feeling empty. I knew if I didn't write something that had lasting value, something that would do more than simply entertain, it would all be in vain."

A committed Christian, Brandt combined his love for the work of writers like Raymond Chandler and Dashiell Hammett with his love for God's Word. The result was Colton Parker.

"I wanted Colton to be an 'every man.' A decent guy who tries his best. He is flawed and makes mistakes. But he learns from them and moves on. And, of course, he gets away with saying and doing things that the rest of us never could."

Brandt comes from a long line of police officers and was employed by the FBI before leaving to pursue his education.

A former United States Naval Reserve officer, Brandt is a board certified podiatrist and past president of the Indiana Podiatric Medical Association. He is a recipient of the association's highest honor, The Theodore H. Clark Award.

He currently resides in southwestern Indiana with his wife and two sons and is at work on his next novel.

Visit Brandt's website at: www.brandtdodson.com.